Lightning Shall Strike

Linda Kay Simmons

For Spike, my confidant and protector,
And to Noelle, always.

Waters of God Believers
Record Book
Page: 107

Hezekiah Moses Simpkins and Ruth Elizabeth Meador
Joined in Holy Matrimony on September 6, 1914
In Hardy, Virginia
On this day they vowed themselves to be a family in the
Waters of God Believers Church and
To raise all children under the covenants of
Their faith.

Thaddeus Polk Simpkins born October 13, 1916
Ida Jane Simpkins born Dec 4, 1918
Joseph Elbert Simpkins born August 20, 1928

Hezekiah Moses Simpkins died on June 24, 1935
Falling from a roof and breaking his neck.
Ruth Elizabeth Simpkins, his wife, followed him
To Glory Land on September 12, 1936
Death by snake bite

In The Beginning

Those who lived in the old farmhouse with the sagging porch and peeling paint were thin-lipped, hard faced, white Southerners, humble yet arrogant in their belief of God. The house breathed in the sins and shadows of generations of Waters of God Believers, but did not exhale for that would be a releasing or letting go. In the darkness of night the house wept sorrowful lamentations with moans and creaking boards.

Thaddeus, the eldest brother, stern faced with blazing eyes quoted scriptures as Ida, his gaunt and haggard sister, let the porch door slam, arms full of chores that would never end. Mamie, the skittish quivering girl taken in as a child of three, peeled potatoes at the kitchen table, watching it all, knowing this life would one day be her own.

Mamie and Joseph, the youngest brother, cowered before Thaddeus. Not in fear, for he did not strike them, but promised an eternity of damnation for misdeeds that went against Holy Scripture only he understood.

Seasons fell upon the house. The swelling pumpkin sun rose and set while moon man shone down his many faces. Farmers called sooee and cows bawled out for their daily milking. The hummingbirds, which had once come around, did not return. Worn down inside and out, Ida, Joseph, and Mamie lay in their beds, their silent aching the loudest sound of all.

You might be asking me how I know these things to be true? Well, I was once Mamie, and Joseph was my one true love.

I've been dead for several years now, so I've had time to think about all that happened while I still had a body. There had been a lot to ponder, and I wonder why I had to die before I had thoughts that things could have been different for all of us.

I lived in Thaddeus's house for over thirty years until I passed away, cold, starved in my own bed, soaked in my own piss, but sometimes things aren't always as they seem; it depends on the teller of the tale. I do not mourn my own death.

Mamie Simpkins is what's on my tombstone. Thaddeus never got round to getting me one, but my daughters, Lula May and Raylene saw that I did.

They waited a full year to see if Thaddeus would take care of it like he said he would, then my girls took up a collection. Sort of passed the hat it was.

Every Simpkins I'd ever known who done passed over got them a real nice tombstone, but they weren't married to the likes of Thaddeus Simpkins.

Ida

As I look back through the years one memory sticks out more than the rest. It was the summer of 1928, and I was ten years old, when I first got a glimpse of the black mare. No one seemed to know from where she came or where she returned. She had been spotted, sometimes in a field or in a high pasture, but no one was ever able to get close to her.

She was high-spirited in the way she carried herself, prancing with her tail held high. Her neck was arched and her legs straight and sound. The men in our church wanted to catch and tame the wild black mare, particularly my brother, Thaddeus, who turned twelve years old that summer.

Thaddeus had seen her on several occasions and itched to tame her, but it was not to be. There was a quickness to her and an unbridled freedom that refused to be caught. Those who knew about horses thought perhaps it was the Arabian in her.

I saw her one more time, from the kitchen window, when she had come close to the house. Thunderbolts had flashed in the sky and thunder rumbled. The cold wind screamed as the mare pawed the ground, nostrils flared, rearing up, throwing her head back letting out a wild neighing. She knew I was watching her as she was watching me. I wiped my hands, damp from doing kitchen dishes, on my dress, then rubbed my arms to dispel the sudden chill that came over me.

"Return to your own kind. Do not stay here!" I spoke to her large brown eyes through mine.

"Do not be caught!" Like a phantom the mare turned and left and was never seen again.

It was a year later my father returned home holding a black colt in the back of his wagon, with Thaddeus behind the reins. Not a word was said from where the horse came, but there had been a caravan of folks who had camped nearby. I thought them to be carnival workers, but Father neither confirmed nor denied.

He gave the colt to Thaddeus as well as a black, right-handed glove that we weren't allowed to talk about. All I ever got from Father was a promise he had me make to be a helpmate to Thaddeus all his days.

Over time Thaddeus and Midnight became like one living creature, dark as thunder and fast as lightning. Sometimes Thaddeus galloped bareback on Midnight so fast it was as if Lucifer was chasing him.

Often I heard the sound of Midnight's hooves running toward the house. After Thaddeus groomed his horse and gave him water, I would hear his footsteps coming up the front porch steps. Looking after Thaddeus was a cross I, Ida Jane Simpkins, dutiful daughter, would have to bear.

PART ONE

"What loneliness is lonelier
than distrust?"

T.S. Eliot

Ida

1935

It was a warm summer afternoon, many years ago, and not too hot for June. A slight breeze made it tolerable for Father to nail shingles on the roof of the recently married Brother Jamieson's new farmhouse. Waters of God Believers helped one another build their houses, barns, fences, and bring in crops. The younger boys were playing leapfrog as the little girls chased butterflies about the yard.

The Sisters called the men to eat. I watched Father as he gathered his tools and placed them in a satchel he hung over his shoulder. As he stepped down onto the rungs of the ladder, it suddenly fell sideways, pitching him to the ground. His hammer lay beside him, and he was surrounded by nails. From the way he laid, I could tell his neck was broken.

Mother rushed to his side, kneeled, and prayed to Almighty God to save her husband repeating the same words many times over.

"Gracious God in heaven, if it is your will spare my husband for he is a good and righteous man."

The rest of the Believers gathered around Father weeping and exalting Jesus while the Elders laid hands upon Father praying for his body to resurrect.

"Help our brother, Lord."

"Spare him to do your mighty work."

"Use him to be a testament to your greatness!"

Standing by the table, still covered with uneaten food, I witnessed two yellow butterflies sweep over Father. Would there be a miracle or were they looking at death? Watching everything unfold, I was frozen and unable to move.

It was late afternoon when the Sisters helped Mother to rise, but she trembled and faltered. Abandoned to her sorrow, she was taken home.

I regret to this day not being able to hold Father's hand when his soul left this earth so suddenly. I had missed my chance to say good-bye. Within our family, pain had taken root.

For days there was disbelief and sadness in our community. Father was an Elder of the church and everyone looked up to him, but life went on. The Sisters came with baked goods for weeks. The Brothers pitched in plowing our fields, and planting our gardens until Mother, Thaddeus, and I could manage by ourselves, with him being nineteen years old and me seventeen.

How I grieved for Father. He always had a kind word and a smile on his face when we greeted in the morning. When I took lunch to him in the fields, he made time for me. We took walks, just the two of us, among the tall pines. Two large maples marked the site of our house. I remember Father standing on the back of his wagon and hanging a tree swing when I was only six. He would push me in that swing after supper.

Mother passed a year after Father died, when a rattlesnake laid claim to her. She had taken the snake from Brother Farley during a prayer meeting, when the snake struck out biting a vein in her neck. Praying and the laying on of hands didn't work. She died soon after. Our brother, Joseph, was seven years old.

It was a sad time in my life, for my friend Caroline also passed away. Just before her death, she'd asked me to care for her young daughter and I agreed. Having one more child wouldn't make any difference. When Mamie got bigger, she would be a help in the garden and around the house.

Being the head of the household was a job Thaddeus took seriously. Even though Father was dead, it seemed that Thaddeus was still trying to please him. Our parents had been devoted Believers with genuine good-ness in their hearts. Thaddeus wasn't like them although he tried to be. I was glad the little ones only saw him at meal times for the most part. While we were eating, Thaddeus was silent. Once his hunger had been appeased he would ask Joseph questions from the Bible even though Joseph was barely eight and had much to learn.

"Joseph, after the flood, what sign did God give that He would not destroy the earth with a flood again?" Thaddeus asked.

"A rainbow," Joseph said timidly.

"How many books are in the Old Testament and the New Testament?" Joseph swallowed hastily and tried to come up with the answer.

"The Old Testament has forty books and the New Testament has less."

"Noah sent out two different kinds of birds from the Ark. What were they?"

"A dove and a crow would be my guess."

"You guessed wrong. Leave this table now and write down all the books of the Bible five times. I want you to know the correct answers before breakfast or you will not be eating."

It seemed that Thaddeus took delight in shaming Joseph for the wrong answers, and it worried me. I was grateful he paid no mind to Mamie.

Mamie

1938

"Don't spill your milk, child," Ida warned me at every meal.

"Yes, ma'am. I'm finished now," I said, lifting my plate to show Thaddeus and Ida that I had eaten all my chicken parts and potatoes when my plate hit my glass of milk, causing it to crash to the floor.

"I'm sorry!" I stood fast, feeling the flush of blood reddening my cheeks. "I'll clean it up."

Joseph came over to help me pick up the pieces of glass.

"She can do it herself, Joseph. Let her be. She has to learn not to be so careless," Thaddeus said in a stern voice.

Shaking, I looked up and met his dark eyes. He sat at the head of the table, his hands folded in front of him with a piercing look on his face.

"She's just a little girl. I need to help her." Joseph was by my side. I didn't want to get Joseph in trouble. I picked up pieces of glass and put them into the dustpan.

"Get back to your seat, Joseph." Thaddeus glowered from under his heavy eyebrows.

I hurriedly swept up the glass, when pain shot through my finger and I let out a yelp. Blood gushed from where the glass had cut me and I felt faint.

"Mamie is bleeding." Joseph spoke up, trying to defend me.

"Ida, see to the girl," Thaddeus boomed. He shifted in his chair. "Joseph, you can go to your room for defying me."

Joseph had stood up for me. He was very brave.

I was forever getting into trouble, like when I was five and tried to climb the tree by my bedroom window to see the mama bird and babies that had just hatched. I couldn't get a good look from my room because of all the leaves. I hadn't climbed very high when my dress got caught on a branch. Ida would be so mad if I got a hole in it! Trying to undo my dress, I lost my balance and fell to the ground.

Thaddeus pushed open the kitchen door. "What happened?" I heard him say, but it was Joseph who scooped me into his arms. I could see the worried look on his face.

"She's alright. Looks like she just got the air knocked out of her," Joseph yelled back.

Thaddeus and Ida didn't come out of the house, and I was glad. I wanted Joseph's help, and he was there. We were a comfort to one another.

Mamie

"Mamie, hurry up with your chores. You haven't collected the eggs, nor fed the chickens, so I can cook breakfast. Don't forget to bring in enough water for me to wash the dishes. We can't be late getting to church," Ida scolded me.

"Yes, ma'am," I hollered back, on my way to the hen house. I didn't want to go to church; it was beautiful outside and church seemed to last forever. I wanted to run and play free of the long dress and apron I had to keep so clean although I had never been allowed to do so.

"Ida, why do the females sit on the right and the males on the left in church? It seems to me families should sit together," I asked, as we walked the half mile to church on the other side of our farm.

"It's been like this as far back as I can remember. I don't have an answer for you, child."

"Ida, will you tell me about my mother and father? I'm eight years old now, and I should know something about them. Please tell me," I said, as I tried to keep up with her long strides.

"Your mother was a good woman, who had a weakness in her blood, and that's what took her life. I have nothing to say about your father and you're not to ask again." Ida said. I knew I had better stop asking questions because of her impatient tone. Ida was never unkind to me but she didn't feel like a mother or even an aunt for that matter. She never hugged me or talked to me the way the other Sisters did with their daughters. She was always after me to do chores.

"I'm teaching you women's work so one day you will be a good and dutiful wife," she said to me more than once. I didn't pay marriage much mind as it seemed a lifetime away. I was grateful to Ida and Thaddeus for taking me in. If they hadn't, I wouldn't have Joseph as my friend.

"Be quiet, now. It's time to go in and sit down and remember, no fidgeting," Ida warned me, when we made it to the white clapboard church. I wished I could stay outside under the maples and oaks that had been planted years ago for summer shade. Today was communion Sunday so the service would be especially long. The Sisters nodded their heads at us when we took our seats. Brother Farley was sitting up front with the box of snakes. Thaddeus and Joseph were already seated, having come earlier in the horse and buggy. Joseph looked at me and smiled. I wished I could sit with him. I knew it was going to be a very long morning.

Every so often I dreamed I awoke, climbed out of bed, and picked up a silver hair brush and ran it through my long blonde hair. A large oval mirror was on the wall and it shone so bright, it was as if lightning wanted to strike out into the room. I did not like lightning. I was afraid of it and I struggled to not look into the mirror. I was fearful if I did I would be struck dead.

Not far from the mirror a red and black rocking horse began to move ever so slowly, coming closer to me, causing the floorboards to creak. As he turned his head toward me, his large painted eyes beckoned me to climb upon his back. I always woke up then. Whenever the dream happened, a strange smell of mustiness and old smoke lingered in the air.

Sometimes during sleep, I cried out. Joseph's bedroom was upstairs, as well, and the closest to mine. He left his door open so he could listen for me if I needed him. He knew about my dream and came to me without Thaddeus or Ida knowing.

One night, when I was nine, I had the scary images again. Joseph lit two candles to cast away the darkness and awakened me from my bad dream.

"Oh, Joseph, it's you!" I wrapped my arms around him. "It was the mirror and the rocking horse again."

"Go back to sleep, Mamie. I won't let the bad dream get you. Your eyes are still squinty with sleep. You just need to close your eyes."

I didn't want to go to sleep because Joseph was with me, and I fought it as hard as I could, but drowsiness was weighing heavily on my eyelids, and I could no longer keep my eyes open.

I was brought back to wakefulness when a cool breeze blew into the room, blowing out the two candles. I sat up, startled.

"What made the candles go out?" I asked in the darkness.

"I don't know, Mamie. I'll relight them."

I heard Joseph strike a match and saw the flicker of light. When the candles were lit, Joseph walked to the closed window. A look of concern crossed his face when he turned and looked at me. I could see he was appearing to be brave and trying to think of what to do next.

Joseph stayed with me until a sliver of the sun caused a wash of pink above the horizon. I wished I could live with Joseph in this twilight world forever.

Mamie

1939

The potato slices were frying in the iron skillet, a pot of beans and fatback cooked, while the coffee boiled. It was just about time to sit down for supper. All I had to do now was set the table.

"Call Thaddeus and Joseph and tell them to wash up. By the time the prayer is said we'll be ready to eat," Ida instructed me. It wasn't but a few minutes until we were all sitting down for our meal.

"Ida tells me you have just turned nine. You are now too old to be friends with Joseph. Males and females are not to mix at your age. It is best you are friends with your own kind," Thaddeus said, barely looking at me from across the table.

"Joseph, I will remind you that you are becoming a man and it is time to put away childish things. Mamie does not need coddling or watching out for. Focus on your chores and the Bible and not on her."

"I heard Brother Frith and Brother Culver talking after church. They said Poland had been invaded by Nazi Germany and our country might soon be at war. Is there going to be a war Thaddeus? Since I'm becoming a man, I need to know," Joseph said.

"God is in charge, and there will be no more talk on the subject." Thaddeus looked at Joseph as he spoke with a face dark as thunder.

Thaddeus's lecturing didn't matter to Joseph or me as we found ways to sneak off and be together after milking cows, feeding livestock and other endless chores. It wasn't as if we wanted to be disobedient; we just wanted to be together, and Thaddeus' endless rules didn't seem fair.

"What Thaddeus doesn't know won't hurt him, not to mention I don't think we're doing anything wrong," Joseph said to me more than once.

Joseph and I had several meeting places, depending on the time of year and where Thaddeus might be working on the farm. Sometimes when I went to slop the pigs, Joseph would follow me and we would visit for a few minutes. Other times we met in the woodshed or piled up loose hay in the barn and hid behind it. We had to be careful as Thaddeus spent time in Midnight's stall brushing him and talking to him in a voice so low, no matter how hard we tried, we couldn't make out the words.

In the summer Joseph and I would sneak away from our work weeding, picking vegetables or shucking corn. We would meet down by the creek at our favorite spot, where the moss was the heaviest and the water the deepest. Joe and I skipped stones, splashed each other, and played hide-n-seek, things we couldn't do in front of Thaddeus or any Believer, for that matter. The only fun to be found was what Joseph and I made together.

Thaddeus didn't like working in the garden when he didn't have to. He had Joseph for that. It seemed Thaddeus always had other chores to do or places to go.

Thaddeus continued to lecture Joseph and me that things of the world weren't important, but I didn't believe it. I wanted to be a girl who could wear pretty clothes and not this stupid gray dress and bonnet. Joseph tried to ask him questions about the war but Thaddeus refused to answer him.

I envied Joseph and other males for being allowed to wear trousers even if they had to wear white shirts, suspenders, black hats, and jackets, except for when they were working in the fields or in their own houses.

I had seen non-believers when they came by our produce stand to buy eggs and vegetables in the summer. The boys and girls talked and were playful to one another. I envied them for the colorful clothes they wore and how carefree they seemed. I wasn't supposed to talk to them, but I watched them while Ida weighed their produce and counted out their change.

One day when I was older, I wanted to be able to sit on a porch swing and hold hands with a boy; a boy who liked me and I liked him back. Maybe that boy would be Joseph. I didn't like thinking one day I would be married to someone the Believers chose for me. I wanted a happy life where Joseph and I didn't have to sneak to be friends and we could wear anything we wanted.

Mamie

1944

The air was sweet with honeysuckle and a sky so blue you thought it was birthing bluebirds. There had been no rain for many days, but I could smell it coming. By afternoon the clouds would be rolling in, full of promise. I had gotten up earlier than usual to get my chores done. I had collected the eggs and fed the chickens. Joseph was doing the milking when I went into the barn to get a bucket full so Ida could make the morning biscuits.

"Looks like you have a helper," I said, as I reached down to pet Tabby, our barn cat who was nuzzling against Joe's legs. Where's your buddy, Clover? She's usually with you," I said scratching behind his ears.

"She's probably up in the hayloft with some poor mouse," Joe said, laughing. "These two barn cats of ours aren't usually far away when there's milking to be done."

"Just put a little in their pans, and they'll be happy," I said, as Joe handed back the bucket of milk to take to Ida.

"I have to finish splitting kindling before Thaddeus, Ida and I can leave for the market after breakfast. I've already loaded the wagon with vegetables, peaches, butter and eggs. If we don't sell everything at the Roanoke market, we'll stop at the general store in Vinton on the way back. You probably won't see us until supper time."

"I wish you could be with me today, Joseph."

"So do I. A day with my brother isn't one I look forward to. I'm glad to be doing my part growing and selling food for the war effort. It's a good thing congress enacted draft deferments for farmers and farm workers; I wished they had taken Thaddeus, though."

"War is a bad thing Joseph. You shouldn't say that, even if it is Thaddeus we're talking about it. Believers are consciousness objectors. You know that."

"I know, Mamie. I shouldn't have said it," Joe said, as I was walking out of the barn.

I washed the breakfast dishes and took to the winding trails with a bucket in my hand after everyone left the house. How I loved walking over the rolling hills that led away from the Waters of God's community. I could see non-believers' farms in the distance. I liked to imagine how they lived, what the inside of their houses was like, and what clothes hung in their wardrobes. I made myself remember not to get lost in my thoughts and daydreams because I had to bring back plenty of berries and herbs lest Ida think I wasn't doing my fair share of work while she was gone.

I needed to hurry to get to the swimming hole before the rain came hard. Girls couldn't swim. We weren't allowed to know how. Sometimes when I knew I'd be working alone in the garden and the sun was full high, I would sneak off to the creek and dunk myself under the cold rushing stream, hoping I would be dried out before someone called my name or came looking for me. Last summer Joseph and I had been alone at the swimming hole when he dared me to put my head under the water. I was scared, so Joseph did it first, then held me by the waist and dunked me like they do at baptisms. Now I wasn't afraid to dunk myself.

It was late afternoon when Joseph found me at the creek. I was surprised, not expecting him to be back from Roanoke so soon.

"I got curious when I didn't see you around the house, so I came looking for you."

"Where's Thaddeus? Won't he be looking for you?" I said, drawing in my breath at the sight of him.

"You won't believe this, Mamie. Thaddeus dropped Ida and me at home, and now he's gone to Brother Farley's to tell him he's relented and decided to purchase a truck!" Joseph's Adam's apple was bobbing with excitement.

"Many of the Brothers have given up on the buggy and at last Thaddeus has given in! The truck is a black 1939 Ford pickup. I saw it today! A non-believer had it for sale at the market. He's selling it cheap because of the gas rationing, and it needing new tires. Thaddeus won't be able to drive it much until after the war is over. He's supposed to get it tomorrow if he doesn't change his mind overnight. As long as I can remember, I've been hearing Believers debating about buying trucks and tractors. I guess times are changing."

"The only thing that worries me is Thaddeus will be able to make more chores for you. We hardly have time to meet up with each other as it is." My eyes welled up thinking about having less time to be with Joseph.

"Don't worry, we'll figure something out. I've got something for you." Joseph shoved his hands deep into his pocket and took out a cat's eye marble.

"This is for you, Mamie. It reminds me of your eyes. I found it on the ground where we were selling our stuff." Joseph took my hand and placed the green marble in my palm, closing my fingers around it. I liked the feel of Joseph touching my hand that way.

Turning our heads in the direction of the woods, Joseph and I heard footsteps coming our way. Thaddeus was quickly approaching. I could tell he was angry as he came toward us with quick and purposeful strides. His right gloved hand was gesturing wildly as he came upon us.

"Joseph, you left without permission. I tracked you here. Do you not remember what I said about you and Mamie being alone together, a girl of thirteen and a boy sixteen? I won't warn you again; get back to the house now. There are chores to be done!

"I'm sure your help is needed in the kitchen, Mamie. I'll be telling Ida to keep a closer eye on you. The Apostle Paul says that idle fingers are the devil's workshop, before you be led into sin. I can tell now I've been too lenient on both of you." As Thaddeus spoke, a vein in his forehead bulged and his nostrils flared.

The rain, which seemed as if it had purposely held back until this very moment, came pouring down and biting hard. Hurrying home, Thaddeus led with Joseph closely following. I could barely keep up with them. An eerie light shadowed Thaddeus as we walked through the downpour. I didn't understand what I was seeing, but felt a sharpness in that light, which one day, would cut Joseph and me like a knife.

Trailing Thaddeus and Joseph in the pouring rain, I tightly held my cat's eye marble in my trembling hand.

Mamie

1944

Joseph and I had to be careful when we planned to see each other such as the day I took a bucket from under the porch to pick blackberries. Joseph went into the barn, then out the other side so no one would see him follow me. He was carrying the walking stick he had just finished carving.

It was the middle of summer and so hot I had taken off my bonnet once I was out of view of the house. My thick blonde hair fell almost to my waist. I hated keeping my hair in a bun, pulling it back so hard and sticking it with pins. Sometimes it gave me a headache.

Joseph caught up with me before we reached the creek. It wasn't long before we came upon a thicket of blackberry bushes.

"Joseph, tell me about your walking stick."

"I started carving, and the head of a horse seemed to come right out of the wood. It's not Midnight, though. I don't want it to be a black horse. It's oak, so it's a golden horse."

"He's beautiful. I like his face."

"He's gonna be free and strong. Some nights I dream about him galloping in the wild, then he stops and looks at me like he wants me to come with him. I wish I could have put the rest of his body on the stick so I could show you what he looks like."

"I like you telling me about him. I'd like to see him, too."

"I'd like to hear your dreams, Green Eyes, hopefully not the scary one about the rocking horse. You haven't had that one for months now."

"It's been a while. I never know when it will come back but I'll pray

21

for a happy dream so I can tell it to you. Right now I can't remember one." Joseph looked at me and smiled. It was like he wanted to say something, but changed his mind.

Joseph and I were careful of the bees hovering around the swollen blackberries that hung shining amongst the prickly tangles. When we were through picking all we dared, we walked to the creek to get out of the summer heat when a large brown copperhead with yellow banding came sliding close to us. I dropped the bucket and stood still with my mouth open, afraid to move.

The copperhead was larger than usual with a big head. It stopped its slithering and lay on our path like it was frozen. Quick as a wink Joseph raised his stick and hit the snake hard, crushing its head.

"I almost didn't see the snake it blended in so well. I could have stepped right on it and would have been bitten!" I said with a quivering voice.

"I reckon the old snake had been sunning himself. I'm glad I brought my stick."

"Thaddeus would have liked that snake for church service. Why didn't you pick him up like a Believer?" I was still shuddering when I spoke.

"I didn't want to risk him biting you. I mean to protect you, Mamie," Joseph replied, his eyes meeting mine.

Something happened to me when he looked at me that way. I became all tongue tied and fumbled for words that wouldn't come. I was glad when Joseph started talking again.

"Even if the snake bit you he wouldn't have hurt you bad. Copperheads don't have as much venom as rattlesnakes, though I've heard it said that a copperhead can have up to twenty young ones at a time."

"Joseph, do you think everything in the Bible is true, like Adam and Eve in the Garden of Eden and the snake tempting Eve?"

"Don't you ever ask Thaddeus anything like that Mamie; he'd beat the tar out of you!" Joseph's face turned ashen.

"You didn't answer my question. I want to know what you think," I asked, rooted to the spot.

"I don't know, Green Eyes, but I often wonder about some of the things that come out of Thaddeus's mouth. I wish I felt different, but I've doubted Thaddeus for a good long while."

Joseph and I were covered in blackberry juice. Stains were on my dress and on his shirt from where I dropped the bucket and we scooped the fallen berries back up. Ida would be mad as a wet hen when she saw our clothes. I was worried.

"If you and I go home with stains on our clothes Ida will know we've been together and will surely tell Thaddeus!"

"Don't worry, Green Eyes. There's an old shirt in the barn I can change into. Ida won't know the difference since all our shirts look the same," he said, and I was immediately relieved.

We lost a lot of blackberries when I dropped the bucket, but I didn't care. Joseph took my hand and held it as we started the walk back home. I liked the feel of his hand in mine; it felt right. We didn't exchange words as we were both lost in thought until it was time to part and for me to walk on alone.

Mamie

Joseph and I snuck off to the spring house in the early afternoon wanting to spend time alone together. Thaddeus had gone to the stockyard with the Elders and hadn't asked Joseph to go with him. It seemed to me, when Thaddeus was with the Elders, he didn't want his little brother anywhere around and that was fine with us.

Joseph and I thought we could get back into the house without Ida noticing, but we were wrong. She didn't say a word when she saw us slip through the front door. Sometimes I wondered what Ida knew, but didn't say.

Joseph and I barely spoke at meal times, and we dared not look at each other least we give ourselves away. The table was long and didn't make it easy to talk, even if anybody wanted to because of the two oil lamps sitting in the middle which I couldn't see over.

If Thaddeus ever caught on to Joseph and me, he might send me to live with another Believer family. Thaddeus wouldn't risk even the hint of me being soiled by any man, especially his own brother. No one would marry me then.

Ida was washing the breakfast dishes and I was drying them, when I got up my nerve to ask her what was on my mind.

"Ida, I've heard whispers about a girl being sent away who wasn't but fourteen. What happened to her?"

"Where did you hear that?"

"A few of the girls were whispering about it after school. They didn't know I was listening. They said she vanished in the night."

Ida looked at me skeptically. "That girl was sent away because she did not fight the nature of her desires. She disgraced her family and does not live in our community anymore. It's probably good you're thirteen and only have one year of schooling left, seeing you girls have nothing better to do than gossip. Go on now, and finish your housework."

I wanted to know more about the girl and what Ida knew about desire that she wasn't telling me. I often wondered what became of the girl, but Ida told me I didn't ever need to know.

I had finished my household work of dusting and cleaning and only had Thaddeus's room to clean when I heard Ida calling me from the kitchen. A folded up piece of paper was lying on the floor by Thaddeus's wardrobe. I could tell there was cursive writing on it and I became curious, so I picked it up and stuck it in my apron pocket, before going downstairs.

"Go find Thaddeus, and tell him we will be ready to eat soon. He's probably in the barn," Ida instructed me.

Thaddeus was standing in the shadows, when I walked toward Midnight's stall looking for him. He looked disheveled and sheepish like I had walked in on something.

"You know better than come to Midnight's stall. Stay right where you are." A change came over his countenance and a hardening in his eyes. I felt a hot stain of embarrassment on my cheeks as if I'd been caught doing something wrong.

"I don't mean to bother you or Midnight. I know you don't want us to have anything to do with him. He's your horse and I respect that. I just came to tell you it's time to eat."

"I'll be there directly. Go on back to the house," he said. I noticed then how dirty and callused his hands were, like he had been digging in the dirt.

The folded up paper was burning a hole in my apron pocked, wanting to be read, but I hadn't had the time or place to read the words.

After we finished the noon meal, I managed to whisper to Joe to meet me behind the outhouse as soon as he could.

"What's this about?" Joseph asked me, when I was finally able to get away and meet him.

"I found this on the floor in Thaddeus's bedroom, what do you make of it?" I said handing the note to him. I stood close enough to Joseph to read what was written as he unfolded the paper.

Our sin was a sickness I didn't plan on catching. No one knows it was you.

"I don't know what to make of it with no names or dates on the paper. You'd better put it back in Thaddeus's room if he should go looking for it."

"It's very strange, don't you think? The handwriting is cursive and it looks like a female wrote it. There's something else. Thaddeus was acting odd, even for him, when I went to tell him it was time to eat. I think there's something going on in Midnight's stall since Thaddeus won't let you in to shovel out manure, although you do it for the other two horses."

"You know Thaddeus doesn't like us paying attention to Midnight. He's mighty particular about that horse. I suppose it's because of his father giving it to him special. I don't want you getting into any trouble with him so promise me you'll stay away from the stall and put the note back in his room."

I didn't do as Joseph said. I kept the note. I wondered if it had anything to do with desire.

I wasn't going to let the story of the disgraced Believer girl stop me from being with Joseph. What if it was just a made up story anyway? I didn't have a way of knowing if it was true or not since no one would say who she was or where she went. Ida might be trying to fool me in case I had misbehaving in my mind.

I started calling Joseph Joe when we were alone. I liked the way it made my mouth pucker when I said it, like my lips were getting ready to be kissed. I loved it when Joe called me Green Eyes, like I had a special name only he knew.

26

Mamie

It was a hot summer day, and I was in the garden hoeing endless rows of weeds when Joe came up to me offering a tin cup of cold water from the spring house.

"Thank you, Joe. It sure is hot out here and it's not even noon yet. I suspect I'll have to quit soon," I said, taking large sips of the cold water into my parched throat.

Joe took the cup from me, then tilted my chin and forced me to look at him directly. He was seventeen and almost six foot to my five-foot one. His arms were muscular and shoulders broad from farm chores. There wasn't an ounce extra on him.

My face blushed red as garden peppers as I looked into his hazel eyes, which were brown with a touch of green and yellow. I had been watching him since we were small children and knew every feature of his changing face. He had a mix of freckles and pimples, but I could see the man he was becoming.

He dropped the tin cup to the ground and pulled me close. My heart was pounding when he lowered his head to mine and kissed me for the first time. It felt like a hundred butterflies were fluttering in my chest when our lips touched. When the kiss was finished, Joe looked into my eyes and I felt my knees go weak. I hoped I had kissed Joe right; I didn't want him to be disappointed.

Things changed between us. There was a yearning in his eyes when he looked at me, and I was sure the same look was in mine. Every chance we could take to be together we did, talking about what was in our hearts.

"I want opportunities, Mamie. Farming is too quiet for me. I'm not afraid of hard work if it's something I want to be doing. I asked Thaddeus why I should make next to nothing raising crops when what I really want to do is work in Rocky Mount or Roanoke, maybe driving a truck or working in a feed store. There are other ways of living life, and I'm not talking about the keys to the Kingdom!"

I couldn't believe what I was hearing. The way Joe was talking made my mind swim. Before long I was telling him about my desires to see more than the farm. I told Joe how I walked to the highest meadow and looked down on the non-believers' farms wondering what life was like inside their houses.

"Joe, I have to confess something. I've snuck into Thaddeus's room and looked around, just being nosy. Thaddeus has a geography book! He also has a book about animals in North America and another about American Indians. I didn't think Believers could have any books but the Bible, but he does! I've studied that geography book when I've had the chance and seen pictures of the ocean and sandy beaches. One day I want to see the ocean, to go in it and feel the waves. I want to feel the sand between my toes. Do you think you and I could go to the ocean someday?"

"Green Eyes, I promise you one day we'll go. I don't know how or when, but it will happen."

I liked hearing Joe's dreams, for he thought of things I never imagined. When Joe talked, I didn't feel like a young girl anymore, and everything felt possible.

Mamie

1945

I'll never forget the warm September morning Joe came up behind me, his hands circling my waist as he kissed my neck. I was in the hen house feeling for eggs in the straw. My breath caught in my throat, and I dropped the eggs I was holding.

"Joe, you startled me," I said, knowing my face had turned crimson.

"Let's you and me take a walk, I got something I want you to see. Meet me behind the sawmill in fifteen minutes," Joe said, squeezing my hand.

As we walked we saw the prettiest flowers blooming with bees buzzing all around them. The squirrels were talking plenty. We passed through the peach orchard and grabbed some ripe fruit, biting it, letting the juices run down our faces.

"Joe, do you think sin and grace bloom like summer flowers?"

"I don't think sin could ever be a flower, probably more of a weed," Joe said, smiling at me.

"The devil is tricky, Joe. I don't think you can ever know for sure."

We walked through the woods that adjoined our property and out the other side. Crossing from one field to the other I couldn't help but notice the daisies showing off their white-petalled dresses. I reached down to caress, but not pick, a few of their golden hearts.

"Joseph, do you think Thaddeus's heart is so narrow and hidden that nothing kind lives there?"

"I don't know, Mamie. You're asking some real tough questions today."

Lost in our thoughts, we walked in silence until Joe had us stop.

"I want you to see that house over yonder; it belongs to the Layman family," Joe said, pointing to a brick, two-story farmhouse in the distance.

"I met Mr. Layman when I went rabbit hunting in the holler between his place and ours. He was hunting, too. He darn near shot me by accident. We got to talking and he invited me back to his house. I helped him with a roof repair while I was there and he gave me this silver dollar," Joe said pulling the coin out of his pants pocket and handing it to me. "It's the first silver dollar I've ever owned. I bet it brings me good luck. I don't ever plan on spending it."

"It sure is pretty, Joseph. I don't have any money, not even a nickel," I said.

"I've squirreled a little away here and there. I've got twelve dollars nobody knows about but you. Sometimes at the market a non-believer will give me twenty-five cents for helping to unload a wagon. Thaddeus lets me keep the money hoping the non-believer will buy eggs or produce from our stall. I do what I can to earn a little money.

"There's something else, Green Eyes. When I'm working the cornfield on the far edge of the farm, I go over to the Layman's house when Thaddeus isn't with me. Mr. Layman and his wife aren't Believers, but they know a lot about us. They're real nice people. Sometimes I'm invited into the kitchen for a piece of pie or cake. I like seeing how other people live, people who aren't Believers."

"Thaddeus will be furious if he finds out what you are doing!" I said, alarmed at his words.

"I don't plan on that happening, and if it does, I'll deal with it then. I don't want to spend my life milking twice a day, clearing fields, planting corn and always being dependent on the fickleness of God and the weather. I want to build things with my own two hands or maybe drive a truck. I've been thinking on that. I can't talk to Thaddeus about any of this, but I can talk to Mr. Layman."

"Thaddeus always says life's lessons are learned by experience, and Believers only need God and each other. He thinks we don't need to deal with the outside world but I want to deal with the outside world, Mamie! I've heard Mr. and Mrs. Layman talk about politics, and I want to vote someday. Thaddeus says voting is choosing between two evils in the world, and it's up to God to put up or take down whoever he chooses for president, but I don't see it that way anymore. There's a war going on and Thaddeus won't even acknowledge it. I've seen the newspapers and listened to the radio at the Laymans. On August 6 our country dropped an atomic bomb on Hiroshima, Japan. I can't imagine how many people were killed. I'm seventeen years old and I have every right to know what's going on in the world."

"I'm worried you'll get into trouble with Thaddeus and the Elders. They might even send you away!"

"I'm learning about the outside world. It will be worth it one day, Green Eyes. I'm sure of it."

Mamie

1946

Winter came and the world seemed to settle down quiet. The tall evergreens and the beauty of newly fallen snow painted a gentle coat of white on the fields and the branches of trees. When the weather was cold like this, the only place Joe and I could meet was in the hayloft.

Brother Farley had come by the house and told Thaddeus and Ida a special prayer service had been called at the church and they needed to be there. Joe and I figured they would be gone for a while. We went to the barn as soon as they left and climbed to the hayloft, snuggling up in old quilts we had hidden in a barrel.

"I can't see the shape of you under that dress. I wouldn't ever dream of hurting you, but I'd like to feel you over your clothes. I won't do it unless it's alright with you, Green Eyes."

I wanted to reveal myself to Joe. Because of this hateful dress there was little of my flesh and bones for Joe to see. I wanted Joe to see if the changes that were happening to my body were normal. Joe would tell me the truth. Ida had said little to me when she noticed the bleeding on my undergarments when I turned thirteen.

"Ida told me I became a woman when the bleeding started, and the pain of cramps was part of a woman's lot in life. She said there was no use in complaining about it. She told me what to do about it, but she wouldn't talk about the changes in my body. Is what's happening to me normal Joe? There's nothing wrong with me is there?"

"You are more than normal, Mamie. You are beautiful and becoming more so each day," Joe said, looking at me like he really understood what I had been saying.

Joe explained what menstruation was. I didn't know how Joe knew, but he did. He explained about getting pregnant, but I knew about that by being around farm animals. It was hard to think about a man and woman doing that kind of thing.

After Joe had finished explaining the birds and the bees to me, he kissed me gentle like. It was different this time as it gave me flutters in my belly and shivers coursed through me. I felt myself flushing with heat and my body trembled. Joe ran his hands up and down my body over my dress. I touched him on his man parts, and Joe let out a little moan as the bulge in his britches grew big and hard. I was startled by what happened to Joe. He laughed gently.

"Don't worry, Green Eyes. What we're doing is normal between men and women. Nothing else is going to happen. I wouldn't ever do anything to hurt you."

When it was time to go, we got up and brushed the hay off one another. Something magical had happened between us. Until that day life had been predictable. One day soon there would be a fork in the road, and I could feel it coming. Thaddeus had been pressuring Joe to be baptized, but so far he had refused, saying he had too many questions and not enough answers.

"I don't want to become one of them, Green Eyes, but I'm not sure what I can do about it. Thaddeus won't put up with me delaying being baptized much longer. We've exchanged some serious words, but I will not buckle. Thaddeus wants to look good before the Elders, and here I am his little brother and almost eighteen and not baptized. I'm not ready to grow a beard and become an Elder like him, and I never will be. I'll leave this place first!"

"I'm worried, too, Joe. I know Thaddeus wants me to be baptized as well, but he's not pressuring me like he is you. I won't be baptized unless you decide to do it, too. What are we going to do, Joe?"

"I don't know Green Eyes, but I'll think of something."

That night I dreamed Joe and I left the Believers together. I awakened and couldn't go back to sleep. Joe had to take me away with him, and I had to make sure it happened.

Mamie

The wind was whistling outside; and the last of the leaves would soon be carried away. Bare fields stretched out, colored yellow by harvested corn. A faint light had filtered through the kitchen window. It was a sad light and made me want to cry. I hadn't seen Tabby and Clover, the barn cats for days and I was worried.

"Don't fret so over those cats. You shouldn't be treating them like pets, they have their jobs to do and so do you. They'll be back soon, wait and see. Now go on and do your work. I want the chicken house and the outhouse cleaned out today." Ida said, as she mended clothes from the rocking chair.

It was late afternoon before I could go to the barn to look for Tabby and Clover. The smell of the pans of milk left untouched, told me they had been gone for days.

I was surprised when I saw Thaddeus asleep, curled up in the hay, with his mouth open. He had been at breakfast, but not come home for the noon meal. Maybe he was sick, I thought, so I gently bent over and touched his arm. A shiver ran to the roots of my hair, when he reached out and stroked my face with his black-gloved hand. I couldn't help but notice the smell that came off of him, or the redness of his eyes.

"What are you doing lurking in the barn, girl. You have no business being here this time of day," he said, with something in his voice I did not recognize.

"I'm looking for Tabby and Clover. I haven't seen them for a while."

"You will not find them here. Bend down here girl, and assist me up."

Thaddeus was unsteady in his legs. I had never seen him this way. As he leaned against me, I noticed what looked to be golden fur through the loose straw.

"There's Tabby, she was asleep right next to you, Thaddeus, and you didn't even know." A frightful silence passed between us as I uncovered the straw. Thaddeus's eyes locked into mine. He knew what I had seen and dared me not to say a word.

I felt the bile rising in my throat as I ran out of the barn, not quite making it to the outhouse, when I began retching up the contents within my stomach. In my head was a strange confusion. Something unknown, yet familiar about Thaddeus had been revealed. Tabby's neck had been broken.

Mamie

I lost count of the bushels of apples that had been picked from our orchard over the past few days. I was tired of picking apples but the good part was I got to do it with Joe when I wasn't washing, slicing, coring and peeling apples with Ida. I loved the beauty of the apple trees in blossom but sure didn't like all the apples that came later.

Thaddeus had peach and apple orchards on the farm as did other Believers. Families helped each other pick the ripe fruit. The Sisters made preserves and canned what they could, and the rest were sold. Keeping an eighty acre farm running was hard work when you were raising a small herd of beef cattle and had several acres of wheat and corn to plant and harvest.

Braving the chill of the early October air, the Sisters were sitting and stirring the simmering contents in the large copper kettle over the open fire when Thaddeus and I arrived at the church. I hadn't wanted to ride over with him since the incident in the barn the day before but he insisted. Neither one of us said a word, but the tension could have been cut with a knife. I wished Joe was with us, but Thaddeus had him in the orchard picking the last of the apples.

The cool weather had put color in the women's cheeks and the girls who were old enough to help were sitting with their mothers. Ida had arrived earlier, and was feeding apples into the kettle, keeping it full, while the Sisters took turns stirring the mixture so it didn't stick. The smell of the cooking apples made my mouth water. I always liked making apple butter with the Sisters and the other girls.

"Thaddeus, you can sit the apples you brought right over there," Sister Clara said, pointing to a spot near the kettle.

"I'll go collect the rest of the apples and be back directly," Thaddeus said, walking back to the wagon.

"It takes three bushels of apples to make a stir and the men are bringing more as we speak. It looks like you brought ripe, soft apples, Mamie," Sister Mary said. "You and Ida did a fine job cutting them up." I liked hearing her praise since I never got any at home.

"It won't be long before we'll all be helping each other with the hog killing but I reckon that comes with life on a farm. It's a good thing we have each other to help out," Sister Flora said to the other Sisters.

"Mamie, I brought some kittens to give away. They're in a box in the church. Why don't you go pick you one out?" Sister Clara asked me.

Thaddeus was carrying up a bushel of cut up apples when he heard what Sister Clara said. Sitting down the basket he placed his hand on the back of my neck and squeezed.

"We aren't in any need of a barn cat, Sister Clara. Don't you agree Mamie?" All I could do was nod but the pressure of Thaddeus's hand on my neck made me recoil.

That evening, at supper, Joe could tell I was upset. My hands were shaking and I didn't say a word. Thaddeus kept staring at me, but I kept my head down as best I could.

Joe followed me when I went to the outhouse. "I can tell something has happened between you and Thaddeus. Tell me what it is."

"I can't tell you, Joe. It's between Thaddeus and me," I said, wanting to wipe the memories out of my mind.

"I'm alright, tired more than anything. I'll be better in the morning." I didn't like lying to Joe but I needed to protect him from Thaddeus's wrath.

"I'm going to get to the bottom of this, Green Eyes. I can tell he's done something to hurt you."

Joe stormed into the barn looking for Thaddeus and I followed behind him.

"Thaddeus, I want to talk to you. Something happened between you and Mamie and I want to know what it is!"

Thaddeus came out of Midnight's stall and walked over to us. Putting his hand on my shoulder, he let it rest too long. "We had a little misunderstanding but everything has been set right. Isn't that so, Mamie?" Once again, I nodded.

"I know there is more to this than both of you are letting on, but I can't make Mamie talk if she doesn't want to. You had better not do anything to hurt her, or you'll have me to deal with," Joe said, warning Thaddeus.

Walking out of the barn door with Joe, I heard Thaddeus laughing.

Ida

"You are wrong to send Mamie away. You need to reconsider this, Thaddeus. Is this why you came to the cellar to tell me this, so no one can overhear?" I let my words come gushing out.

"You cannot order me about, Ida. I am doing what is best for this family. I have already told Mamie she is leaving."

"She's done nothing wrong. By sending her away all will believe she has done something shameful, and she has not. She will be disgraced and it could be the ruin of her," I said, trying my best to convince him to let her stay.

"She is not our flesh and blood. I owe her nothing."

"Tell me what Mamie did, Thaddeus, for you to treat her this way," I said, gripping a wash board close to my chest.

"I have only just decided. I will be making the arrangements this afternoon. The sooner she leaves here the better."

"Does Joseph know about this?"

"This is no concern of his."

"Thaddeus, think of our parents. They would never do such a thing as this." I said with my voice raised, and my body trembling.

"I will not discuss this any further, Ida. I didn't mean for this information to upset you so. After the noon meal, I will be leaving but will be back before dark."

I stayed in the cellar sobbing as I finished running the wet laundry through the wringer.

How dare Thaddeus send Mamie off like she was a dog or a mule. He never was one to listen to reason and I knew my pleading had fallen on deaf ears. Wiping the tears from my eyes, I climbed the cellar stairs. It wouldn't do Mamie any good to see me upset.

Mamie was sweeping the porch, looking somewhat dazed, when I found her.

"Mamie, what has happened? Please tell me if you know," I asked.

"Thaddeus knocked on my bedroom door before the sun was up and told me to pack my satchel; that I would be leaving here tomorrow before breakfast. Thank you for caring for me, Ida, I will miss you and Joseph."

I could tell by looking at Mamie, she was seething inside as was I. This was cold and mean even for Thaddeus. Mamie was family and she had done no wrong.

Mamie

J oe had to be told I was being sent away. It was early yet and I still had chores to do before Ida could start breakfast. Standing by the hen house, I scattered feed, talking soft and low to the chickens. *What am I going to do? I don't even know where I'm being sent to live. Why does Thaddeus hate me so, I haven't done anything to him.* I wanted to tell Ida and Joe about Tabby and Clover, but Thaddeus would call me a liar and take me before the Elders. I had seen the look in his eyes, and thought him capable of anything so I had said nothing to them.

My hands were shaking when I went to the barn for milk. Thaddeus wasn't in Midnight's stall so I had a few minutes to talk to Joe undisturbed. I couldn't help but notice how the birds had been roosting and digging holes in the straw stacks and the mice had gotten into the feed since there were no barn cats to stop them. Thaddeus would never be allowed to be an Elder in the church if it was known what he had done. Mistreating animals was not tolerated among Believers for they were God's creatures, much less killing. I wouldn't mind saying farewell to Thaddeus or Ida if Joe was going with me; leaving him behind would be worse than chopping off my legs.

"Joe, I've something to tell you and I want you to stay quiet until I'm done." I said, handing him the empty milk bucket.

"What's wrong, Green Eyes? Are you ill?"

"Thaddeus is sending me away tomorrow and he won't say where. I can no longer live here. I have more to tell you but I don't want to be overheard."

"What do you mean he's sending you away," Joe said, turning red with rage.

"Joe, calm down as best you can, at least until after we can talk. I don't want to make things worse. Hopefully you and I can come up with something. Please don't let Thaddeus get the best of you at breakfast. He's going to goad you into fighting with him. Don't let him do it. Promise me you won't. It will only make him look right in sending me off."

"I can't promise anything, Green Eyes. I want to beat the tar out of him and I just might."

"Meet me this afternoon at the willow tree. We need time alone so I can tell you more."

"I'll be there Green Eyes, won't nothing be able to stop me."

Sitting at the breakfast table, Joe stared hopelessly at the eggs and fried potatoes Ida had prepared. "Is something bothering you, Joseph?" Thaddeus asked. Joe glared at him hard and said not a word. He kept his promise to me.

The morning crept along ever so slowly as I waited for the right time to steal away from the house. Thaddeus finally took off on Midnight, and said not a word of where he was going. It was the hottest hour of the day when I ran through the woods and fields, with the folded paper in my pocket. Ida didn't try to stop me from leaving. I'm sure she knew I was meeting Joe. The willow tree was on a far off field where we couldn't be seen. I arrived winded and out of breath. Joe was waiting for me.

"I can't let you go, Mamie. There must be something we can do to stop this," Joe said, as he held me close.

"Surely there is," I whispered. "I might have a way."

"You are leaving tomorrow, Mamie. We have to do something now!"

The evening meal was eaten in silence. A feeling of doom caused none of us to look up from our plates. I retreated to my bedroom having not eaten a bite. I was restless and knew sleep would be impossible. When the house was quiet I tiptoed down the creaky stairs carrying a candle and a box of wooden matches. The night was still and the plow horses stayed quiet, except for Midnight, who let out an impatient neighing, as I entered his stall.

"Whoa, steady there," I said trying to sooth him. "What goes on in here, Midnight, can you tell me?" By candle light I searched the stall. Nothing seemed out of place. Frantically I felt among the shadows, but found nothing. Thaddeus's overalls were handing on a hook. Searching the pockets I found two mother-of-pearl buttons. They were unlike the buttons, Ida used in sewing. Ida said they were too fancy, but a few of the Sisters used them on their dresses even if it was vanity.

Climbing the old wooden ladder into the hayloft, I sat down and tried to make myself think clearly. Running my fingers over the buttons, I wondered whose they had been. How did they end up in a pocket in Thaddeus's overalls? I felt on the verge of collapse. All of this was due to Thaddeus's cruelty. If my plan failed, I wanted to die.

The next morning Thaddeus had hitched the horse and buggy to take me away. Ida and Joe were standing in the yard watching him in disbelief.

"Get in the wagon, girl. It's time to go," he said, without looking at me.

"Let Mamie eat breakfast before she goes," Ida pleaded with her older brother.

"Thaddeus, before you leave there is something you need to hear. Mamie, come stand beside me." Joe's face was hard as stone as he spoke.

In unison Joe and I repeated with as much authority as we could muster what we had practiced under the willow tree.

"Our sin was a sickness I didn't want to catch. No one knows it was you." Then I held the note up so Thaddeus could see it and let it fall to the ground.

Reaching my hand into my apron pocket, I pulled out a mother-of-pearl button and placed in my palm. Joe walked toward Thaddeus showing him the button I had given him just moments earlier.

"Recognize these?" Joseph asked.

Thaddeus's face turned a ghostly white. Our bluffing had worked.

Joseph took my satchel out of the wagon. Thaddeus unhitched Mid-

night and retreated to his stall.
    I wasn't going anywhere.

Mamie

1947

It was Joseph's nineteenth birthday, and the azaleas were blooming. Believers didn't celebrate birthdays. I thought this was wrong. Joe had told me how non-believers celebrated. He had been at the Laymans and seen the birthday cake and presents for the party Mrs. Layman had for her husband earlier in the year.

I packed a picnic, knowing Joe was busy picking vegetables to take to market. Tomorrow Ida and I would start canning food for winter. I didn't like standing over the hot wood stove for hours preserving green beans, tomatoes and everything else we grew. I'd rather be in the garden picking beans.

Today I was going to take Joe to his surprise birthday place. Ida wouldn't miss me for several hours. She was helping Sister Frith with canning, and then she was going to a meeting at the church.

When I cooked supper the night before, I put back a couple biscuits, two pieces of chicken, and two eggs from a jar of pickle juice before I served everybody their food so I would have something for today. I didn't have any cake, but had a bit of honey to put on the biscuits to make them sweet. I gathered a towel, some clothing items, and put them into my sewing satchel.

"Mamie, I'm letting you stay home because you say you're having heavy cramping because of your woman time. I expect you to have dinner done by time I get back just the same," Ida told me.

Thaddeus would be at a council meeting. The meetings could take all day, depending on what had to be discussed. Thaddeus was being allowed to more meetings as he was growing in favor with the Elders. He tried not to show his pleasure, but I could tell he was proud, and being proud was a sin. I was glad Thaddeus had more meetings. I was uncomfortable around him. I didn't like how his eyes followed me. Today no one would be around to see me and Joseph take off to the creek.

I had been practicing for this moment in my mind over and over again so everything would go right. I wanted to do something special for Joe on his birthday. Something he would always remember.

"I have a surprise for you and you must do exactly as I say and don't ask any questions," I said, surprising Joe in the garden and taking his hand.

When we got to the bank of the creek I made Joe close his eyes. When I told him he could open them, I had taken off my bonnet and was undoing my braids. Joe's eyes never left me as my hair fell low and loose around my shoulders. I had taken off my undergarments before I left the house and had nothing on but my oldest and thinnest gray dress.

I walked into the water and indicated for Joe to follow me. As I did, I unbuttoned the top buttons of my dress, so the swell of my breasts showed. I turned around and looked at Joe. He came forward, took me in his arms, placed his hand on the small of my back, and lowered me into the water as I asked him to do.

Raising my legs, I let myself float as I gently pulled my dress so it came up high on my legs. My crown of glory floated around my head in the currents as my nipples, cold from the water, pushed against the thin gray fabric of my clinging garment. Joe pulled me up, and as he did, I placed my arms around his neck and kissed him slowly and deeply. He didn't pull away. I knew he wouldn't.

Leaving the water, we lay on the creek bank looking at each other as if for the first time. We stayed that way for as long as we dared, exploring each other in body, heart, and words.

"Thaddeus wants me to do farm chores twelve hours a day, if I'm lucky. He's never satisfied. I don't want to take over the farm someday. In fact, Green Eyes, I don't want to be a Believer. Mr. Layman has been a good friend to me. We talk about all kinds of things when I can sneak away. I try to do little things for him in his house, so no one will see me and he insists on giving me a little money for it. I'll never be able to accept the Believers and all their rules. I've listened to the radio and seen the telephone at the Layman's house, and I don't see harm in any of it. I want to live in modern times."

How had Joe gotten away with all this and not gotten caught, and to be with a non-believer at that! Joe got me thinking I didn't want to be a Believer either. I wouldn't have to wear this stupid dress and bonnet my whole life. I wanted to live the rest of my life with Joe.

We had stayed away as long as we dared. Standing, I took off my wet and clinging dress and stood naked before him.

"My God, Green Eyes, you're so beautiful. If only you knew how beautiful." Joe stood and held me in his arms. His male part was hard and pressed against me.

"We better go, Joe. It's getting late." I pulled away from him taking a gray dress and undergarments from my sewing satchel and putting my wet dress into the bag.

I combed my hair out and put my bonnet back on. It was time I got to the house and started supper. I needed to light the stove and get the potatoes peeled for the meal to be ready on time. Joe and I clung to each other and kissed before we started back.

"Thank you, Green Eyes. I can't believe what you did for me today. I'll never forget. I promise one day we'll have more times like this, and we won't have to worry about Thaddeus."

I felt a huge lump in my throat when we parted. Joe left before me and went back to the garden to work like any ordinary day.

The table was set and the meal almost ready when Ida and Thaddeus got home. Ida kept her eyes downcast as she walked through the kitchen door.

Joe came in from the garden and washed up for supper. We pretended like nothing had happened between us. We were good at keeping secrets. Joe and I seldom spoke to each other in the house as not to raise any suspicions of our feelings for one another.

Thaddeus took his seat at the head of the table. Joe and Ida took their places as I went about serving them. Thaddeus said the meal time prayer as I stood with my head bowed. The prayer wasn't as long as usual, when Thaddeus cleared his throat as if he had something else to say.

"It's time, Mamie," Thaddeus said as I placed his food in front of him.

"Time for what?" I asked, as my knees wobbled and my breathing stopped.

"For you and I to marry. I was given approval at the special council meeting today. It's time for me to start a family of my own. I have prayed and gotten a message from the Almighty One to marry you."

I stood there cold as stone and couldn't utter a word. My worst fears were upon me, but only worse. I was to marry Thaddeus, Joe's brother. This couldn't be happening! Joe's eyes were full of pain and misery. He knew better than to speak. It would only make things worse.

Thaddeus hadn't asked me if I wanted to marry him or not. In fact, he didn't look at me or say another word while he ate his pork chops and greens. Ida's eyes never left her plate as she moved her food around with her fork. I wondered what she was thinking, what she might know, but wasn't saying. I made myself get through supper, although I couldn't force down a bite. While clearing the table and washing the dishes, I felt as if I might pass out before making it to my room. There had to be a way out of this; there had to be.

I paced the floor in my bedroom wanting to die. My head was spinning. I couldn't marry Thaddeus. It was after nine when I heard rocks pelting against the side of the house. Looking outside, I saw Joe making motions for me to open the window.

"Mamie, get a few things together and meet me at the edge of the woods quick as you can. We're leaving!" Joe said, and then he was gone.

I crawled out my bedroom window on the second floor. Luckily, the tree beside my window had strong branches. I threw down the pillow case that held nothing more than my hairbrush, nightgown, and toothbrush. I wanted to leave everything behind, but I did as Joe said.

I ran toward Joe as fast as I could, throwing myself in his arms when we met. We ran through the woods and fields, arriving at the Layman's house tired and out of breath. The Laymans ushered Joe and me into their house.

Mrs. Layman had us sit at the kitchen table and gave us a glass of ice tea before she began to speak. "Mamie, we feel like we know you from the things Joe has told us, and we're willing to do for you kids what we can."

"Why are you willing to help us?" I asked, looking at the couple. Mr. Layman placed his hands on my shoulders and looked deep into my eyes before speaking.

"We have some experience with Believers. It's not a life for everyone born into it. Joe is a fine boy and deserves a chance to be his own man. If you're sure you want to leave the Believers and be Joe's wife, we'll help you. If not, you better speak up now, girl, and I'll take you home."

"I've never been surer of anything in my life." Mrs. Layman smiled when I said this.

"Well, if everybody is in agreement with what we're about to do, my wife and I will drive you to a motel on Williamson Road in Roanoke we know about. Tomorrow you can go to the courthouse and get a marriage license. Here's thirty dollars to help with the expenses. We want you to consider it a wedding gift," Mr. Layman said, pressing money into Joe's hand.

"You have to agree to get married as soon as possible. Otherwise we wouldn't be doing this," Mrs. Layman piped in.

"Before I forget, let me give you the phone number of someone who can help you. Levi Ferguson is a good man and a friend of mine. We fought in the war together, and I think you kids have a lot in common with him. I'll call Levi and explain everything to him tonight. He'll be expecting to hear from you in the morning. Now let's get going before it gets any later," Mr. Layman said as he wrote the number down and handed it to Joe.

We walked out of the kitchen to the shed. "This sure is a nice car. I've never seen anything like it," I said climbing into the backseat.

"It's a 1940 Ford. One day you and I might have a car just like this one," Joe said, getting into the car behind me. I'd never been in a car before, only Thaddeus's old truck. We drove for almost an hour without anyone speaking much. I couldn't think of any words to go with what I was feeling. Joe put his arm around me and held me tight during the drive. I was excited, but scared, but my Joe would know what to do.

Getting out of the car in front of a green cinderblock motel with a vacancy sign in the window, Joe and Mr. Layman shook hands.

"Good luck, you two. Look in on us when you are settled in your new life," Mr. Layman said as his wife gave me a long hug. The Laymans stayed outside with the car running until we were registered in the motel, then they drove away.

The clerk behind the desk, a fat older man with big lips and greased back hair, looked at us funny. I remember thinking he had probably never seen people like us checking into a motel. He handed us the room key after Joe paid him six dollars and we found our room, 112, on the backside of the motel. Joe opened the door and checked out the room before he let me come in, then, taking me by the hand, he led me into the room, closing the door behind us. The walls were dingy and the carpet dirty, but I didn't care. I was with Joe, and no one would find us here.

For a while Joe and I sat on the edge of the bed just looking at each other and not speaking, then Joe got to his feet, pulling me up with him. Slowly he unbuttoned my dress. He took his time undoing my undergarments and let them fall to the floor. He stood there staring at me, a soft expression on his face as if he was under a spell, then he was kissing me with parted lips. My desire became so strong I couldn't breathe as I undressed Joe. Gently Joe picked me up, cradling me in his arms, and laid me in the bed, then climbed in beside me.

The next morning, as I lay awake watching Joe, I noticed there were no pictures on the walls. Our clothes were strewn all over the room and the bedspread lay in a heap on the floor. There was blood on the sheets from what we had done. I know we should have gotten married first, but as far as I was concerned we already were, running off the way we did. I hoped Joe and I wouldn't have to pay money to buy new sheets.

I got up and pulled open the drapes. I should have been exhausted but I wasn't even tired. I couldn't believe what Joe and I had done. We had slid away from the Believers. Looking back, we were little more than children.

Mamie

Joe called Levi Ferguson as soon as he woke. Joe had seen Mr. Layman use a phone, but never used one himself. It took some figuring out, but it wasn't long before we got it to work. It wasn't but a couple of hours when Mr. Ferguson and his wife, Violet, came and picked us up in their car and took us to the courthouse to get our marriage license.

By late morning we arrived at the Ferguson's home, which was run down with peeling paint. I could see there was an outhouse in the back yard and a water pump on the front porch.

"Welcome to our home. Come on in and take a seat at the kitchen table while I fix us coffee and something to eat. You must be hungry by now." Violet smiled warmly as she spoke to us.

I was glad to see they had electricity. The kitchen was pretty, with lace curtains on the windows and a red and white checkered tablecloth on the table. Pictures of flowers and mountains hung on the walls and a quilt was folded over the sofa.

Violet made coffee, biscuits, and scrambled eggs for us, although I couldn't eat a single bite, there were so many thoughts racing through my head. Joe managed to eat his fill and then some. As I recall, we spent a long time in the kitchen talking.

"Jimmy Layman and I had a long talk last night. He's a good fellow and feels bad for you kids. He told me everything he knew about your situation. I'm glad he called me. Violet and I want to help," Levi said as Violet nodded in agreement.

"What Jimmy Layman didn't tell you was I used to be a Believer myself."

I knew my jaw dropped when he said this.

"Do you know Thaddeus and Ida?" I asked.

"I knew their parents from church meetings mostly. Thaddeus was always a different one and hard to get to know. It seemed he wanted to be just like his father, always preaching, and being important. I only knew Ida to nod to her."

"Would you mind telling us why you left the Believers?" Joe asked, with a look of amazement.

"You don't have a beard either," I said without thinking. Levi smiled at us.

"After the military I decided to stay clean shaven. Violet prefers me this way," Levi laughed and continued to talk.

"When I was a young man there were rumblings and talks of war. I snuck off to Rocky Mount every chance I got and bought newspapers and magazines. I read everything I could to learn about what was going on in the world. It wasn't long before I became outspoken with the Believers, telling them it was alright for us to defend our country even if it meant fighting. As you can well imagine, the Elders were not happy with me.

"When Pearl Harbor was bombed in 1941, I couldn't sit back and let others do all the fighting. I had neither wife nor children to leave behind, so I enlisted in the Marine Corps. It was hard telling my folks what I had done. I knew I broke their hearts, but it was something I had to do. When the Elders came to dissuade me, I had second thoughts, but it was too late; I had signed up. Believers don't join the military, much less fight. I knew I was leaving behind the only life I had ever known and I felt sad about that. I did my share of fighting in the Pacific and got wounded in Guadalcanal. That's how I lost my leg. That's the short version of my story and why Jimmy Layman called me about you two."

"I can't imagine how hard that was for you to do. Did you ever go back and see your family?" I asked.

"Only twice. My parents and I sat on the porch and tried to talk, but the distance between us was too great. Mama cried when she saw my leg was gone. After that I figured it was for the best I stayed away, and my father agreed. Besides, I have all the family I need with Violet. I met her in the Maywood Restaurant. She was the prettiest thing I'd ever seen with her smiling dimples and wavy brown hair, pretty as a picture she was and still is." His eyes twinkled and his hand reached out to cover hers.

"Violet didn't make any comments about my missing a leg; she treated me like any other man, and I sure appreciated that," he said.

"I never would have met Levi if he hadn't left that church, so I'm glad he did. He never tried to get me to join the Believers. I'm a backsliding Baptist through and through. I thought Levi was real handsome the first morning he sat at the counter and ordered his breakfast from me. The Maywood is close to his house and he needed someplace to eat. We have good coffee, pie, and a blue plate special, so Levi kept coming in."

"That's not the only reason I came in, Violet, and you can't be telling Joe and Mamie it was!"

Violet let out a big laugh. "Levi Ferguson, you're a good man and that's why I love you. I'm sorry to break up this conversation, with it getting interesting, but we have to get a move on if we're going to get you kids married tomorrow. I have the perfect blue dress for you to wear, Mamie, because that dress and bonnet you're wearing will never do. Levi, go find something Joe can wear. We can't have them getting married looking the way they do now."

Violet took me to the bedroom she shared with Levi and sat me down at her vanity. She brushed my hair out long, then pinned it back on the sides with pretty clips. I felt awkward having her do this for me. I don't recall anyone brushing my hair except maybe Ida when I was small.

"I'm going to put a touch of pink lipstick on your pretty face and a little mascara. Oh, girl, that looks so good on you. Let me get the dress now," Violet said while removing it from her closet.

"I married Levi in this dress back when I was a size nine. Now I'm a healthy fourteen. Levi never says anything about the weight I've gained. He knows when to stay quiet. That's why I love him."

Violet helped me get out of my Believer dress.
"Child, you don't have a brassiere on!" she said with an amazed look.

"The way the dresses are made with the big collars, we don't wear one. They would have to be store bought," I said, blushing crimson.

"We have to do something about your black shoes and stockings. I think we should throw them out they're so ugly," Violet said holding a shoe in each hand.

I couldn't help but laugh because I felt the same way. I couldn't believe I was standing before this woman with nothing on but my underwear and cotton slip. I felt modest in front of Violet, but for some reason it was alright and I didn't feel ashamed.

"I'm glad I didn't get rid of my clothes when I outgrew them," Violet said as she pulled a large suitcase out from under the bed.

"Let's go through this and pull out what will work for you," she said, unzipping it.

"Well, look here. A brassiere! And here are the matching shoes to the dress. Try them on, Mamie."

I slipped on the high heels she offered me and the brassiere.

"It looks like we're going to have to stuff toilet paper into the brassiere and the shoes," Violet laughed.

"I don't know if I can walk in these," I said, taking a few steps and stumbling.

"With a little practice, you'll be just fine. Try walking around the room," Violet said.

In a few minutes, I was able to walk in a straight line. Violet helped me into the blue dress and zipped it in the back. It fit perfectly, although it barely covered my knees.

"I've been keeping this dress for something special and here it is. In case no one has ever told you before, you're a beauty with those high cheekbones and cat eyes. No wonder Joe is smitten by you. Now go look at yourself in the mirror on the bedroom door."

I could barely believe it was me in the pretty dress with my blonde hair lying soft and long around my shoulders.

When I walked into the kitchen Joe about fell onto the floor.
"Mamie, is that you? You look like a full grown woman!"

Everybody laughed hard, including me. Joe and I didn't look like the same people at all. Joe had on a new plaid shirt of Levi's and a pair of brown pants that were two inches too short. He never looked more handsome.

"I bought that shirt for Levi two years ago. It's been hanging unworn in his closet since then. He won't wear anything but a blue shirt or a white one. I guess that shirt was just waiting for you, Joe.

"Since you and Mamie are outfitted for the wedding in the morning, we'd better plan the rest of the day. Levi and I have some regular clothes you two can wear until you can afford your own. Right now we have to see about your blood tests. You can't get married without them," Violet said.

"I've never had blood drawn. Won't it hurt?" I asked.

"Nothing to it," Levi said.

"But why do we need it? What's it got to do with getting married?"

Violet took me to the bedroom and told me why. I couldn't believe the things she was saying. Levi was in the kitchen explaining the need for a blood test to Joe. Believers never got a blood test, but then they didn't get married at the courthouse either.

Getting blood drawn wasn't so bad. Joe looked like he would faint when they took his, which made me laugh a little, but only to myself. Violet and Levi took us into a grocery store afterwards where Violet purchased food for dinner. I had never seen so many canned goods in all my life.

Violet made a nice roast and we had biscuits that came out of a can. Violet had to tap it on the edge of the sink before it popped open, then she baked them. They were good, too! We sat up until nine o'clock talking, then Violet told me I needed to get my beauty sleep.

That night I slept in the guest bedroom in one of Violet's flannel nightgowns while Joe slept on the fold-out couch. I was restless thinking about the events of the last two days. I wanted Joe to hold me in his arms, but I could wait. After tomorrow, we'd be married and all would be different. Joe and I would be together always.

Mamie

The next morning Violet came into my bedroom with a breakfast tray of coffee, juice, toast, and eggs. "After you're finished eating I'll help you get cleaned up and ready for your wedding day. Yesterday was just a dress rehearsal. Plus, I was told to keep you occupied as Levi and Joe are up to something," Violet said as she smiled at me.

After eating, and a trip to the outhouse, Violet fixed my hair and makeup.

"I'm so glad we tried on the wedding clothes yesterday and everything fit you so good. We wouldn't have had time to get everything ready otherwise," Violet said, as she sprayed me with *Tabu Perfume*.

"You look beautiful, Mamie. I guess we can go see what the boy's have been up to now," Violet said, ushering me out the bedroom door.

Joe and Levi were sitting at the kitchen table with big grins.

"You have a surprise, Mamie. Wait until you see our car! Violet insisted on decorating it, so it's all her idea. Joe and I just did what we were told to do by a bossy woman!" Levi grinned.

Levi and Joseph had tied tin cans to the back of the car and written *just married* in shaving cream on the side windows while Violet helped me dress. I had never seen such a thing before, and it made me giggle so hard I couldn't stop.

"There's no use in waiting. Everybody get in. We have a wedding to get to!" Violet said, and I was still laughing.

Levi drove us to a florist on the way to the courthouse. Joe and Violet went inside, leaving Levi and me in the car. When Joe came back, he was carrying red and white flowers with a cloth band around them.

"It's just beautiful, Joe. I've never seen anything like it before."

"It's called a corsage, and the flowers are carnations," Joe said, looking happy and proud.

"Let me pin it onto your dress," Violet said when she came around to my side of the car.

"Now doesn't that look pretty on you? I'll help you press the flowers later so you'll have a keepsake from your wedding," Violet offered.

"I'd like that, Violet. I never want to forget anything about my wedding day."

Everybody tooted their horns as Levi drove us to the courthouse. Violet and Levi stood proudly as our witnesses as Joe and I took our vows before the Justice of the Peace.

Going down the courthouse steps, Violet and Levi threw rice at us. People we didn't know were waving, smiling, and yelling congratulations. Joe and I were married!

Mamie

Violet and Levi took Joe and me to the Maywood Restaurant after our wedding. Violet and Levi spent time talking to the man who owned the restaurant so we couldn't hear. He looked to be a good friend of theirs.

"We'll be back to pick you up in a little less than two hours," Levi told us.

"I thought you were going to stay and eat with us," I said, looking first to Violet, then to Levi.

"A bride and groom need to have time alone. Besides we're leaving you in good hands," Violet said, kissing me on the cheek.

She didn't think I saw the big wink she gave to the owner just before they walked out the door.

The owner, who introduced himself as Harry, took us to a booth in the back of the restaurant and gave us menus to look at. Neither Joe nor I had ever been in a restaurant before. We didn't need to worry because Violet and Levi must have told Harry about us. He made suggestions for our dinner. I ordered meatloaf, green beans, and potatoes. Joe ordered pot roast, carrots, and potato salad. We each had two forks, a water glass and sweet tea. The waitress kept coming by, smiling at us and asking if we needed anything else as she refilled our glasses. Joe and I grinned at each other when our food came.

"You look so pretty, Green Eyes, I like seeing you so happy."

"We've gone and done it, Joe. There's no going back now." I shuddered thinking about what would happen to us if we did.

"This is the way it was meant to be for us." Joe reached out and squeezed my hand.

"I'm glad I'm your wife, Joe. It could have been so different if you hadn't met Mr. Layman."

"Let's not think about that. Today is our first day as a married couple and I don't want us spoiling it with unpleasant thoughts."

"This is where Levi met Violet. He must have come in and sat at the front lunch counter we walked by. Now here we are, you and me. Don't you think it's romantic, Joe?"

"There's been enough happened in the last two days, that's for sure. It makes me think God is smiling on us."

People continued coming into the restaurant, and it seemed almost full. I couldn't believe folks lived like this, with other people doing the cooking and serving. When the meal was over, I thought I should get up and help clear the table, but the waitress just laughed and smiled.

"It's alright honey, I'll do that, you just sit back with that good looking husband of yours." She acted like what I had done was real funny, though she didn't say so. I just wanted to be helpful.

I thought Harry was coming back to talk to us but instead he stood in the middle of the restaurant and clicked his glass with a spoon.

"Everyone, I have a special announcement. We don't often have two young people dining with us straight from getting hitched at the court-house. If you would, please raise your glasses to the bride and groom, Joseph and Mamie Simpkins! Let's toast to the newlyweds for a long, healthy, and prosperous life!"

Everyone took a sip of their beverage, cheered, and clapped for us, then our waitress came forward with the biggest piece of coconut cake I'd ever seen.

"Feed him a piece of cake, honey, then let him feed you," our waitress said, and that was what we did. I never felt so happy. As people left the restaurant, they stopped by our table to congratulate us. It didn't seem any time had passed before Levi was back to get us.

Violet and Levi had been busy fixing up their bedroom for us to spend our wedding night. The room was real pretty, with burning candles and flowers I knew came from Violet's front yard. The bed was made up with a different quilt from earlier in the day; this one had the wedding ring pattern. Beside the bed was a water pitcher and basin. There were little packets called Trojans there, too. Joe said he knew what they were for when I asked. Violet and Levi insisted on staying in the other bedroom for our first night together as husband and wife. Joe and I protested, but gave in.

The next morning Violet knocked on our door. "I'll give you a few minutes to get decent, then Levi and I are coming in. There's no need for you to get out of the bed." I was confused by what she said.

"We need to follow the lady's instructions," Joe said, smiling at me.

Violet and Levi came into the bedroom carrying a breakfast tray of pancakes with blueberry syrup, orange juice, and coffee. More flowers were on the tray.

"Oh, this is so nice. Come in and talk to us," I said.

"Not a chance, young lady. We just wanted you two to have a little sustenance. We'll see you at dinner time." Levi and Violet left the room, shutting the door behind them. I heard Violet and Levi laughing through the closed door. We didn't leave that room all day except for a couple of trips to the outhouse.

Joe and I stayed on with Levi and Violet at their insistence.

"We have a spare room, and we like your company. This isn't forever, just until Joe gets a job and you two get your feet on the ground. Besides, one day you two will have little ones, and there's sure not room enough for all that, not that I would mind one little bit." Violet grinned from ear to ear.

Mamie

1948

When Violet and I were alone, we shared our secrets. I loved those times. I told her what it was like to live with Thaddeus and Ida, and how Joe and I depended on each other as children. Many cups of coffee and pieces of pie were devoured during our talks about me, Joe and the Believers. Sometimes we laughed, but more often there were tears.

"Enough about me. Tell me about you and Levi. I want to know everything." Violet was more than willing to share.

"Levi started coming to the restaurant. Pretty soon he got to be a regular, always sitting where I would be the one to wait on him. I thought he liked me, but I wasn't sure. One day I just out and out asked if he'd like to take me to a picture show and he said yes. It took months of going to picnics, movies, and fancy dinners before he would so much as take my hand. At first, I admired his restraint, then I thought it was something about me; he lacked desire for me or maybe it was because he had an artificial leg. One day I had enough and pressed him about it.

"Levi Ferguson, you're gonna kiss me or else!" I told him as I pushed him over on the picnic blanket and lay the smoochiest kiss on him you've ever seen, just like in the movies. Do you know what happened then?"

"He kissed you back?"

"No, he cried and started telling me things that should stay private between a man and a woman. But I knew he wanted me, and there were unmistakable signs. We got married by the Justice of the Peace soon after and things changed for the better. Levi had no problems to succumbing to the desires of the flesh. As time went on he was able to stop brooding about the Believers and build a good life with me. It hurt Levi deep in his heart to leave the Believers, but he stood strong in his conviction to serve his country.

"Being in the war, he saw things that made him question his very belief in God. Levi's never been able to get over what he was forced to do in order to survive. He still believes losing his leg was a punishment from God for things he had done. I don't think he will ever be able to accept taking a life."

"Can I ask you, Violet, why you and Levi live like this instead of a house on the road with a bathroom and running water? I can tell by the way you dress and the jewelry you wear you're used to nicer things."

"Levi had been through enough. He bought this house and five acres when he came home from the war with his pension from being wounded. Levi didn't know what else to do but a little farming and he sure felt lost. He eventually got where he could get around pretty good with his artificial leg and could do more things around the place, although he paid no attention to the inside. You should have seen this place before I moved in. It was like an old hermit man lived here. At least now it's got a woman's touch.

"Not long after we were married, Levi got a good job at the Weaving Mill, and I had already been working at the restaurant for several years. We've got money in the bank now, so maybe one day we'll buy us a nicer house, but to tell you the truth, as long as I have Levi I really don't care."

Mamie

I had been wearing Violet's clothes, but no matter what we did to them they just didn't fit me right. Violet was a good bit bigger than I with a bust on her that could have been a shelf; that's what Levi said anyway. To me, Violet was truly beautiful and I knew Levi thought so, too.

I was happy to have the clothes and never complained, but Violet said it wasn't right I didn't have a few nice things to wear that were bought new for me. Joe could have gotten a job at a saw mill or lumber yard, but he decided to work on the looms at the Weaving Mill. Levi put in a good word to the boss about him.

When Joe got his first paycheck he gave me $15 to spend on myself. I was so excited. I never had cash money before.

Downtown Roanoke was full of cars on that Saturday afternoon when Violet drove me to shop. I was surprised Violet could drive.

"I've had a driver's license for ages. Levi and I share the car. Today I took him to work so I could have it. Sometimes when he needs it, I take the bus. It's real handy and you can get all over town in it. In case you didn't know I'm 33, so I have age and experience on my side. After we're through shopping I'm taking you to eat at Woolworth's lunch counter." Violet turned her head at me and grinned.

Violet was showing and teaching me things I never dreamed about nor thought possible. A woman driving a car and making her own money! I had been to Roanoke only twice before when Thaddeus and Ida needed me to help sell eggs on the city market, but I had never been in a department store.

Violet must have had me try on twenty dresses before we decided on two. I got a beautiful pink dress that Violet said set off my complexion and hair, whatever that meant. I looked deep into the mirror trying to figure out what Violet meant by her comment. Pretty soon I had my nose pressed right up to the glass. Violet got tickled at me staring into that mirror. It got us laughing so hard we had to sit on the floor in that funny dressing room. The salesgirl stuck her head through the curtain asking us if everything was alright, and that made us laugh even more.

Violet took me to the shoe department where I got a pretty pair of beige pumps. I didn't want black ones, as they would always remind me of Believer shoes. Violet said my new shoes would go with almost everything, and I was happy about that.

After I had paid for my purchases, we went to Woolworth's. I was wearing one of my new dresses, having put what I was wearing into the shopping bag.

"Violet, they have birds in this store and fish!"

"They're parakeets and goldfish, Mamie," Violet said. We laughed at everything as she led me through the store by the hand. I had a grilled-cheese sandwich and an ice cream sundae at the lunch counter. It felt so right being there with Violet. I was starting to feel as if I finally belonged in this new world and that I had left the Believers behind.

When we got home, Joe whistled at me and gave me a big wink. He liked what he was seeing, and I felt proud to be his wife. That night after supper Violet took me aside.

"While you were paying for your purchases I slipped off and bought you something else. This is from me."

I opened the bag and saw the prettiest black lace nightgown you could ever imagine.

"I can't take this from you, Violet. You've done so much for me already."

"Yes, you can and you will. I love doing this for you and Joe. You are family now." She squeezed my hand.

Joe almost went out of his mind when he saw me in that nightgown. The next morning at breakfast Joe grinned from ear to ear thanking Violet profusely for her gift.

Mamie

After Joe had saved up several paychecks, we rented the upstairs of a house on Dale Avenue, near the Weaving Mill, in Roanoke. Violet and Levi didn't live but a short drive away. I did babysitting and took in sewing from a few of the neighbors for extra household money. My love for Joe grew deeper every day, and I could tell by the way he looked at me he felt the same. Violet and Levi were our best and dearest friends. I felt so blessed some days I cried with joy.

Violet came by almost every day and taught me how to make biscuits as good as hers. Ida had taught me to make biscuits but they usually came out thick and hard. Violet's biscuits were light and better tasting. She also gave me the secret to her special fried apple pie. I had so much to learn and Violet was always willing to teach me.

One day I was in the kitchen brewing coffee when Violet came by before her afternoon shift at the restaurant. Joe left for work earlier, but made me stay in bed as I had been feeling tired and run down. He thought maybe I was coming down with something. Violet and I sat at the kitchen table to drink our coffee. I took the first sip and ran to the bathroom and threw up. I heard Violet laughing. When I came back to the kitchen, I was pretty mad.

"How can you laugh at me when I'm sick?" I said, pouting.

"Have you missed any of your lady times?" Violet quizzed me.

"It has been a while, maybe a couple of months, now that I think about it."

"Mamie, I think you might be expecting."

I couldn't believe what she was saying, but a little voice inside me said it was true.

"I'll make you an appointment with my doctor unless you have one you like better," Violet offered.

"I've never been to a real doctor before."

"Well, we're going to take care of that. Expecting or not, you need a checkup. Sometimes I'm still baffled by the backward ways of the Believers. They take better care of their livestock than they do themselves."

Violet got me an appointment the next day. I didn't say a word to Joe about my suspicions.

Dr. Gibson's office was up a long stairway over a dentist office in Vinton. There was a frosted pane of glass with his name on it, Dr. Gibson, M.D. He was an older man, at least fifty. He wore his gold wire-rimmed glasses down on his nose when he talked. The top of his head was bald, but he had hair on the sides. Violet stayed with me during my physical, mostly because I wouldn't let her leave the room. I was scared and ashamed to let a man, even a doctor, see me partially undressed.

Dr. Gibson was nice and very patient with me. He could tell that I was nervous, cause of the way I kept looking at Violet instead of him.

"I think your suspicions are right, Mamie. I put you about three months along. If you want to be tested, we can take a urine sample and send it to the lab. Your urine will be injected into a rabbit. If the rabbit dies, then the test is positive and confirms you're in a family way."

"I don't feel good about killing a rabbit if we don't have to," I said, dismayed by the idea of killing a perfectly healthy rabbit.

"I don't think it's necessary. I'm usually right about these things. You're young and healthy. All expecting mothers need a lot of rest during this time. Be sure not to lift anything over your head. It could cause the umbilical cord to wrap around the baby's neck."

I was worried I would do something to hurt the baby without meaning to, but Dr. Gibson assured me everything would be alright if I took good care of myself and followed his instructions.

"Oh, she will, Dr. Gibson. I'll make sure of it myself," Violet said as she hugged me tight. Dr. Gibson's nurse set up a time for the next appointment and gave me a pamphlet to read and share with Joe.

Violet took me to the grocery store afterwards, then came home with me and helped me make Joe his favorite meal, chicken and dumplings with lemon meringue pie that was five inches high. I picked up a baby bottle at Garland's Drug Store and filled it with beer.

"Wish me luck when I tell Joe at dinner," I said, hugging Violet.

"He should pick up on the news when you give him that baby bottle to drink from," Violet said through her laughter. "This has been some day. Now it's time I get out of here."

That night when I gave Joe his beer in the baby bottle he about fell out of his chair.

"This is wonderful, Green Eyes. A baby!" I lifted my glass of milk, he lifted the baby bottle, and we cheered. After dinner, we read the pamphlet together.

"This sure is different from how our mothers had babies. I never knew there was so much to worry about." Joe said, turning pale as he read.

From that night on Joe did everything he could for his future child and me, waiting on us hand and foot.

Mamie

1949

It was past my due date, and it seemed my little darling didn't want to come out into the world. Violet, Joe, and I went for my doctor appointment. Dr. Gibson let everybody into the room after he finished examining me.

"After supper, I want you to take Mamie on a long drive, a few bumps in the road couldn't hurt," Dr. Gibson said, giving Joe a wink.

Levi drove us around for two hours on the bumpiest roads he could find. That night I went into labor. Violet and Levi drove Joe and me to Jefferson Hospital. I was knocked out cold during delivery given something called an anesthetic. My baby girl entered the world just before midnight on May, 18, 1949.

My little girl wasn't a day old when Joe came into my hospital room carrying a big bouquet of flowers.

"Joe, they are so beautiful," I said.

"Not as beautiful as the baby in the nursery," Joe said, as he leaned over and kissed me. "There are a couple of people waiting in the hall. Are you ready for company?"

"I can see Levi and Violet's head peeking around the door. We better let them in," I said. Levi entered the room carrying the biggest teddy bear I had ever seen.

"For the baby," he said, grinning.

"I thought as much," I said, laughing at Levi.

"I'm not to be outdone," Violet said, as she handed me a book of baby names. "I come bearing gifts. It's time this child has a name. We'll come back tomorrow and look at the book."

I was tired and full of emotions. Tomorrow we would name my little girl.

The next morning I started looking at the book with Joe standing over my shoulder. Levi and Violet came over that afternoon.

"I see a lot of pretty names in here but nothing feels right," I said to Joe, Violet and Levi.

"Look at the meanings and not so much the name," Violet said.

"I like Lula. It means abundance, lady, princess. This is what I want for my little girl. I want her to always have what she needs and to be treated like a princess."

"I like it to, but she needs a middle name," Joe said. "How about May because that's the month she's born in."

"It's perfect. Our little princess will be named Lula May Simpkins," I said happily. Her name felt just right to me.

I stayed in the hospital bed for a full week. The nurses brought Lula May to me for bottle feedings. I thought I would be breast feeding. That was what the Sisters did, but the nurses told me baby formula was better.

A week later we were able to take Lula May home, but not before the hospital doctor told me visitors weren't supposed to come into our home until our baby was two months old because of germs. I put my foot down on that one. Violet and Levi weren't visitors. They were family!

What happiness and delight Lula May brought to us. Joe couldn't get enough of his baby girl. Violet and Levi spoiled her rotten. Joe and Levi painted the nursery pink while I was in the hospital. I had wanted to wait to paint the nursery until I knew if I was having a girl or boy.

Violet and I had purchased lots of baby things beforehand. I never knew there was so much for babies!

"Violet, I want to thank you and Levi for all you've done for me and Lula May. Believers don't fix up special nurseries for their young ones, just a cradle and some hand-me-down clothes."

I had loved every moment of what we created for Lula May. Pictures of baby animals were on the walls, stuffed animals and a Mother Goose storybook was on a shelf, along with cloth diapers and baby clothes. She had everything a baby girl could need, and more.

Joe and I fell into the ways of the world, so gradually I didn't see it happen. We bought a record player and danced in our living room. Every time Joe got paid, which was once a month, we bought a new record album to add to our collection. We had a radio and a Kodak box camera. We took pictures and had our pictures taken. I loved the photographs of my baby girl and husband.

I thought of how the Believers wouldn't let pictures be taken. I loved my photographs so much. I shuddered every time I thought about the Believers and put them out of my mind.

Mamie

1952

It didn't seem any time at all before Lula May turned one, two, then three. I was blissfully happy with my life. Joe was promoted to supervisor, and I had turned twenty-one years old.

"Are you ready to have another baby," Joe asked me one night after supper.

"Not yet. I want to enjoy Lula May for another year or two."

I liked the idea of another child, but everything was so perfect the way it was I didn't want to risk changing anything for a while. Joe was fine with my answer, saying we had lots of time to have another baby.

Violet came over almost every day after she dropped Levi off at work. We drank sweet tea and played with Lula May. Violet was always bringing her gifts like story books or stuffed animals. When Levi came to the house he liked nothing better than to make faces and animal noises at Lula May, making her laugh. It was her daddy she loved best of all. He made the best horsey. Lula May rode on his back as he galloped, the best he could, on his hands and knees.

Joe had taken up learning the flute and had gotten quite good at it. He found the silver flute in a pawnshop when he and Levi were looking for tools. Joe bought a tambourine for me and Levi already played the harmonica, learning it in the hospital after he was wounded. Violet played the banjo which had belonged to her grandfather, but she needed a lot of practice. I'd give Lula May a cooking spoon and my washboard. You

73

never heard such a racket in your life or seen so much fun!

During the summer we went swimming at Lakeside Amusement Park. Can you believe I had a bathing suit? Lula May had a cute one with ducks on it that Violet and I bought when we went shopping in Roanoke. It took everything in me to wear the navy blue one piece bathing suit in public the first time.

"Violet, I can't be baring my legs for all to see. Only Joe should see me this way," I said, holding a large beach towel around my body in the ladies room.

"Tell you what, Mamie, let's take our cover-ups off at the pool at the same time. That way no one will pay so much attention to you."

No one seemed to notice when I unwrapped the towel from around me, and took off the cover-up. But I sure was glad Violet was with me wearing a bathing suit, too.

Joe and I played gin rummy with Violet and Levi when we weren't in the pool with Lula May; or at least I attempted to play, having a toddler in my lap. Joe had a wild laugh when he won and always teased me about playing strip poker, though I knew, without a doubt, he would never let it happen.

"Joe, let's get in the swimming pool. Violet can watch Lula May for a few minutes. I want to lie in your arms and play baptism like we did when we were Believers."

Lying in Joe's arms I remembered our special day at the creek, which seemed a lifetime ago. Whispering in my ear, Joe told me he was remembering that day, too.

At the end of the day we took Lula May to the merry-go-round. The lights and the way the horse went up and down on the poles had her entranced. Pointing and giggling, it was always the golden horse she wanted to ride.

Mamie

One of my favorite things to do with Lula May was to take her to the library. I knew this was more for me than her since she was only four. I dressed her for whatever the weather was, put her in her stroller, and off we went. Sometimes I got chills from all the possibilities of learning that were in library books. I was so excited when I got my library card I could barely contain myself.

Lula May loved cuddling in my lap or her daddy's and having us read to her. Joe was great at making funny animal noises, making her go into fits of laughter. Often as I went about my chores she would follow me holding a storybook for me to read to her. I hardly ever said no.

I was looking through the magazines at the library when one caught my eye. It was the August 8, 1952 issue of the *Saturday Evening Post*. On the cover was a man enjoying the sand and waves of Myrtle Beach. I read every word in the magazine twice and wrote down notes.

I thought back to the books in Thaddeus's room and Joe's promise to take me to the beach someday. I checked out a travel book on South Carolina which had a lot of information about the beach. That night after a special supper I brought up my idea about going.

"Joe, let's you and me sit down. I have something I want to talk to you about," I said as we made ourselves comfortable on the couch.

"Do you remember we talked about going to Myrtle Beach a long time ago? Well, I think it's time we go."

"I think it's a good idea, Green Eyes, but we'll have to wait until the week of July 4 next year. The Weaving Mill closes down for a whole week then."

"That will give us plenty of time to plan the trip. Levi will be off since he works at the mill. Violet can put in for vacation time, and Lula May will have just turned five. It'll be a perfect time to go," I squealed in delight.

"It's settled then. We'll make this the honeymoon we never went on," Joe said, as he gave me a big hug.

"Except we'll be taking our friends and child on this honeymoon," I said as we snuggled up to each other on the sofa.

Violet was almost as excited as I was. I told her I wanted to stay at the Dunes Golf and Beach Club because it was on the cover of the magazine. Violet and I sent for brochures.

I checked the mailbox every day looking for them. Finally, the day arrived. I spent all afternoon looking at the brochures I had laid on the kitchen table. I could barely contain my excitement when Joe came home from work.

"A dream, Joe; this is going to be a dream come true!"

Since it was early, we didn't have any trouble getting reservations for five days and four nights at the Dunes Club. I would have liked to have stayed all week, but it was pretty expensive. I must have made twenty lists of what I would need to pack for the trip.

Before I knew it, we had loaded Levi's car for our adventure. I never had so much fun as on that road trip. We stopped along the way and ate sweet peaches at the roadside stands, sang songs with the radio, and picked at and teased each other as Lula May dozed on and off. Levi and Joe sat in the front seat. Us girls, spread out in the back.

I couldn't believe the beach when I saw it the first time. I stood transfixed, watching the waves while holding Lula May in my arms. Sitting Lula May on the sand, I took off her shoes and mine. We ran to the edge of the water with Joe, Violet, and Levi close behind.

"The salt air is wonderful," I said loudly, not taking my eyes off the waves. "This is the most magnificent thing I have ever seen!"

Lula May squealed in delight as I put her feet into the water, allowing it to splash onto her little legs. Joe and I each took one of Lula May's hands and walked down the beach, stopping often to pick up shells. By the time we got back to the hotel our pockets were full.

The day had grown hot, and I wanted to jump right into the ocean and I would later, but Lula May was a happy but tired little girl, with a blush of sun on her sweet face. We would all go swimming after Lula May had taken a nap. We still needed to settle into our rooms and unpack our bags.

"Tonight Levi and I are babysitting so you and Joe can have the honeymoon you never had. There's no saying no, either," Violet said, standing at our open hotel door.

"I wouldn't dream of it," I said, giving Violet a big hug. "I don't know how it is I deserve such friends as you and Levi."

That night Joe and I walked hand in hand on the beach, under a full moon, and then returned to the hotel. Our room was beautiful and we could see the beach from our small balcony. Opening the glass doors wide and seeing the ocean filled me with delight. I couldn't help but think of the only other motel I had been in, the one on Williamson Road the Laymans took us to. So many wonderful things had happened for Joe and me since we left the Believers.

"I have a surprise for you, Mamie. I bought us a bottle of champagne. Neither of us has ever tried it and I thought tonight should be the night," Joe said, popping the cork and filling our glasses.

"I don't know if I like the taste, it sure is different, but the little bubbles are cute. Maybe the second drink will taste better than the first," I said, offering my glass to Joe for a refill.

I liked the way the champagne made me feel, all light-headed and giggly. Joe and I made the sweetest love and awoke to a gentle breeze coming through the screen in our window. Joe and I had the most romantic honeymoon night possible.

The first few days were spent swimming and sunning, covering each other in suntan lotion. I had bought sand buckets and shovels, and we built sand castles with Lula May, which she promptly kicked over. Twice we went to eat at fancy seafood restaurants. One night we ate in the Dunes dining room, which had actual air-conditioning. It was the best food I ever had in my life.

On the last day I was sad to leave, but put on a sunny face. Levi and Joe had decided to play golf. Neither had ever played before, and they were getting a lesson. Out of politeness they invited us, girls. We declined, as they knew we would, wanting to stay on the beach and play with Lula May. When it was time to go, we packed the sand buckets and beach balls and loaded the car. We were all suntanned and smiling. We had made perfect memories.

Mamie

1954

S uddenly and without any warning my entire world fell apart.
Mac Hallowell was a friend of Joe's from the Weaving Mill. Sometimes he drove Joe home from work, other times Joe walked as it didn't
take him any more than fifteen minutes. I didn't think anything about Joe
being a little late coming home because sometimes Mac and Joe stopped
off and had a couple of beers.

By ten o'clock I was frantic with worry. Joe had never gotten home
past 7:00 p.m. It had started snowing hard around seven and icy patches
were forming on the road. I managed to get Lula May to sleep, but she
could tell I was worried.

"What's wrong, Mama?"

"Nothing, my baby, you go to sleep now," I said, rocking her until
she fell quiet and I placed her in her bed.

I was pacing the house when the police came knocking at the door.
There had been an accident. Was my husband Joseph Simpkins? Was
there anyone they could call for me?

I had no memory of fainting, but before coming back to consciousness, I saw a golden horse rear up on his hind legs. The solid whites of
his eyes showed nothing but emptiness as he looked at me, turned, and
galloped off into the clouds. I tried to scream, but no sound would come
out.

The next thing I remember Violet and Levi were there. They tried to explain to me how Mac's car slid, spinning around and around on the ice in the black night. Joe was sitting on the passenger side when the car went down an embankment.

A single pine tree was all it took. There had been an open kerosene container in Mac's car from where he did house painting on the side. Mac was barely alive with fire burning thirty percent of his body. A couple walking in the snow had seen the crash and were able to pull the men from the burning car, but Joe had been killed instantly.

Why did you leave me Joe? Our marriage had been full of laughter and every day a dream come true. Now you have gone to an unseen place where I cannot follow. Where are you? This very morning I awoke in your arms. We had coffee, scrambled eggs, and toast. Lula May and I kissed you goodbye like we did every day as you left for work. By evening you were gone. Our little girl has wept inconsolably, calling out for you, not understanding what Levi and Violet have tried to tell her. My heart has been torn open, and I am no use to Lula May.

I believed our happiness would last forever. I believed the Holy Spirit mingled in our lives and created a new world for us to live in with our friends Violet and Levi. I believed this until the moment you were stolen from me. Now I no longer believed. I would have to carry on alone and do what was right for Lula May.

Mamie

I sat in my rocking chair and stared as the snow continued to fall throughout the next day. I stared until the sun set and came up again. I survived, but knew my tears would last as long as God made me live.

The Waters of God Believers had protected Joe and me from the evil of the world, but we had chosen not to be led by the Spirit, but by the flesh, and had done wrong by our daughter. We hadn't taken her to church or read the Bible to her. She knew too little about Jesus.

Joe and I had the potential to be as bad as any sinner, and we took it. Joe's death was a judgment on his life and mine, and now my punishment was to exist without him. Joe and I tasted alcohol, danced, played cards, and had our photographs taken. We did not follow the Word.

"Please, forgive me my sins. Take the accident away and bring Joe back to me," I beseeched Jesus through the darkness of the days and nights that followed. I don't remember making funeral plans leaving it to Violet and Levi.

Violet held me up as we walked into the funeral home. I wouldn't let Lula May see her father in the casket. I was afraid of what it might do to her seeing her father's body so badly burned, although Violet told me his face had been spared. I wanted Lula May to remember her father as he was. Lula May stayed with Levi, his arms around her, protecting her as I made my way to my husband. Seeing Joe's body was more than I could stand.

"It's not him. It's not my Joe. There's been a horrible mistake," I cried out when I saw him. Violet took me in her arms as I sobbed.

"It is Joe. Look close and you'll see it's him. Look at his hands. You'll

81

recognize them. Do this, Mamie, before it's time to close the lid. Kiss your husband one more time."

Again I looked. It was not my Joe.

The next morning there were howling winds as we buried Joe in Evergreen Cemetery. I was surprised to see Thaddeus and Ida there. Later that day Violet told me she had put a notice of Joe's funeral in the *Roanoke Times* obituaries. Somehow Thaddeus had gotten word.

Violet and Levi stood with me and Lula May, their arms around us, holding us up. Joe's friends from the Weaving Mill were there. I prayed for Jesus to come to us, to be with us as we buried my husband, but He did not answer and gave me no sign. If Jesus did not care for me, Joe or Lula May, I would not care for Him.

After the final words had been spoken and everyone had given their condolences, Thaddeus came forward and asked me to step away from the others so we could talk privately.

"Are you alright with speaking to Thaddeus without us?" Violet quizzed me.

"It's alright. Keep Lula May with you while I talk to him."

Thaddeus took my elbow and led me far enough away so the others couldn't hear us talking. He cleared his throat before he began to speak.

"Mamie, it is my duty to provide for you and your daughter since my brother is dead. You're a widow now and need a man to look after you. Come back to the home we once shared and we'll begin life again, as husband and wife, the way God intended it to be. All I have is but one requirement for you, and that is to bear me sons."

Lula May was almost six years old, and we had no place to go. I couldn't expect Violet and Levi to support us. It was wickedness that caused Joe's death, and I would not bring my darkness into their home. Maybe this was the sign I was looking for.

Mamie

Violet and Levi begged me not to leave, but I knew I must. We were in the kitchen and Violet was trying to get me to eat but I could not. Lula May was finally asleep having been up most of the night crying for her Daddy.

"If your mind cannot be changed leave Lula May with us. We will raise her as our own," Violet said, pleading with me.

"I am leaving and taking Lula May with me. It is best that we go." I did not want to tell them the reasons. I wanted to spare Violet and Levi the horrible thoughts that ran through my head.

"Dear God, Mamie, don't you know what you will be doing to Lula May? Levi sat up most of the night, rocking her and drying away her tears. He is almost as close to her as Joseph was. You can't do this to her or to us!" This was the first and only time Violet ever raised her voice to me.

"Lula May will always have a home here, the same as you. You have become family and the door is always open," Levi said, his voice deep and trembling.

"Lula May and I will be gone soon. Thank you for all your kindness," I said, turning away from them. I couldn't bear to see the pain in their eyes.

I would not risk Lula May's eternal damnation, being raised with non-believers, when my very soul was at risk. I had been like Eve, tempting Joe with my flesh making him fall in love with me. If I hadn't left Thaddeus's house and married Joe, he would still be alive. I hoped eventually Violet and Levi would become like a dream to Lula May, but I knew

I would never forget them.

Three days after Joe's funeral I moved into Thaddeus's house, the same one I had left years before. Since Joe and I ran off, Thaddeus had continued to study scripture and grown in authority with the church. I wondered why he hadn't married and if he felt shame that I had left him for his brother. Ida still lived in the house attending to his needs. She was now thin as a board; her black hair was streaked with white and pulled back so hard in a bun it stretched her skin. The years hadn't been kind to her.

Ida told me my household duties which were few and gave me three gray dresses which set me apart from the world and reinforced my place in the church.

"Your apron is always to be worn for protection from soilage and as a symbol of service to God and to the Believers, Mamie. Don't be forgetting that. I'll be making dresses for the child and give her small chores to do."

It broke my heart when I saw Lula May in the dress, bonnet, and apron for the first time.

"Mama, I don't like it. Take it off me." Lula May pulled at the bonnet and started to cry. "Daddy, come help me. Please, Daddy. I don't like it here."

Leaving Lula May with Ida, I rushed to the downstairs bedroom, I was to share with Thaddeus, and cried in my pillow. I was but a small child when I came to live here, and now it was the same for my little girl, but rather this life for Lula May than what could happen in the outside world.

I wasn't there a week when words were spoken over Thaddeus and me by Brother Adam Farley at a Wednesday night prayer service.

"It is not good that man should be alone; I will make him a helper fit for him. For he who finds a wife finds a good thing and obtains favor from the Lord. Thus say the readings from Genesis 2:18 and Proverbs

18:22."

It was done. I married Thaddeus Simpkins, the very man from whom I'd run.

Preparing for bed, I hung my gray dress in the wardrobe aside the other two. I folded my undergarments carefully and laid them in their proper place in the top drawer of the dresser I would share with Thaddeus. I tried to delay the moment of my near nakedness should Thaddeus come into the room.

"Please, God, don't let Thaddeus touch me tonight," I prayed.

With a shiver I pulled my nightdress over my head. Slipping into bed, I turned on my side and closed my eyes.

Thaddeus did not bother me on our wedding night or for the next week either keeping on his side of the bed. How I hated this! It was Joe I wanted lying with me, but eventually the inevitable happened. There was no kissing, no arousal, nothing like when I was with Joe. I only wanted it over with. I wanted to sleep and to dream about Joe.

Time went on and I did not conceive and this weighed on Thaddeus. He believed it my fault for my womb not accepting his seed. Every night Thaddeus made me kneel with him beside our marriage bed beseeching God for a son.

"Pray, pray to Jesus," he implored me while we were on our knees.

"You must be purified from your past, for the ways of the flesh are sinful in God's eyes. Through the will of God my son will come through you."

I thought Thaddeus's prayers would last throughout the night, and some nights they almost did. When Thaddeus felt right with God about what we were about to do, he would allow me to get into bed. Lifting my nightdress over my hips, Thaddeus did what had to be done.

Mamie

Lying in bed with Thaddeus, I thought I would lose my mind. I thought of Lula May and what I had done by bringing her here. I could barely look into my child's eyes, not wanting to see the hurt in them.

Seeing Lula May in the gray dress and bonnet was like seeing my ghost, when I lived in this very house. It was better I kept my distance from Lula May so she could fit into this world and forget what she had before. Thaddeus had no idea how much I suffered by coming back to live with him. He thought being his wife should satisfy me.

When Thaddeus fell asleep and his breathing became heavy, I arose from bed and traveled in the darkness with my wakeful candle. At first I didn't venture far, but as time passed I ventured farther into the night. Sometimes I walked up the creaking stairs to Lula May's room and watched her sleep. Kissing her forehead, I would pray that she would find the strength to survive this life and find the same kind of happiness I had with her father.

Thaddeus didn't know I left his bed, even when I timidly climbed back in before daylight. He was a heavy sleeper, worn out from farm chores, but he arose at daybreak, and for this I was grateful. He always slept in his bedclothes and I in mine.

Joe and I had slept with nothing on. At first we were modest with each other and never would have dreamed of such a thing, but it wasn't long before Joe's skin was my skin.

I didn't like the room I shared with Thaddeus. With Joe there were summer roses at the bedroom window. Framed pictures of Joe, Lula May, and the three of us together hung against wallpaper with small yellow flowers that graced the walls. I wondered what happened to the pictures. Were they tossed aside when the landlord took back his property? Were they stored away in cardboard boxes in the basement of the house?

It did me no good to dwell on the pictures and what was. I took great pains to control myself, but it did little good. I was forever anxious and resentful for losing what I had before.

I lay in bed, night after night, trying not to scream. I hated it when Thaddeus touched my nipples with his black leather glove, tracing my body until his fingers were between my legs. He never took off the glove, and I wondered if it was to hide a deformity, but I dared not ask.

I had made a terrible mistake by coming here and could no longer bear it. On one such night Thaddeus came to me, desiring for me to conceive his son, I refused to get on my knees and pray for my purification. My once good manners could take it no more, and I ran into the night screaming for Joe, my true husband.

"I don't know what to do. I cannot live this life. Help me. Joe! No sooner than I called out to him, a flash of lightning showed a golden horse rearing up, shaking his mighty mane. How I wanted to jump onto his back and ride! Just like the lightning, the horse was gone.

A voice softly came into my mind; *I am nearer to you than you are to yourself.* I understood the message. Joe and I were one in spirit and soul and always would be. Thaddeus couldn't come between us. He was not my husband and never would be. A downpouring of my tears came as hard as the rain. I had experienced a cleansing and was making friends with the night.

Mamie

1956

It had been over two years since I came back to this house of sorrow, yet it felt like ten. From my bed, I could see the oval shaving mirror on the opposite wall. I had paid no attention to it before, but this morning a shaft of light from the window caused clear but shining colors to reflect from it.

I was sure not many faces had been reflected from that mirror. Maybe Joe's mother glanced at it a time or two, or a young male who had stayed in this room had used it, maybe even Joe. The mirror caused me to reflect on the silver-looking glass and hairbrush Joe gave me for our first wedding anniversary. H loved to watch me brush my long hair one hundred strokes.

"You're so beautiful, Mamie. I want you to see yourself the way I see you. It's not a sin."

I didn't look the first few times Joe asked me to, but left the mirror face-down on the dresser. Joe was delighted when I finally picked the mirror up and held it close to my face. I felt silly for not doing it before. I had looked into a mirror when I was with Violet in the dressing room buying clothes, and there was a small mirror in the bathroom above the sink, but it wasn't large enough to see my whole face. I didn't want to peer into a looking glass only to see myself.

Rising from the bed, I stood in front of the oval mirror, then lit the candle I kept on the bedside table. I always wanted a candle burning for

Joe. Thaddeus blew out the flame when it was time for sleep. I hated him when he did this. If he only knew why I burned that candle! Always I had secret candles and a box of Diamond Matches hidden for my night time wanderings.

I stood and gazed into the wavy reflection in the shaving mirror. A different woman had replaced the young woman who once was. Since I had been in this house as Thaddeus's wife I had only seen my distorted reflection in pools of still waters after heavy rains.

Mesmerized, I stood before the looking glass as a beam of light began to shine on the mirror's surface. It wasn't the candle flame! My face began to change in shape and features, as if my old self was being slowly cleared away.

Before my very eyes Joe appeared, staring and smiling back at me, his eyes so full of love and serenity that I was overcome by tears. There was no mistake. Joe had come to me. I heard him speaking, his voice inside my mind.

"Beloved wife, draw on food, water, and rest. I need you stronger and clearer, so it will be easier for me to come to you."

Quickly as he came, he was gone. This wasn't my imagination. This was real.

No one would be able to understand, so I would not say a word. I dared not speak. My life with Joe was in this mirror. My suffering flew out of me like fluttering doves the moment I saw his face.

The morning breeze moved through the window causing the curtains to move, but it was Joe sending the clear circles with white edges to dance in the room. As I looked toward the morning sky, I saw my true husband's image shining in a shaft of light. He was with me. I was sure of it.

Mamie

A movement in the air, a sparkle of light let me know when Joe was with me. I smelled the *Old Spice Cologne* I bought for him the first Christmas we were married. Joe always wore it for me. He was coming more often now, usually in the evenings or early morning hours as I was just awakening. I would feel a brush of my hair, a gentle touch to my shoulder, or a feather light touch on my face which I knew to be a kiss from him.

My heart beat faster and my stomach dropped when I sensed him near me. My arms and face tingled when he was close and the room turned cool. I would see a whitish wispy film, then there was nothing. He was gone. I became mixed with happiness and despair, then I noticed it. A fingerprint beside the candle which I burned for him on the bedside table. I shall no longer dust. Joe was here. He was! I wondered how Thaddeus couldn't sense Joe around me. How could he not feel his brother in the room with us?

I was always in the bedroom well before Thaddeus. When twilight darkened I prepared for bed. When darkness had settled within the bedroom walls, I often grew restless. Leaving the bedroom I would look into the kitchen and see Thaddeus sitting at the table, hunched over his Bible, in the lamplight. I would return to the bedroom, willing Thaddeus to bed and sleep, for I needed to leave and meet my Joe.

Thaddeus eventually became aware I wandered in the night, as I would come back to bed shivering from the cold of winter. Being quiet was the price Thaddeus paid to get a son from me.

Months passed, and I didn't feel Joe around me. I lay down to rest one unbearably hot August day, weary from worry that he wouldn't come again. Waiting for the dog day afternoon to pass, asleep or awake, I do not know; my body and eyes became frozen. I couldn't move, but I could see Joe staring at me from the foot of the bed. There was a troubled look on his face.

"Please, Joe, take me with you!" I tried to cry out, but my mouth wouldn't move and in an instant Joe was gone.

Once more my body moved and my eyes opened. What was he trying to make me understand? Heartbroken, I stayed in the bedroom waiting for him to reappear until Ida insisted I come downstairs and sit with her in the kitchen.

That evening a storm began brewing. Outside my bedroom window, the far off lightning flashed, and I could hear the thunder coming closer. Soon the dark winds would be blowing and spirits knocking, but come tomorrow there would be a full moon shining its yellow glow, and I would again search for Joe.

Mamie

1957

It wasn't right that the sun kept rising, the snow kept falling, and one day should follow the next. I felt that the darkness should stay forever. I walked at night. I couldn't help myself. Again and again I went to the creek, walking across the stony river bed remembering my beloved. I felt closer to Joe there. I could not hide my true nature, so there was no reason to try. Ida said I must stop this foolishness, but she couldn't stop me. I never knew how much I loved Joe until he was gone, fast as chimney smoke.

A hard and icy snow had fallen. It was a night like this when my Joe left me. As I walked among the tall evergreens lining the road, tears rolled down my face. The sliver of moon in the night sky offered little light as the pine trees creaked their wooden bones. Lost in thought, I did not sense the slippery slope. Falling down the embankment, I rolled to a place so dark there were no shadows. Trying to get up, I lost my footing again, twisting my right ankle. Covered in snow and twigs, I tried to walk, dead branches and undergrowth hampering me as I limped. I was grateful I had taken the time to put on heavy shoes and not bedroom slippers as I sometimes did. I no longer was on a path, but in heavy woods.

Moving slowly through the forest, I tried to find my way without stumbling or falling. I was shivering cold, wearing little more than my nightgown, robe, and the shawl Ida left by the kitchen door. Coming to a clearing, I noticed an unnatural light in the distance. Unafraid, I hurried toward the light, tripping on branches, almost falling in my eagerness to reach it. A man's shadowy figure was signaling for me with a lantern.

I followed the distant light, limping and shivering. The house was dark and all were asleep when I arrived. No one knew I was gone, and there had been no lantern. Joe had shown me the light.

Mamie

Summer had come, and for this I was glad. I put my nightdress on and climbed into the feather bed. I made sure there was room for Joe and that his pillow was properly placed beside mine. Joe told me to always make a place for him. I knew if he didn't come to me tonight he would surely come tomorrow. I giggled with anticipation.

Sinking into the warm, sweet darkness of the night, I thought of the plan I had for the next day. More times than not, Thaddeus did not sleep with me, but stayed in the barn with Midnight. I wished he would stay in the barn every night and leave me alone. I didn't like to think what Joe was seeing when Thaddeus made me mate with him, touching and fondling me, his hand in the black leather glove.

I awoke before sunrise. Joe hadn't come, but I knew I would see him today. I dressed quickly. No one was up as I went into the kitchen. I gathered a piece of cornbread, wrapped it in a dish towel, and placed it in my apron pocket. Joe liked it when I ate. I was doing this for him.

I watched as the sun came up. It was going to be a warm day, a perfect day, with a gentle breeze. I couldn't contain my excitement. Why had I not thought of this before?

Walking through the woods, I had a strange pounding in my heart from anticipation and yearning for my beloved. Finally I came upon a heap of white rocks where a chimney had once stood so I knew my path was right. I hadn't been to the swimming hole where I had given Joe his birthday present so many years ago. It was much too far to go in the night.

Having walked so fast I had a stitch in my side I sat down to rest for a moment. Then I heard the creek calling me, and I was upon it, or it upon me, I didn't know which. Walking toward the water, I removed my gray dress. On the embankment, I removed my undergarments and placed them where I could find them later. Slowly walking into the creek, I began to call on Joe.

"I'm here. Come to me now, my beloved. I've prepared the day for us."

Naked on a large smooth rock, warming by the sun, I pulled the pins from my hair, letting it fall down loose around my shoulders the way Joe liked. I laid back on the rock and closed my eyes. My hands and feet were in the water, and I felt the currents wash and splash over me. From the depths of the water Joe came to me, made love to me as I knew he would. All day I stayed, even after he left, still feeling his hands, his manhood inside me, his sweet kisses all over my eager and receptive flesh.

Darkness would be coming soon, and I hadn't thought to bring a lantern. How I wish I had for I did not want to leave. During our love-making, Joe whispered we could return here again and again. Still, sadness filled me at the thought of leaving. I wanted to become the mossy shadows under the trees so I could stay here forever. Rising, I caught a glimpse of something in the crevices of the large smooth rock I lay upon with him. A green cat's eye marble!

PART TWO

"The Snake which cannot cast
its skin has to die"
Nietzche

Lula May

Sometimes it's hard to recall the way Mama and Daddy were when I was a little girl. How hard I try to remember. Mama was a laughing woman then with soft flowing hair, the color of sunflowers. Her eyes reminded me of Tabby, our barn cat, as they both had the greenest eyes. Mama always had something pretty in her hair that sparkled like silver.

Daddy had a smile as big as the moon and was so tall he could almost reach the stars. Many the nights he played his flute while Mama sang. They would take turns whirling me around the room to Daddy's playing or Mama's singing. I was the spitting image of Mama, Daddy said, and what a lucky man he was to have two such beautiful gals in his life. How I adored those nights!

I remember Mama screaming the night Daddy was killed. I couldn't understand what had happened. Violet was there holding me tight as I sobbed. I couldn't stand to hear Mama wailing. I was scared. Where was Daddy? I don't remember much else that happened except for Violet and Levi taking me and Mama to their house.

Violet and I were playing dolls and having sugar cookies and milk when a horse and buggy pulled up to the house. Mama was sitting in her rocking chair holding Daddy's flute, not saying a word. It had been three days since Daddy's funeral when Thaddeus came for Mama and me. Dressed all in black he walked into the house and took me and Mama away from the only people I had ever loved. I was six years old. Violet tried to reason with Mama.

"Mamie, you don't have to do this. There's no need for you to go off with him; stay here and live with me and Levi. We don't want you to leave. Think about Lula May. She's like our own daughter. Please don't take her with you! You know what it will be like for her," Violet said, her eyes darting from one of us to the other.

Mama got out of her chair, took my hand, and walked toward Thaddeus. It was as if she was staring, but not seeing. Violet cried when Thaddeus removed the silver clips from Mama's hair and took Daddy's flute.

"Musical instruments are never used by Believers. Females dress modestly at all times, not with flowing hair, gold or pearls but adorned with good deeds. Woman, take these things away as they will not be tolerated in my household," Thaddeus said, as he handed the flute and jewelry to Violet.

Mama didn't do anything to stop him.

"Thaddeus, don't do this, please! Wait and talk to Levi. We can reason this out!" Violet screamed these words over and over as he walked Mama and me outside, lifted us and placed us in the buggy.

"We are a separate people from the world. The scriptures uphold how we should live, in meekness. God's will is being done this moment."

"Wait while I put a few of their things into a bag. There are items Mamie and Lula May will need."

"Be quick about it. I will not wait long."

I was scared by the sternness of Thaddeus's dark eyes, the blackness of his hair parted in the middle, the long beard and his thin lips. I didn't let go of Mama's hand. While waiting for Violet, he turned his attention to me.

"Child, I am your Uncle. It is my duty to lay claim on you. From this day forward your name is Sarah Ruth Simpkins, as decided by the Council of Elder. Sarah Ruth is a solid Christian name fitting for your new life. Your grandmother's name was Ruth. You would do well to remember that and strive to like her. Before long you will forget what came before this day. The Believers are now your people."

Violet returned with the cloth satchel Mama used for her sewing. Violet handed me the Raggedy Ann doll she had made me for my fourth birthday. The man took it from me and handed it back to Violet.

"The doll is unnecessary," he said, taking the satchel from Violet's hands.

Violet was still screaming at Mama not to go as we drove away. I don't recall anything after that as I fainted dead away.

Lula May

I don't remember much about the following months, except for Violet banging on the door demanding to see Mama and being sent away.

"Lula May, I won't forget you and don't forget me," she called out each time she came. I heard male voices arguing and knew Levi was with her.

There was no one else who lived in the house with Thaddeus except for Aunt Ida. I hated she made me call her that. She was always stern, never smiling, and quick to correct me. Aunt Ida made me two gray dresses. I hated these dresses and did not want to wear them.

I wanted my Raggedy Ann, my stuffed pony, and tea set. I wanted Daddy to come and snuggle with me, and for Levi to put me on his big shoulders and tell me silly stories, while Violet fed us animal crackers. Most of all I wanted my old mama back again. It wasn't my mama in the gray dress and bonnet! It was not! I had lost my real mama and didn't know how to find her. Where was she? Where had she gone?

Violet made more attempts to see me and Mama over the next couple of years. If Violet showed up while I was outside, Aunt Ida quickly got me into the house and locked me in my upstairs bedroom. I heard raised voices, then Violet's words would sound farther and farther off. A car door would slam, and I knew Violet was being sent away.

"Mama, let me out of this room. Please, Mama I want to see Violet!" I yelled, but she did not answer me. Eventually I would fall asleep, worn out from crying and pounding on the door, only to awaken to a plate of food on a chipped blue plate beside me.

Sometimes in the darkness of night, I heard the sounds of whimpering and someone walking in bare feet. My door would creak open and Mama would come in and sit on the edge of my bed.

"Mama, don't go, stay with me."

"I came to tuck you in. You need your sleep," Mama said, as she kissed my face and pulled up the covers. I could feel the wetness of her tears on her cheeks.

"Give me a big hug, Lula May, then I have to go."

I held tight onto Mama and she held tight to me.

Then she left me and went out into the night.

Ida

1957

I felt bad for Mamie and Sarah Ruth coming here to live. How I hated calling that sweet child another name rather than her own. I always knew no good would come of Joseph and Mamie running off the way they did. Joseph had a mind of his own even as a child. He wasn't about to bow down to Thaddeus as he grew to be a man. Not like I'd always done. Joseph was a sweet but stubborn child. I cared for him the best I could after our parents died. I never tried to take the place of our mother, an outspoken God-fearing woman. I was Joseph's big sister, and let it go at that.

I've often thought if Thaddeus had treated Joseph more like his younger brother, shown him a little kindness, maybe Joseph wouldn't have felt the need to run off with Mamie.

I was at the special prayer meeting when Thaddeus told the Elders God had spoken and told him to marry Mamie. No one said anything to dispute Thaddeus's revelation. How could they? To me it could have been a little hocus pocus. I had seen how Thaddeus looked at Mamie. He was a man, after all. Thaddeus could have married someone else. There were plenty of women to choose from; it didn't need to be her.

Joseph and Mamie should have been married in the church and things would have worked out fine, and Joseph would still be alive. You couldn't tell Thaddeus anything, and there wasn't any use in trying. My opinion never mattered to Thaddeus, and I stopped giving it to him years ago. Thaddeus talked to God, and God answered. God didn't talk to me; never did.

Lula May

"Get up Sarah Ruth, it's almost sunrise. You have plenty of chores to do before breakfast and today's Monday, so it's wash day," Aunt Ida called out to me from the kitchen.

"Can't I stay in bed? It isn't even light outside," I hollered back, knowing I'd soon be worn from a day of hauling water, scrubbing on a washboard, and wringing out the clothes.

"Don't be sassing me, girl. Do you want me to send Thaddeus to get you?"

"No ma'am."

Every morning was like this. Aunt Ida was nothing like my Violet, who was always laughing and fun, wearing bright colors and giving me lots of hugs. Violet and Mama played games with me, like tiddley winks or checkers while we ate ice cream cones. Sometimes I spent nights at Violet's house on the fold-out couch in the living room. We giggled and ate popcorn as late as we wanted.

Uncle Thaddeus was seldom at home, except for meals. It was hard to believe my father and this man were brothers for they looked nothing alike. My father's hair was light, like mine, and he was clean shaven with twinkly eyes and a big grin. Uncle Thaddeus was tall and stern with a full dark beard, splotched with gray, dressed always in the same black clothes, unless he was working in the fields, then he wore overalls.

He would come in for breakfast after having done chores since sun up and say the morning prayers, which lasted for the longest time. I kept my eyes closed, head down and hands folded on my lap as I had been told to do but I didn't listen to him.

104

I made myself think about Mama and Daddy and the breakfasts we shared, all of us fixing it together. I didn't have chores to do then. Daddy said there was a lifetime of chores ahead of me, and I was to be a child for as long as I could, and wouldn't I soon be ready for first grade? That's where the work really began, and Mama would laugh and agree. We didn't go to church either. Daddy said he had enough church to last him a lifetime. If he wanted church, he would walk in the woods and talk to God directly. Thinking about Mama and Daddy helped me keep their memories alive and the stern voice of Uncle Thaddeus out of my head.

After breakfast I cleared the table and Aunt Ida did the dishes.

"Lula May did you memorize your Bible scripture for today. If so tell it to me now."

"In the beginning was the Word, and the Word was with God, and the Word was God," I quoted to Aunt Ida.

"Where's the verse from Lula May?"

"From the book of John," I said.

Aunt Ida had me memorize a Bible scripture every day. When I made a mistake I had to write the scripture ten times. She also tried to teach me sewing and wanted me to help her cut the fabric to make clothes just like hers, long to the floor, with stupid bonnets and aprons.

"I don't want to learn to sew. I can't stand it that you want me and Mama to dress just like you. These ugly black shoes look just like men's," I said, pointing to my shoes and hers.

"Everything in this house reminds me of gray skies and thunder. There are only gray dresses, gray bonnets, black beards, and heavy moods. It feels like a bad storm is going to break every day. I hate it here! I won't become one of you. I won't. My name is Lula May Simpkins and no one will call me by it. I am not Sarah Ruth!"

Aunt Ida didn't say anything while I continued with my ranting. It was a good thing Uncle Thaddeus was gone.

Ida

I brought Thaddeus's Bible to him like I did every single night, the dutiful sister, always doing as she was told. Sarah Ruth sat at the table, timid as a church mouse, as Thaddeus read the scriptures. There was more to that child than she let on. I had seen it in her many times where Thaddeus had not.

Mamie sat in her rocker saying and doing nothing. There were more chores with two extra people living in the house. I was tired and worn out with a bad case of nerves. I felt so blue I thought I'd changed colors.

Listening to Thaddeus read the Bible, going on and on, I wanted to scream, but I didn't dare. I never dared. Mamie rocked back and forth, sometimes slowly, then faster, then slow again, thump, thump, thump against the wood floor. Her eyes stayed focused above Thaddeus's head, toward the window, as if there was something out there besides darkness. Sarah Ruth would eventually fall asleep with her head on the table. The heaviness in the room was too much for a child.

On a cool September night, the evening wore late with Thaddeus spewing words. I thought my eyes were playing tricks on me when I noticed his teeth and tongue were growing as I watched, horrified! His white teeth turned into the biggest I had ever seen, and his hair became darker than coal. Before my very eyes, Thaddeus turned into his horse Midnight, now a Bible reading horse! Maybe he was the black horse in Revelation! I stared in disbelief, afraid to speak.

It was late into the night before the Bible reading horse stopped reading and allowed us to go to our beds. I prayed throughout the night that I should live in the Book of Genesis, in the garden with Adam and Eve, before the snake was let loose into the world and not in the book of Revelation!

Just before sunrise I got out of bed and peeked into Thaddeus's bedroom. He was sleeping like nothing had ever happened. I lit the stove and made coffee before the others were up, thinking upon the night before.

After cooking breakfast I went for a walk toward the cemetery looking for black-eyed susans to make me feel better. I knew I wouldn't find any because it was too late in the season. Most of the leaves had fallen. Continuing to walk I saw snake track crossings on the dusty path. It was unusual to see so many. Staying on the trail I noticed how the buzzards were swooping in big circles; a dead deer probably.

I tried with all my might to push the image of the Bible reading horse out of my head. I knew I should be talking to Jesus, but I couldn't take much more of Him either. He never did what I asked and did terrible things to me instead.

"Stay away from me Jesus, and don't come back. You've cursed me with visions and I don't like it. You are fickle and uncaring. I do not like you!"

Chores were waiting, so I had to go home. When I walked in the house I saw that a small brown bird had made its way through the crack in the kitchen window, his wings beating frantically against the ceiling.

"*Free me from this place,*" I heard him plea.

"How can I free you when I cannot free myself?" I said back to the small creature.

I opened the kitchen door wide, and he found his way outside with help from my broom.

What was he a sign of? What was to come?

I was putting wood into the stove, when a wind blew through the door like an unwanted visitor, causing the kitchen door to slam.

"Who are you that entered this house?" I cried out.

A soft voice spoke. "It is me, Joseph."

107

Lula May

1958

The Council had voted and now Uncle Thaddeus was an Elder. It was official. He was one of them. Aunt Ida said it was an honor to be on the Council of Elders.

"Your Uncle Thaddeus has studied for years and now the council has found him worthy. I'm sure our father would be pleased." It looked to me like Aunt Ida was forcing a smile and I wondered if Uncle Thaddeus's father was rolling over in his grave.

"I know I've been pushing you hard to learn special prayers and scriptures. You're almost ten, Sarah Ruth, and behind the other girls in school since they started younger than you. I've talked to Sister Irene about your staying after school for an extra hour. She has agreed to help you with your Bible reading, arithmetic and writing so you'll be able to catch up quick. It won't be long before you will have to stand before Brother Farley and be questioned about the Bible. Brother Farley makes sure all the children are learning what they are supposed to."

I didn't mind staying after school. I liked being away from the house and Sister Irene was nice. I wished school was every day, but girls only went three times a week, and not at all when it was planting time or the crops were coming in. Sister Irene made me laugh when I worried I wasn't learning quick enough.

"You are a smart girl, smarter than most. Your arithmetic and reading are getting better every day. As fast as you are learning, maybe you'll be teaching here instead of me."

I liked the idea of being a teacher but was sad girls could only go to school until they were fourteen.

The day came for my meeting, and Aunt Ida, Mama and I arrived at Brother Farley's at the appointed time. Aunt Ida had Mama come with us, saying it was good for her to get out of the house for a while and be among other people.

Sister Farley opened the door and let us into the house. She had lines in her face, and dark circles under her eyes. Her shoulders were stooped like she was all worn out. I knew she wasn't very old, but she looked it. I had heard the Sisters talking about her after church. It was wrong to gossip but they still did it when the Brothers weren't around.

"Come on into the kitchen. My husband will be with you directly," Sister Farley said.

Aunt Ida placed Mama in a rocking chair in the kitchen, where she rocked back and forth in a state of agitation. I could tell she didn't want to be here, and neither did I. Her eyes were closed and her hands gripped the chair. Mama hadn't spoken a word in days.

Brother Farley had cruel blue eyes, and I didn't like him even if it was a sin. When quizzed, I stood before him and recited back the scriptures he asked for. He never asked me if I would like to sit or have a drink of water. More than that he never asked me what I believed.

One day I had enough of him. I was mad and agitated at his endless questions and I could not contain myself.

"Brother Farley, I have but one question for you. Can you tell me my real name?"

"You have the name the good Lord gave you. You are Sarah Ruth Simpkins. Just like Saul on the road to Damascus, your name was changed, lest you ever forget," he said, looking at me with piercing eyes.

"My name is Lula May Simpkins and it will always be!" I yelled, then stormed out of the room. I would always be Lula May, no matter what anyone thought or said.

For over a year, I went to Brother Farley's house to be quizzed. During that time his wife passed away.

"You must be especially kind to Brother Farley and say special prayers for him. It will be hard for him not having a wife and a helpmate," Aunt Ida said. I hoped Brother Farley did not find another wife. I would pity the poor woman if he did.

I was surprised when Brother Farley stopped our meetings and recommended to the Council that I be baptized. Why wasn't it up to me to decide if and when I wanted to be baptized? It should be my decision. Why was Brother Farley making decisions about my life?

Lula May

1959

I wasn't sure what I thought about being baptized. Since I had little to say in the matter, I decided to go along with it. To my way of thinking, I didn't figure baptism could hurt me one way or another, and it wasn't worth making a fuss over.

There had been thunder, lightning, and hard rain for days. The creek was swollen and the ground was wet with red mud. On the day of my baptism, the sun shone bright and the smell of honeysuckle was in the air, making me sneeze. Aunt Ida said it was a good sign and God was smiling.

It took longer than usual to walk to the part of the creek where baptisms were done. We were slowed down, because of the mud, and Mama having to be prodded to walk by Aunt Ida. When we got there, most of the Believers had already gathered.

I took a long look around knowing my life would be changed after I was baptized, but I wasn't sure how. I would soon be eleven, not that Mama nor anyone else would remember.

Through the trees on the creek bank I could make out a barn that had about disappeared except for the rusted tin roof. A house was well hidden by a row of saplings, with leaves and branches thickened about it. I wondered what happened to the people who had lived there.

By mid-morning the sun was blazing hot and the Brothers' dark, sweat-drenched shirts stuck to them like second skins. The Sisters were busy watching over the children, yet all eyes were on the proceedings.

Blankets had been spread out for the picnic that would occur after the baptisms. This was one of the few times children were allowed to play together. I looked forward to that.

Brother Farley began the service by praying for peace for all mankind. I liked those prayers, the peaceful ones. When the prayer was over Brother Farley walked to the water, turned, and spoke to the crowd:

"Today three young people will enter this creek. By doing so they agree to live and share all they have with other Believers and draw no attention unto themselves. The Holy Scriptures tell us Christ is coming soon to get His church, His bride. Will we be ready? Today John Troward, Elizabeth Troward, and Sarah Ruth Simpkins will commit themselves to Christ and to the church."

John, a tall lanky boy of thirteen, walked into the water first. Brother Farley put his arm behind John's back and lowered him into the creek. When he brought John up, Reverend Farley said something to John no one could hear. I saw John nod in agreement. John walked out of the water and rejoined his family.

Brother Farley came back to the rest of us and took Elizabeth Troward by the hand and led her into the creek. She was a shy girl of ten and small for her age. I had seen her at meetings. She always hung close to her mother.

The water was high on Elizabeth, almost up to her waist. Brother Farley was protective of her, picking her up and holding her in his arms like a baby. He lowered her into the water. When he brought her up he said something to her, and like her brother, she nodded in agreement. Brother Farley helped her out of the water and came for me.

Taking me by the hand, he led me into deeper water than the others. The current was stronger than I expected and my dress was heavy, like a weight pulling me down. I didn't feel brave; I felt scared. Brother Farley laid his hands upon my head and prayed for the Holy Spirit to fill me.

Holding me in his arms, he lowered me into the water and quickly pulled me up again. Brother Farley looked me in the eyes, searching for I know not what. Was I saved? I didn't think so. If he saw anything in my eyes, it was doubt.

I had barely caught my breath when Brother Farley lowered me into the water again, keeping me down longer this time. Would I see Jesus now? I hadn't held my nose, and water had entered in. I struggled against him, needing to come up for air. Again, I didn't see Jesus. Brother Farley's penetrating blue eyes scanned my face as he brought me up. He didn't ask me a question or talk to me; and I knew why; he could see the anger in my face. Sara Ruth would not submit to this ritual and neither would Lula May!

Brother Farley tried to dunk me the third time, as I struggled in his arms to get away. I didn't want him to submerge me again. Stop, I tried to yell, but he placed his hand over my mouth. Panic entered my being as Brother Farley held me under and wouldn't let me go. I fought to come up, but Brother Farley was too strong. I couldn't breathe, yet he forced me to stay under. At last he let go of me, and I came to the surface. I struggled to breathe and coughed up water.

"Praise God, for Sarah Ruth Simpkins has surrendered to the Almighty. Today there has been a mighty victory for the Lord!" Brother Adam Farley yelled from the creek.

While underwater I visited someplace I had never been before, and I did not see Jesus.

Lula May

1959

I was barely eleven when Mama gave birth. I would always remember that night. Just before dark I found a coal-black feather, fallen like a leaf, beside our house where two crows hunched on our chimney. I felt their eyes following me. I had seen them there many times before. They watched me like they knew me, and maybe they did.

Water was boiling on the wood stove, and Aunt Ida was scrubbing her hands when I came into the kitchen. "The baby will be coming soon. Stay close at hand should I need you, Sarah Ruth."

I was excited and scared at the same time. What would Aunt Ida expect me to do? I wished we had electricity and running water at a time such as this. I wished Mama could have real lights and not just a kerosene lamp, and candles in her room, like we had when we lived with Daddy. Sometimes I was spooked by the shadows on the walls, even at my age, and maybe Mama was, too.

I often dreamed of the house I lived in with Mama and Daddy. I remembered the single-bulb kitchen with Ball jars of blue glass shining beautiful from the window light. Mama's canned beets, which she was famous for, and I hated, lined the wooden shelves with other canned food. We had running water and an indoor toilet. I wanted to return back to the way it was then, but with Daddy gone and a baby coming I knew I wouldn't ever be able to go back.

The mantel clock ticked off the moments to Mama's moaning as she lay in bed upon a tattered brown quilt. Several of the Sisters came and went, laying hands on her, but it was Aunt Ida who never left her side. "Sarah Ruth, I want you to go to the barn and stay until the birthing is over. It shouldn't be long now. I'll call for you then," Aunt Ida said, pushing me from the bedroom.

I was glad she had me leave. I hated seeing Mama in pain and I was only in the way. Thaddeus's mind was on the baby, so he didn't stop me from going into Midnight's stall and brushing him, wanting the time to pass. Midnight wasn't young anymore and I wasn't allowed to give him the same attention I did the plow horses but tonight was different. Thaddeus was busy talking with Brother Farley and Brother Frith and not paying any attention to me. Several times I heard them praying for the safe delivery of Thaddeus's son.

Moon Man had dressed himself as a silver sliver in the sky while the two crows sat sentry on their chimney post wanting to bear witness to my brother's birth, on the 23rd of July, 1959.

The sun was just coming through the cracks in the hen house when Sister Charlotte came to get me. I had been throwing the chickens their grain and had collected nine eggs for my trouble. When I was allowed upstairs, I had a baby brother.

Mama looked tired and worn out, I had never noticed how frail she looked before. I went over and kissed her cheek as she nursed the baby. Looking into my eyes, she whispered to me so the Sisters couldn't hear, "love your little brother, Lula May." I felt so happy; it was if I had Mama back again. I hoped this time the real mama would stay.

When Mama and the baby were ready for visitors, Thaddeus went into the bedroom and took his son from Mama. I quietly followed behind Thaddeus wanting to know what he was going to do with my brother. He went into the kitchen, placed the baby in the cradle he had been making for days, and called for Ida to join him. Standing in the pantry, they did not see me when Thaddeus began speaking.

"I want Mamie to nurse the child for only a few days. I'll be going to Rocky Mount tomorrow to buy the necessary bottles for my son. I want you to do the feedings, Ida. Talk to the other Sisters about the best way to do this."

This wasn't what Believers did, even I knew that. Thaddeus didn't want Mama to breastfeed his son. Aunt Ida was to take over my baby brother's feedings, not Mama, and that wasn't right.

I loved my baby brother from the moment I laid eyes on him and wanted to hold him whenever I could. I hated it when I heard him cry and wanted to comfort him. Thaddeus and Aunt Ida scolded me, saying not to spoil him. When Aunt Ida didn't think anyone was around, I saw her pick my brother up and cuddle him. She never knew I saw her.

Mamie

"We shall wait to name the child until it is ordained by God," Thaddeus instructed me. I knew I had no say in the matter. Ida had been taking care of the baby while I recovered from childbirth. She and Lula May brought me food on a tray. It was such an effort to do the little I was able to. Three weeks had gone by when Ida insisted I go outside.

"Mamie, you need some fresh air, you're far too pale. Take the baby outside and I'll bring his cradle. I don't want him in the kitchen while I'm canning; it will be too hot in here. I've already hung up the wash. If you're up to it, you can take it down when it dries. I'd have Sarah Ruth help me, but Sister Charlotte's been feeling poorly, so I sent Sarah Ruth over to help out."

There wasn't any use in arguing with Ida, so I did as I was told.

I laid down on the quilt Ida had brought outside and placed under the hickory tree. The baby was lying in his cradle beside me. How I enjoyed seeing his little fingers and toes. It wasn't long before the baby and I were both napping. When I woke, the sky was getting grayer by the minute. In the far fields lightning had begun flinging flares of light, with thunder sounding like gunshots. I prayed there would be no fire.

I didn't want to upset Ida, so I would need to hurry and get the clothes down. As fast as I could I picked up the clothes basket and ran toward the clothesline when out of nowhere, a bolt of lightning hit the clothes line wires, becoming a ball of fire striking the hickory tree under which my new born son lay in the cradle. The bark flew off the trunk and limbs went a flying.

Rushing to my baby, I saw him in the cradle, unhurt and cooing!

117

Picking him up, I held him close to my pounding heart. He was alright. He was safe.

Within minutes, Thaddeus and nearby neighbors arrived. The group was silent as Thaddeus took my son from my arms.

"This is the sign I have been waiting for!" he declared.

His voice became deeper and more commanding as he continued to speak before the crowd that had gathered.

"From the sign of the lightning bolt, I name my son for the Apostle Paul. We will call him Ray, for the ray of light he will be in the world. My son's name is to be Paul Ray Simpkins, and he is a messenger of God!"

I almost fainted; not from heat or weakness, but from what I saw in my infant son's face which I hadn't seen before.

"My son is Joseph's child!"

The words came out of me loud and clear. Thaddeus heard me, as did everyone else. People began to murmur, and I was overcome with a ringing in my ears.

118

Ida

Thaddeus was swelled with pride over the birth of his son. It was like the child's mama had no part in it at all. The child wasn't but a month old when Thaddeus wanted him dedicated in the church. Mamie seemed weak and wasn't coming out of her room much. I think she was affected by the lightning bolt striking so close to her. She told me she still had ringing in her ears and bouts of dizziness.

Mamie had gotten where she didn't ask about the baby or Lula May, but kept to herself with the door shut. Thaddeus planned to go on with the dedication when he could have waited for Mamie to get better. I couldn't help but think he wanted it that way, particularly with her saying the baby was Joseph's child. She was right on one account; her boy was the spitting image of Joseph.

I got the baby ready for his big day, bathing him in a washtub on the kitchen table. Thaddeus, who didn't take notice of clothes, had me sew a white gown for Joseph.

"White is for purity; make something fitting for my boy," Thaddeus told me.

The gown came out real nice, with the special stitching I put around the neck, with blue thread. Once the baby was fed and dressed, Thaddeus took him from me. He wouldn't wait for me or Sarah Ruth to get ready, but walked to the church carrying his son.

When Sarah Ruth and I arrived at the dedication, we sat on the third row. I didn't want us to sit in the front with the Elders. I didn't want any attention to be on me or Sarah Ruth. This was Thaddeus's special day, and I didn't want no part of anything that might go wrong.

119

"Where's Sister Mamie today? I didn't see her come in," Sister Thrasher asked me. She and several of the Sisters were sitting in the row right behind me and Lula May. I felt as if they were all ears as they waited for my reply.

"Sister Mamie is too ill to be here today. I imagine she will be better after a few more days of rest."

All eyes were on Thaddeus when the dedication began. The majority of Believers were there, for this was a day of great importance to the congregation. It wasn't every day a son was born to an Elder. All eyes and ears were upon Thaddeus as he spoke while holding the baby.

"I come before you with my first born son, Paul Ray Simpkins. I prayed and the Lord granted me what I asked of Him for it is He who opens and closes the womb. I have been given the duty to raise this infant. Today I dedicate my son to the Lord by reading Psalm 127:3-5.

Lo, children are in the heritage of the Lord:
And the fruit of the womb is his reward.
As arrows are in the hand of a mighty man;
So are children of the youth.
Happy is the man that hath his quiver full of them;
They shall not be ashamed,
But they shall speak with the enemies in the gate."

After the final words were spoken, Thaddeus continued to hold Paul while each of us came up, one by one, to bless him and accept him into our community.

Sarah Ruth and I quietly walked home afterwards while Thaddeus stayed behind with the baby. It wasn't right his mother wasn't there. It wasn't right at all.

The next morning the Elders came with their sons to build another outhouse. Thaddeus would no longer share one with women, nor would his son. All morning they dug the hole, by noon time they were done.

Lula May

I liked having a baby brother. Uncle Thaddeus smiled more, but Mama smiled less.

"We will call the boy Ray until he can accept his rightful place within the church. At that time he shall be called Paul," Thaddeus told me and Aunt Ida after he finished the breakfast prayer. Mama was in the bedroom and hadn't come to eat. I thought it sad Thaddeus didn't consider Mama or care how she felt when he picked the baby's name.

Uncle Thaddeus made a highchair for Ray, and it didn't seem like any time at all until he was able to sit with us at the table, eating the mush Aunt Ida made him for breakfast. Mama seldom ate breakfast with us and wasn't there to see Ray take his first step. I took Ray to see Mama whenever I could unless Aunt Ida or Uncle Thaddeus kept me from doing so.

Taking Ray to Mama, I stood him up by the bed, stepped away and called his name. He took three steps before he fell down and started to cry. I picked him up and put him in Mama's lap. She smiled at her boy, held him and comforted him.

Sometimes when Mama took Ray a contented look would come upon her face. Just as often confusion came over her and she would push him away.

"Look, Mama, Ray's got his arms out for you to hold him," I said, placing Ray on her lap.

"Take the boy away, Lula May, for one day I will lose him too."

"You haven't lost me, Mama, I'm right here. Don't you care?"

Mama didn't answer me, so I took Ray and left the room.

Lula May

1961

"Sarah Ruth, take your mother a cup of coffee and ask her if she's coming down to eat. If not, I'll fix her a boiled egg and toast and you can take it to her," Aunt Ida said as she filled the dishpan with hot water from the wood stove. Mama hadn't come down for breakfast, but I'd thought little of it.

Thaddeus was still in the kitchen having breakfast and spending time with Ray, who had recently turned two years old. For over a month Thaddeus had been taking Ray to the barn, hoping he would get used to Midnight and stop his crying at the sight of the horse.

"Ray will not sit on Midnight's back even as I hold him," Thaddeus said to Aunt Ida, clearly frustrated by his son's behavior.

"Give him time, Thaddeus. He's just a little boy. It will happen," Aunt Ida replied, trying to placate her brother.

Mama was still in bed when I went into her room. I yelled for Aunt Ida to come quick. Mama heard my voice and looked up. Her hair was matted and her face flushed with sweat. I was scared and stood there helpless to do anything. I was relieved when Aunt Ida came rushing in.

"How long ago was it when you started leaking fluids?" Aunt Ida asked Mama.

"Don't know," Mama said as she rolled to her side, moaning in pain.

"Go downstairs and gather a sharp knife and a fresh sheet. Then put water on to boil and come back here," Aunt Ida ordered me.

When I came back to the room I saw Aunt Ida had pulled Mama's nightdress up around her hips and there was blood on the inside of Mama's legs.

"Sarah Ruth, you're old enough to help. I want you to time your mother's contractions. I'll show you how."

"They're seven minutes apart, Aunt Ida," I said, having watched the mantle clock and followed her instruction exactly. An hour passed, more blood came, but no baby.

"Go find Thaddeus and tell him to ride Juniper hard, and bring Sister Harriet here. I'm going to need her help."

Thaddeus was in the barn with Ray, waiting for news of another son. I stayed in the barn with Ray as Thaddeus rode off on Juniper. He was soon home, followed by Sister Harriet in her horse and buggy. I thought it fortunate how we had acquired Juniper from Brother Lyle's family, seeing how the elderly Brother had passed away and they had no need for an extra horse to feed.

The baby didn't come, although the full moon did. I heard Aunt Ida say the word breach and I knew that wasn't a good thing. I couldn't stand the sounds Mama made as she screamed in pain. Thaddeus went into the house, telling Mama she neglected proper self-control with all her carrying on.

"Thaddeus Simpkins, you leave this house and do not return until I send for you!"

I never heard Aunt Ida stand up to Thaddeus, and I was proud of her. I saw Aunt Ida in a way I never had before.

During the night, lightning flashed nearby, and it sounded as if thundering horses were snorting and stomping their hooves against the roof. Still, the baby didn't come but Brother Farley did. Mama's screams terrified me, and I wondered if she was reminded of how lightning struck when Ray was born.

Thaddeus stayed in the barn with Brother Farley praying as I watched over Ray trying to comfort him as best I could. After a long crying spell

I took him to the hayloft, rocked him in my arms and sang to him until he finally fell asleep. Mama's cries had become weaker and fainter as the night wore on, and that scared me more than her screaming did.

On September 30, 1961, just before sunrise, my baby sister arrived. Aunt Ida let me into Mama's bedroom so I could see her. She was tiny, but had a mighty cry. Aunt Ida laid her in Mama's arms, but she couldn't hold her. Sister Harriet held the baby against Mama's breast, and my little sister latched on.

"Your mother is weak from loss of blood and will need much care. I'll need your help more than ever," Aunt Ida whispered to me. "I want you to gather the bloody rags and sheets and take them to the wash tub to soak."

Thaddeus didn't go to see Mama or the baby. He didn't hold his daughter like he did Ray. He wasn't given the son he wanted and did nothing to hide his disappointment. With the difficulty of the child's birth, Thaddeus would not be given a quiver of sons. He would have only Ray.

It took Thaddeus several weeks to name his daughter. I was beginning to wonder if he ever would. We were sitting at the supper table, except for Mama, who was eating in her room. Thaddeus stood from the table and picked Ray up from his chair. Holding Ray in his arms, he drew in a deep breath, then made his announcement.

"I am naming the girl Raylene, after her brother. As she becomes older she will be a helpmate to him as he goes about God's work. As is fitting with Mary and Martha, in Luke 10, so shall this child be a Martha. Raylene Martha Simpkins is to be her name from this day forward."

Thaddeus looked each of us square in the eye, letting us know we had no say in the matter. I felt bad for my little sister. I hoped her life wouldn't be like Aunt Ida's; cooking, cleaning, and doing backbreaking chores, while always caring for Ray.

Raylene was a colicky baby where Ray was a happy one. She cried night and day. It made me think she didn't want to be born. Only her big brother Ray could comfort her. Raylene became her big brother's shadow as soon as she learned to walk. Ray never seemed to mind and was always watching out for her.

I couldn't understand how Mama could just sit in her rocker and pay no never mind to Ray, Raylene, or me, for that matter. The Mama I remembered would never have been like this. My old Mama was beautiful in spirit and flesh. At least that's my memory of her. It seemed a long time back when Mama came into my room to tuck me in.

There was sadness in Mama's eyes and a kind of darkness that played upon her face. Sometimes when you least expected it her lips would turn up and she seemed almost happy, but it didn't last for a moment. I was always sad when it happened because it was never us, her children, she was smiling at.

If Mama would have let me place my hands on her cheeks, I believed I would have felt the extent of her sorrow and somehow drawn it into myself and out of her. Maybe then I could have gotten her back, or at least a piece of her, but I was scared to try.

Mamie

1962

I had been a brood mare and nothing more. I had served my purpose. Thaddeus allowed me an upstairs bedroom of my own. He left me alone, thinking I was crazed. He was right; I was crazed from the loss of my beloved.

I kept a candle burning for Joe as I had always done, but now Thaddeus wasn't there to blow it out. My children's rearing had been taken over by Ida, so I wasn't needed by anyone. Thaddeus had his son and that was all that mattered.

Lying in bed for days, I became too weak to get up. There was no sleep, because my heart was angry. I worried for Lula May, Ray, and Raylene endlessly. There was no tenderness nor affection in this house. What they received had come from me. Now they would have to be there for each other. Love and acceptance was what they needed, and I had no strength to give it to them, nor was I allowed to do so. One day this house would fall to ruins, and I would be glad for it.

How I envied the moon and stars, for they had the sky to hang on to, but I was suspended like a spider dangling from a thread, without my Joe. A great heaviness had hold of me in body and mind. My thoughts had gone to live in the dark, deep woods where no light shone in. My eyes which once gazed upon my children's faces, red gladiolas, and the silver sparkles in quartz rocks now saw only grayness. I prayed for death to take me, but I wasn't wanted. I was nothing more than a gray dress that should soon disappear.

126

Mamie

A high fever and a prolonged delirium; brain fever was what Ida called it. I do not remember anything except the scent of Joe in my bed. How could Joe be here when he was nothing but bones and dust in a box? A strange feeling came over me when I noticed the silver dollar lying on the bedside table beside my water glass. It was warm to the touch, a strange occurrence, to be sure. Joe was gone, a car wreck. How could this be?

I lay in bed holding the 1888 silver dollar Joe carried in his pocket. It was the first dollar he made. He thought the silver dollar brought him luck. Joe and I were going to dinner with Levi and Violet when he noticed a hole in his pants and had me put the coin in my purse for safe keeping. The next day Joe was dead. The purse and silver dollar disappeared a long time ago. I stayed curled up in the bed pondering the silver dollar. Joe must have brought it to me, as a sign.

Pulling myself up on my elbow I noticed the imprint of a head upon the unused pillow. Joe had been in bed with me as well. I felt giggly, like the young girl I was when first Joe kissed me. Was I dreaming within my dreams? I did not believe so. Maybe I was going insane. If so, may insanity take me now!

Mamie

My tears wouldn't let me rest. Wishing Joe would come back to me kept me from sleep. I would have no companion but him. Without Joe I had no beginning nor end, no night, no dawn, nothing but burning sorrow. I prayed to God to take me so I could go to Joe, but He did not answer me. I was a prisoner of myself.

My hair had turned gray and there were lines on my face. Would Joe know me since my illness made me old? Ida washed my hair and made me sit in a chair before the fire in the kitchen, as it dried. She tried to make me eat, but I wanted no human nourishment. Ida forbade me from running into the woods in my nightdress, with my hair hanging wild. She had seen me as I stared into the moonlight calling Joe's name.

"I am afraid for you, Mamie. Something terrible will happen to you if you don't stop this foolishness at once. Joseph was my brother and I can tell you he is not here!"

I didn't listen to Ida. I left the house in the dead of night. I liked seeing the critters' eyes shining yellow and hearing the dogs howl as they hunted for coons. I would go to the cemetery and stare at the stone beds until the sun peeped up over the mountain. I was envious of those who had gone to their eternal rest and wondered what it was like. I could almost hear dead lips moving trying to tell me things I couldn't understand. If I was lucky I saw crows gliding in circles. The crows were closer to Joe than I. How I wanted to be one of those crows!

Thaddeus did not try to stop me from my nocturnal wanderings as Ida did, for I no longer existed to him. Should Thaddeus ever come to me wanting another son, I would drown myself in the creek or take the rat poison in the barn.

My nights were passed in vigil, waiting for Joe to take me away from this house of sorrow. He was the only road I would travel on. I wanted no one but Joe. He was my only salvation.

Lula May

Brother Farley attended the snakes, feeding them rats and mice the boys caught as part of their duties to the church. The snakes were kept in a plain wooden box behind the pulpit. I had seen the dark diamonds on the rattlesnake's back, and heard its tail rattle when others handled it.

I had been told many times how my Grandmother Ruth handled serpents, drank poison, and talked in tongues. The last time she was bitten was different. The snakebite killed her quickly. No one bothered to get medical treatment because that would have tampered with God's will. Believers still talked about my grandparents' faith and how the Holy Spirit came upon them at meetings.

"Sarah Ruth, it was your grandmother's time to meet Jesus and be with her husband again, that's why she picked up the snake that bit her. Try to be more like your grandmother and live by her example," Brother Farley said to me after church.

"If what you say is true, then my grandmother was a fool," I said back to him.

When Brother Farley preached he glared at me from the pulpit, daring me to come forward. I glared right back, for I had nothing but contempt for him since my baptism.

"Come to the pulpit, Sister Sarah Ruth and prove your faith," he taunted me.

I never went forward. I had not experienced the signs and knew I never would. Thaddeus was disappointed in me, but I didn't care. Aunt Ida never handled snakes. Perhaps she never felt the anointing, although many Believers did. Often members spoke in tongues, and some lay in death-like trances while others jerked about on the floor.

During these meetings I prayed for Ray and Raylene to never receive the Holy Ghost. I never wanted them to handle serpents nor drink strychnine. I wanted them to stay safe. One day I might not be around to watch over them.

I feared for Ray because Uncle Thaddeus had a burning desire for Ray to believe as he did. Most of all he wanted my little brother to speak the word.

Lula May

1963

I ran away over and over again, but never had a well thought out plan. It was hard to run away in the daylight, in a long gray dress and bonnet. I was always found and brought back to Thaddeus, where there was hell to pay. He made me write scriptures for hours and deprived me of sleep by giving me endless chores. The only thing that kept me going was keeping an eye on Mama, Ray, and Raylene. I knew I had to get away as soon as I could, because of Thaddeus's crazy talk, which was scaring me and giving me nightmares.

"Sarah Ruth, you are fourteen. It won't be long before I find a suitable husband for you, an older man who can handle you and make you a respectable wife. You need discipline so you will know your place in life."

I had seen the older Brothers and their younger, but haggard wives. I shuddered to think of what would become of me if Thaddeus had his way.

I was fifteen when my luck changed. It was summertime and the days were long. Aunt Ida was busy cleaning up the kitchen and Thaddeus had gone to a meeting. Ray and Raylene were in the garden picking beans. I didn't know how much time I had until Thaddeus returned.

Sneaking into Aunt Ida's room, I took off my bonnet, apron and dress and hid them under Aunt Ida's bed. Taking a pair of Ida's sewing scissors I cut a hole in her bed sheet and pulled it over my head. I wrapped a piece of a rope around my waist for a belt which I had found in Thaddeus's room along with a five dollar bill. Picking up one of Aunt

Ida's unfinished quilt tops, I wrapped it around my shoulders like a shawl. It didn't look like a real dress, but it would have to do.

Mama was sitting in her rocker by the window when I went in to say goodbye. I gave her a kiss on her forehead and looked into her sad eyes.

"I'm leaving, Mama. I hope one day I can see you again when things are different."

Mama reached out and touched my face. She understood what I was telling her. I had no time to stay with her, and was sad I couldn't see Ray and Raylene and explain to them why I was leaving. One day I would try to make them understand.

Climbing out my bedroom window, I ran to the barn. As I looked back at the house, I saw Mama standing by her window. She raised her arm in a wave of goodbye. I felt a lump in my throat. Was I wrong in leaving her? What would become of her and Ray and Raylene without me to look out for them?

I had no time to dwell on my actions. I had to continue on, even if it was wrong, because there was no going back, not even for Mama. Married to someone Thaddeus chose for me wouldn't help them, or me, one bit.

Running through the fields and woods, I took the path that forked to the left, then another left, and I was on the main road. I planned on hitchhiking in which ever direction I could get a ride. I didn't have any plans beyond that.

Several cars passed me and didn't stop. When I saw a black pickup truck coming, I turned my back to it and walked off the road, not wanting to be noticed. It was mostly Believers who drove black trucks. A big blue car came down the road. I could tell there was a man driving it and nobody else was in the car. It pulled over.

"Young woman, what are you doing hitchhiking? It's not safe," the older man said, his bushy eyebrows raised in concern.

"There's nothing wrong, sir. I have friends waiting for me in Vinton where I'm starting a new job," I said, looking at the ground.

"Get into the car. At least with me, I'll know you're safe. My name is

Layman. James Layman," he said extending his hand.

I never had shaken anyone's hand before, least of all a man. Mr. Layman didn't lecture me any further about hitchhiking. He asked me my name as I got in and shut the car door.

"Tell it to me straight, young lady. I don't mean you any harm. If you're in any kind of trouble maybe my wife and I can help."

I told Mr. Layman I had two names, Lula May and Sarah Ruth Simpkins. I saw his knuckles go white as he grasped the steering wheel.

"I knew your Father well. He was good man. I'm not going to drive you anywhere but to a pay phone. I helped your parents before and it seems their story has some more telling to do."

Mr. Layman handed me the change he had in his pocket and drove me to a pay phone at the Hardy post office. I dialed the number with Mr. Layman's help. A woman answered.

"Who are you?" I asked.

"Who are you?" she asked back.

"Lula May Simpkins." I heard a gasp on the other end of the line.

"Stay right there, girl. I'm coming to get you!" I handed the phone to Mr. Layman.

Lula May

Violet and Levi Ferguson cared for me as if I were their very own daughter. Violet and I shed many tears when I was ready to talk about what it was like living under Thaddeus's roof.

"It's alright to grieve for your mama, Lula May. You love her and I would expect nothing else. I want you to get the tears out," Violet said.

"I left Ray and Raylene behind and they are so young. I'm afraid Thaddeus will punish them for my leaving. I know how he is, Violet. He'll make them do all the milking, slopping the hogs, and washing on top of the many other chores they already have. Thaddeus will make them stay up way too late memorizing and copying scriptures when they are barely old enough to write."

"I know it's hard not to feel guilty about leaving but Ida is there with them. Somehow things have a way of working out in the end. Look at me and Violet for example," Levi said, putting his arm around my shoulder. "Have some faith girl, and take each day as it comes."

I still couldn't help but wonder what Thaddeus said to Ray and Raylene about me. I knew it wouldn't be good. I thought about Mama, Ray and Raylene day and night and prayed Aunt Ida would do whatever she could to protect them all.

It didn't take but a few days before Uncle Thaddeus figured out where I was. Violet was shelling beans on the porch when she saw an old black truck driving very slowly towards the house. I was in the bedroom reading, and Levi was napping on the couch when Violet came running into the living room. Memories came flooding back to me from childhood, and I began crying and weeping like a little girl. This time Levi was ready for him.

"Violet, you and Lula May stay in the house and don't come out," Levi said as he picked up his hunting rifle and walked into the yard.

"Thaddeus Simpkins, get away from this house, before I shoot your ass."

"I've come for the girl."

Violet and I were staring out the open window as Levi raised his rifle and aimed it at Thaddeus. Taking a few steps back, Thaddeus gave a slow, disbelieving shake of his head. He got into his truck left, and did not return.

Lula May

1964-1967

"Tomorrow morning I'd like for us to go to Jefferson High School and meet with the principal and guidance teacher to figure out what we need to do for you to attend public school," Violet said, at the break-fast table. I became nervous thinking about being with students my own age. Would I fit in? Would they all be smarter than me? I was up early still worrying about going to school with non-believers and won-dering what they would think of me. I couldn't eat a bit of breakfast.

"Non-believers aren't so different from us, Lula May. When I was in the service I met some really fine men and now I have plenty of friends through my work. You'll be just fine, girl," Levi said, patting my hand.

"That went well," Levi said, as we left the guidance counselor's office the next day.

"The books on the suggested reading list look interesting. I might have to read a few of them myself. We can stop on the way home and get you a library card. I know you'll do well on the placement tests once you've had time to study." Violet said, shifting a pile of books over to me while she looked for the car keys. Flashes of Mama taking me to the library came into my head and I wished she was with us now.

Violet and Levi tried teaching me math and geography when they came home from work. We would sit at the kitchen table and go over my assignments together.

"Lula May, Levi and I can help you with your studies but only up to a point. I think we had better get a homebound teacher. I remember the guidance counselor saying she knew of a good one for you. Math has never been my strong suit and I've taken you as far as I can go."

Mrs. Burnett, a retired high school teacher, started coming to the house twice a week. She was a good teacher and I worked hard. Sometimes Violet took me to the Roanoke Public Library on Jefferson Street where I would check out books about different countries. I liked reading about distant places and dreamed of going to Europe and Australia one day.

The following fall I was able to attend high school. I took business classes, learned to type and take shorthand. After school and on weekends I worked with Violet at the Maywood Restaurant serving endless cups of coffee with a smile.

You never saw two people prouder when I graduated from Jefferson High School. Violet wanted me to go to National Business College in Roanoke and get my secretarial degree.

"With a little more training you could be a secretary at the Norfolk and Western Railroad in Roanoke. It's a good job, honey, with good pay. You'd be secure if you worked for the railroad."

I had other ideas. I wanted to travel and see places. I read every moment I could. Literature was my favorite subject. When I turned eighteen, I applied for a job as a stewardess with Piedmont Airlines.

I was so excited when I got a letter asking me to come for an interview I could barely stand it.

"Violet, I'm going on an airline interview! What can I do to make sure they hire me?"

"I've been thinking on it ever since you mailed in your application. Tomorrow we're going to the airport and see what the stewardesses are wearing when they walk off the airplane."

Violet and I watched several flights come in, making mental notes on what we should buy, such as shoes and handbags that looked like uniform pieces.

Leaving the airport, Violet took me to Crossroads Mall and we went shopping in JC Penny and other stores. After trying on several outfits, Violet bought me a dress, shoes, and a purse that looked as close to the uniform as we could find. Several days before my interview we went back to Crossroads Mall, and I went to a fancy salon where my hair was cut and styled and cosmetics purchased for the full effect. I looked like a stewardess!

I boarded my first airplane at Woodrum Field in Roanoke and flew to Winston-Salem, North Carolina for my interview. I spent the night in the Holiday Inn, not sleeping a wink.

The next day, I took all kinds of tests and was interviewed by several different people. All sorts of pretty girls came in to be interviewed, but I knew I looked as good as they did. I could tell all of us were nervous, but who wouldn't be? When the testing and interviews were finished, I still remained while many of the other girls had been sent home.

I was hired on July 14, 1967. Sarah Ruth was finally put to rest that day, and Lula May was reborn.

PART THREE

"With Lightning, the past is
but a prologue to the future."
Unknown

Ray

1969

"You were born for a special purpose, Ray, and it will be revealed in time. Come to me with your questions and I will guide your path," Father said as we were walking home from rabbit hunting. I hadn't managed to shoot anything, but Father had so we'd be having rabbit stew for supper.

As far back as I can remember Father had been telling me this and I still didn't understand what he meant by it. I often wondered why Father wore a black glove on his right hand when no one else did. I asked him once and he just looked at me hard. I never asked again.

When I was a little boy I remember wanting to sit on Mother's lap, but Aunt Ida always took me away from her. I had an older sister, Sarah Ruth, who went away. I wasn't allowed to mention her name. Luckily I had my little sister Raylene. I liked being a big brother and watching over her. I didn't want her to go away, too.

I started milking cows with Father when I was five. He and I worked in the garden side by side growing everything we ate, as well as harvesting acres of corn and hay on our eighty acre farm. We had apple and peach trees which I liked to climb when Father wasn't looking. Aunt Ida raised broiler chickens and fryers. Sometimes we had as many as thirty beef cows.

We had several horses besides Midnight. Father never allowed me or Raylene to ride his horse, saying he was special and only his. Molly and Ben were plough horses, and we had Juniper as well. It was my job to shovel the manure from their stalls and put it in the vegetable garden.

Father shoveled Midnight's stall himself.

Field work started early, with feeding and harnessing Ben and Molly. This happened after I filled the wood box. I liked plowing the fields and the damp smell of overturned soil.

When I was nine I was old enough to watch Raylene so Aunt Ida could go with Father and sell eggs and produce at the market in Roanoke. She had a regular route she walked, going door to door in neighborhoods with her big egg basket while Father sold from the market stalls.

Raylene and I had chores to do while they were gone, but I made sure we had time to play, plus it was the only time we were alone with Mother. Raylene and I tried to make Mother laugh. Sometimes we could coax a little smile, but more often than not there were tears in her eyes. Why couldn't she be like the other mothers? Didn't she know she had children who needed her?

Raylene always had questions for me when no one was around. Father and Aunt Ida couldn't be bothered with a little girl's nonsense. I didn't see it as nonsense, not if the questions were important to Raylene.

"These blue and yellow iris's sure are pretty, aren't they Ray?"

"Not as pretty as you, Raylene," I said, and began chasing her around the front yard. When I caught her she became all serious. I hadn't expected that.

"Ray, where does the thunder go when it leaves?"

"Back to heaven, Raylene. God sends the thunder because he wants to remind us he's up there watching over us."

"Do you ever hear the music in the wind, Ray?"

"I sure do, Raylene. What you're hearing is leaves passing stories between each other, just like people gossiping."

"Do lightning bugs really have lightning in them?"

"God made them that way so they can always find their way in the dark."

"You'll always be with me, won't you Ray? Say you won't ever leave me."

"I'll never leave you, Raylene. I promise."

Ray

I had been out searching for a wayward cow since after breakfast and it was almost noon. I found him finally in the high meadow toward the woods. I had a few minutes to myself when I got back to the barn so I went about finishing my surprise for Raylene.

"Come here and see what I've made for you," I hollered out to Raylene. I knew she was nearby but I didn't see her anywhere. Finally I caught a glimpse of her near the tool shed, close to where a large patch of violets grew.

"Thank you, Ray," Raylene said, taking the doll from my hand, breathless from running. "She looks like the mama to the other dolls you made me since she's bigger and wearing a dress."

"Aunt Ida gave me one of her quilt squares and I painted on a face with barn paint. I'm glad you like her."

"I love her Ray, I really do," Raylene said, as she gave me a big hug. "You are the best big brother ever."

Sometimes Raylene and I went into the woods searching for chinkapins. We liked the taste of the tender nut. When we found some Raylene would laugh and laugh excited about roasting them in the fire and having a sweet treat. I felt bad because Raylene didn't get much of Mother's love. I worried for her because I had seen the light in her eyes. She was drawn to light. At nighttime Raylene gazed at the stars and the moon. Often she stared at the fire in the cook stove and didn't hear her name being called.

When Raylene was but a tiny girl she was taught to pull weeds. By the time she was six she was picking beans, shelling beans, then cooking those beans and putting them on our plates at suppertime. It was Ray-

144

lene's job to collect eggs. When she was old enough she churned the milk I brought to her after I had strained it. I worried for her because it was hard work for such a little girl. There was always something to be done on a farm.

Sometimes when Mother was in her rocking chair, Raylene and I would look at her wondering if she was thinking of us. At times Mother's face would take on a different look and a smile would cross her face. It was like she was seeing something or someone, and it would give me a shudder. Raylene made the mistake of touching Mother's face during one of these times and, quicker than lightning, Mother's face became a storm cloud and raindrops rolled down her cheeks. Raylene became scared like she had done something bad when all she wanted was her mother.

Aunt Ida attended to Mother's needs, making her take a good bath once a week. Mother didn't have the desire to take a bath herself, but Aunt Ida made sure she got one. Hauling and heating water was a hard job, but a necessary one. I didn't mind hauling water for Mother, Ida and Raylene's baths. I knew that women liked to stay especially clean.

We were always coaxing Mother to eat as she had little interest in food. Sometimes she ate and dressed herself. Usually it was a sign she would be leaving the house in the dark of night, coming home with a wild look in her eyes and twigs in her hair. Many nights I climbed out my bedroom window and followed her until Father found out.

"I'll lock you in your room if you ever follow her again," was his stern warning, and I knew he meant it. I stopped following Mother, but watched out my window, hoping she returned safely from the night.

Raylene

1970

It seems as far back as I can remember I've been ornery and full of doubt. My earliest memories are of Father taking Ray and me into the woods and making Ray stand on a stump and pray. Father wanted Ray to be anointed by the Almighty One, to pray and speak in tongues. Ray couldn't get off the stump until Father said he could.

Father would be on his knees beseeching God to enter his boy and wouldn't stop while Ray stood on the stump. I had to ignore my empty stomach as this went on for the longest time. I tried to imagine myself making daisy-chain jewelry since I couldn't wear any other kind, but it was hard not to notice Father. When he was talking to God his voice was louder, deeper, and measured out with a boldness that caused the hairs on my arms to rise. Eventually Father would stop and Ray could, too, and we would go home together.

Every night Ray had to read to us from the Bible until Father said he could stop, then he would have me read a few chapters, mostly from Proverbs. We never read anything except the Bible.

"The only things we need to know comes from the good news of the gospel," Father said over and over again.

Sometimes I felt Mother was almost with us during the Bible readings, but not really. Mother barely smiled, talked, or cried. She didn't do much of nothing.

"Raylene, I want you to notice when the moon is full, Mother will start talking real soft, like someone is with her. She does it other times but mainly then."

"Who is she talking to, do you know, Ray?"

"Mother was married before Thaddeus. His name was Joseph. He was Sarah Ruth's daddy. I think it's him she's talking to. Remember, Raylene, just because Mother isn't right in the head doesn't mean she's crazy. There's a difference."

We went to church every Sunday and Wednesday. Most meetings Believers came right up and accepted the invitation when it was offered. People would commence to praising the Lord and hugging each other as they were being saved. I remember hoping I didn't die because I hadn't been saved. I had never been anointed and didn't want to be. Sometimes people were marked black and blue from serpent bites. Brother Farley got bit bad handling a rattlesnake as I watched on at a church service.

"If it is the perfect will of the Almighty One, evil will be cast out and you will be healed," Father said preaching over Adam Farley's outstretched body, as two Elders knelt by his side. For days Brother Farley was in a fever, thrashing around, while members of the congregation laid hands on him and prayed.

Brother Farley didn't die although his arm rotted, then withered away and had to be cut off. God was never blamed, for it was Brother Farley who misjudged Spirit when he picked up the rattlesnake. Brother Farley had his personal experience of salvation and a spiritual wound to show for it, which he wore like a badge of honor.

I kept quiet in church, particularly when Father preached. I didn't want him to look my way and call on me to come forward. I had seen him do this to Ray over and over again, making Ray quote scriptures from memory and to praise the Lord with all the excitement he could muster.

"The Holy Spirit's not in me, Raylene. I haven't felt the anointing, handled snakes, or drank poison and I'm almost fourteen! I don't want to be a disappointment to Father. I want to feel the Holy Spirit more for him than me. Do you think I should pretend it happens?"

"If you want it more than anything, it's bound to, particularly if you wish it on a falling star," I said, even though I had my doubts. I hated Father for putting Ray through this like a hunting dog he was training. Ray's pretending didn't feel honest to me, and I felt sorry for him. I was glad I was a girl and Father didn't expect much of me.

Father paced back and forth when it was his turn to preach. He took off his Believer's jacket when the anointing came upon him, and that was a sure sign it had. It was unseemly for a Brother to be in church with his white shirtsleeves rolled up and his collar open. Opening the box, Father would take out a copperhead or a rattler with his black gloved hand and drape it across his shoulders as the serpent writhed around. People would leap up and shout with their tongues on fire. Sometimes prayer meeting would go for hours on end, and I would get so tired watching it all. I never felt any different on these nights and wondered what was wrong with me.

I remember sneaking out on one of these nights. The room was in a fevered pitch. I knew no one would notice I was gone. I walked to a grassy patch beside the parking lot and lay on the soft green grass. I was hoping to see a falling star and make Ray's wish for him. Heat lightning was flashing and became so bold it lit up the sky. The smell from the feverish white bolts screamed and cracked the night sky open, filling my nostrils and the rest of me with a blessed white light. The lightning came so close I thought a bolt would come crashing down on me. I wondered if Ray's wish would come true.

Ida

1971

I barely remember when I started doing it; it was such a long time ago. I couldn't take Thaddeus eating mouthful after mouthful of sweet potatoes, scraping his little pitchfork against the sides of his metal bowl trying to get every last morsel. I thought I'd lose my mind with that scraping sound. Ray and Raylene were sitting at the table, good little children.

It was just a little D-Con I mixed up in Thaddeus's sweet potatoes, not enough to taste. Thaddeus loved sweet potatoes like no person I'd ever seen. I gave him a little hemlock tea to wash it down with.

Thaddeus took poison regular at church meetings in the name of the Lord. I was sure the little extra I gave him wouldn't hurt him none. I fixed his plate special. I never gave D-con to the children. They didn't need it. They didn't scrape the bowls with their forks.

Ray

1973

"Ray, I want you to understand the workings of the church. You are four-teen now, and because I am an Elder, you are allowed to attend council meetings with me. You can observe but you cannot speak," Father said, as we drove home in the wagon, hot and dirty, after a full day of shuck-ing corn. I felt honored Father thought me worthy to attend meetings with him.

I sat quietly at the meetings, with four other sons of Elders. We lis-tened as church doctrine was discussed as was the price of feed and who needed the next barn built. The meetings went pretty much the same from week to week and I waited outside with the other sons if church business went in a personal direction or something had to be voted on.

"We are always to be obedient to the laws of the nation unless they conflict with the laws of Jesus," Brother Frith said at a meeting. When we got home I asked Father for clarification.

"An Elders' job is to protect our families from the evils in the world and this includes being called to fight if our country should go to war. In order not to be caught up in the outside world we do not own radios, read newspapers nor consort with non-believers. Our mission is to keep our families in faith and it is the Elders duty to instruct by word and by example, for the pressure of the outside world is always with us," Father said, with his hand on my shoulder.

I hoped one day I would be found worthy to be an Elder, as had my father and his father before him.

Ray

1974

It was the first Friday in October when I snuck out of the house and drove Father's truck to the carnival just a few miles outside of Rocky Mount's town limits. I'm ashamed now to admit how I gave in to temptation. I had seen the flyer for the carnival when Father and I went into town to buy nails and barbed wire. Tonight was the last night of the carnival, then it headed on to North Carolina.

When Father and I got back from town we did some fence work where a few of our cows had gotten out. Father decided to leave the truck there overnight and we walked back to the house so we could check the rest of the fencing. I knew I could get by with taking the truck.

It was a foolhardy thing to do going to the fair. It would be another year before I could get my driver's license. I'd been driving Father's truck on the farm for several years so I wasn't worried about driving so much as Father finding out. He went to bed before dark in the summer time and got up at the break of dawn. Aunt Ida went to her room and didn't pay no never mind to what I did after supper.

When I got to the carnival, every parking spot in the field was full except for the very back. I left my hat in the truck and put a flannel shirt on over my suspenders so no one could tell I was a Believer. There would be no good coming from drawing attention to myself.

Paying my money to the dark-haired, shadow-faced woman in the ticket booth, I entered through the gate, wondering why I came. I had no business being here. It was just curiosity, and I knew better, but still I wanted to see for myself what a carnival was like. Father would be ashamed of me and wouldn't let me attend council meetings with him if he knew, but I had come this far and didn't want to turn back.

Walking around for a full hour, I watched how the sounds and smells bewitched people, causing them to throw good money around on needless trinkets and carnival food. Sweethearts walked by me arm in arm and other folks screamed in terror and delight from the lifts and falls of the rides as a funny looking man walked around on tall stilts. Little children stared at the lights on the merry-go-round as they rode the circus animals around and around. I didn't talk to nobody, and nobody spoke to me.

I was watching a man throw balls at milk bottles when I noticed an older white-haired man with heavy lines etched in his pock-marked face hawking a side show. He was waving his black-gloved hand wildly about, trying to get folks' attention. He wore a glove on his right hand, exactly like Father! I couldn't help but walk closer to the man.

"Son, come on into my tent and witness the sword swallower, the tattooed man, and the bearded lady. Tonight's the last night as we'll be rolling out before dawn and won't be back until next year."

I was so taken back by the man's green eyes all I could do was swallow hard as I paid him my twenty-five cents. Entering a world of freaks of nature and a maze of distorted mirrors, I wondered again what I had done by coming here. Never had I seen such things as these.

"Well, what do you think, son? Was it worth the price? Mysteries and more mysteries, wouldn't you agree, boy?" The man's green eyes were on me as soon as I came out of the tent.

"I can tell by looking at you, you're naive to the world. You wouldn't be one of those Believers now, would you?"

I felt goose bumps all over me.

"How did you know?" I asked in astonishment.

"You have the look. Once upon a time I knew some Believers from these parts. My parents were Believers. I tried my hand at being one myself, matter of fact. I had a wife and a little girl, I've been told. I wasn't around to see her born. Living the life of a Believer was like living in the night with no dawn coming, so I took off for parts unknown and ended up here in the traveling side show."

The man was spinning yarns, he had to be! I wanted to ask why he wore that glove, but it weren't no business of mine. The green-eyed man began to speak again as if reading my mind.

"I can tell you're wondering about the glove. Curious you are. Pure hands have no need to be covered. I've done unforgiveable things with this right hand. I attempted to kill the body and spirit of one of God's finest creatures, a beautiful black mare like no other. I carry the burden of what I did and for other cruelties, too, yet I feel no guilt for my actions. It says in Revelations, 'and lo a black horse; and he that sat upon him had a pair of balances in his hand.'

"I was to be the rider of that black mare and the Bible was speaking to me, boy. The mare wouldn't let me ride her so I punished her, just like we're punished here on earth. Do you want to hear more of my story, or for another twenty-five cents I'll tell your fortune."

I backed away without a word. Feeling a terrified elation, I left the devil man standing there conjuring up lies with a curled up smile on his lips as he hawked others with his wildly gesticulating black-gloved hand inviting them into his tent.

What I had seen at the carnival made me fearful for Raylene and for myself. There were many ways to be tempted in the world and so much evil. If Raylene was to see the bright colored lights of the merry-go-round with zebras, horses, and goats she would want to ride and eat the cotton candy and candied apples as the other children did. She wouldn't have no chance at all to live the life she was born into. I left the carnival seeing all I needed to. I wouldn't ever go back.

Turning down our road, I cut off the headlights. I didn't need them because the moon was full, and I didn't want to risk Father seeing them, though I knew he'd been asleep for hours.

It was just after eleven p.m. when I caught a glimpse of something ghost-like near the edge of the woods. It was Mother in her nightdress, her hair shining like a white flame. Behind her, an orange flicker of light was glowing near the barn; fire!

I parked the truck and went running to the big metal bell, just outside the kitchen door and rang it over and over. Father came running onto the porch pulling up his suspenders while Aunt Ida followed. Nearby Believers came running to the prearranged signal, and we did what needed to be done to smolder the fire.

Mother had been outside with a candle and nestled down among the old oaks. The flame from her candle caught fire in the leaves. Mother hadn't fallen asleep or been burned. It wasn't a big fire and hadn't been going long. The flames were easy enough to extinguish, but wore us all out. Before daylight we were all back in our beds, smoky smelling and covered in ash.

It wasn't no time before the cattle were bawling from the pressures in their udders and I was back in my overalls. I was thankful we were all safe, and Father never knew I took his truck, though it was a good thing I did.

Standing on the front porch, I breathed in the smells of manure, silage, and smoke still in the air. I said a prayer for all of us that the fire wasn't worse. We had all survived and the carnival was leaving town.

Father and Aunt Ida made sure Mother didn't leave the house by putting a lock on her bedroom door from the outside. It wasn't long before her eyes became dull, like she wasn't there at all. She would sit for hours in her rocking chair not even rocking. When the weather turned cold, Aunt Ida had her sit by the wood stove in the kitchen. Mother didn't seem to care one way or another.

Time passed and she got to wringing her hands and mumbling under her breath. Father relented and took the lock off her door. To my way of thinking, Father got spooked by Mother's strange ways. It wasn't long before she was going back out at night, and nobody stopped her.

Raylene

The wind was blowing, and the smell in the air told me more snow was on the way. Mother looked contented. Her white cheeks were flushed, having been out in the cold for the better part of an hour. She left the house before breakfast, without any of us knowing, to walk who knows where. Ray followed her tracks and brought her back. She hadn't gotten far because of the depths of the snow. Now she was sitting in front of the stove, ignoring a plate of stale biscuits and gravy, while her big toe wiggled through the hole in her stocking. I tried to get Mother to acknowledge me by tickling her toe but her mind was like melting snow.

Aunt Ida and I had been quilting since early morning. "Raylene, help me pull this quilt into the frame and then I'll show you where to stitch. When you're done with that I'll show you how to put the binding on," Aunt Ida said.

Aunt Ida let me pick and choose the fabrics and patterns for the quilts now that I was almost thirteen. I liked these times with her and Mother. Without Father in the house we could relax in each other's company. Even in the snow Father and Ray had cows and other chores to tend to.

"Aunt Ida, how many quilts do you think you've finished all together?"

"Fourteen or fifteen. One never got finished."

"Why not?" I asked.

"It was the quilt top Sarah Ruth took when she ran away. I'll talk no more about it."

Turning away from me, she picked up a pan, filling it with beans for supper.

Ray

1976

On a Tuesday night in March a special council meeting was called and Father insisted I be there. Brother Farley opened the meeting.

"Times are changing and we are fewer in number as our young people are leaving, not wanting to farm, and needing to make an income to provide for themselves and their families. Many of us are older and need help with the farming and tractors are expensive. Our Brothers in Ohio are similar to us, but there are differences as they work in carpentry more than farming and freely deal with non-believers. As we all know, the church divided on these issues years ago. Perhaps if we laid our differences aside, relented, and allowed carpentry as our Brothers in Ohio do, some of our young people may not leave."

"Ray, you've been coming to Council meetings for a while and you've had your driver's license for almost two years. Isn't that right?" Brother Frith asked me.

I nodded yes in agreement wondering why he was asking about my driver's license.

"We've been talking among ourselves and have decided to send you to Ohio for us. We will give you letters to take to the church in Carpers Town. Perhaps we can start a discussion on how we can continue in God's work together. We are asking that you be allowed to stay for a season and learn their ways. While you are there perhaps you can find a young woman who is suitable for you to wed when the time is right," Brother Culver said.

I couldn't believe this was happening, that I would be allowed to do such a thing!

Over the next two months I was prepared for the trip. The Brothers obtained maps for me, marking the best and quickest routes.

Father and I made day trips in the truck practicing for when I would be on my own. As his confidence in me grew, I went alone to Christiansburg, then crossed into West Virginia where I got my first motel room. I saw a place where truckers were staying so I thought it would be a good, safe place to stay.

It felt so strange entering a room with a radio and telephone. I didn't tell Father, but I turned the radio on. I listened to a news program then turned it off. I had entered the non-believer's world, and so far it was going well.

Ray

I was finally ready for my first trip to Carper Town, Ohio, a trip of 400 miles. I had extra oil and a new tire in the back of the truck. Aunt Ida fried a chicken for my trip. There was a pound cake for me to give to Sister Carper when I got there as well as several bushels of peaches from our orchards.

I drove through West Virginia, passed Columbus, Ohio where I got a motel room for the night. The next morning I drove another eighty miles before arriving in Carper Town. I saw signs for Mansfield, Ohio another thirty miles away. At the time Mansfield meant nothing to me.

Following the handwritten directions from Brother Tobias Carper, I turned down the road to the Carper farm. It was 9:00 a.m. on a Saturday when I arrived. I drove up to the house and Sister Carper came out to greet me.

"Welcome, Ray. I've been expecting you. Come on into the house and wash up. I had my daughter, Amy, bake some fresh cookies for you."

Walking into a large kitchen, I could see Amy was busy washing dishes. Drying her hands on a dish towel, she picked up a large blue platter and offered me cookies.

"Oatmeal, my favorite," I said, smiling at her as I took one from the platter. Amy gave me a shy smile, then offered the tray to her mother. She was a pretty girl. I guessed her to be about fourteen or fifteen.

"My boys aren't around right now. They're driving a team of draft horses to the market. We always have plenty of fresh eggs and milk to sell and its good experience for them. I need to stop talking now and let you settle in; you must be tired from your drive. We have a nice bedroom for you upstairs. You don't even need to share," Sister Carper said, smiling at me.

I was taken with her warmth and friendliness. At home women would never talk so much nor look a man in the eye as did Sister Carper.

At supper the boys, ages ten and twelve, sat with us as did Amy. The round oak dinner table was one Brother Carper had made as were the other furnishings in the house.

"The desk in the corner is very nice," I said to Brother Carper.

"It's a writing desk, made out of cherry. You might say cutting and sawing wood are in my blood," he said with a chuckle.

While our meal was being eaten Brother Carper began telling me about the business, the other families I would meet, and the church. Sister Carper made sure my plate was full of meatloaf and mashed potatoes while her husband talked.

"Most of the Brothers work in the carpentry shops or in the store. Other families have dairy farms and work the land much the way your family does. People come from all over to buy the quality furniture we make. I would like you to apprentice with me Mondays through Saturdays and I will teach you how to be a carpenter. Do you agree, Ray?" Brother Carper asked, looking at me kindly.

"Thank you Brother Carper. I'm more than willing to learn."

Brother Carper and his wife had taken me in like I was one of their own. I felt blessed to be in this home with these fine folks.

Brother Carper and the others were always helpful, showing me what I needed to learn, and I enjoyed their company. At the end of the first week I had made a small table with an oak stain.

"You're catching on quick, Ray. You'll be a fine carpenter before you know it," Brother Carper told me.

I wasn't used to praise, and I promised myself I would be worthy of his trust and set about learning everything I could.

I was surprised the children went to public schools, with many of them graduating. When school let out in the afternoon, the boys came to the shops and went about practicing the skills they needed to be crafts-men, while the girls went home. On Wednesday evenings we went to church and took communion. Usually there was foot washing and an Elder would speak on grace and acceptance. I didn't see any snake han-dling while I was there, not even once. On Sundays there was anointing of the sick and scripture reading. Afterwards there was a shared meal and fellowship. I liked Sundays best of all.

Most days when work was done I went to the barn and watched the children play wolf in the empty barn stalls before they were called for supper. Several families lived close by and the children all seemed to collect in the Carper's barn. The wolf chased the children, tagging them until they became wolves, too."

"Ray, would you be a wolf and chase us?" The littlest boy in the barn asked me. He looked to be no older than six.

"You had better run and hide because this wolf is coming to get you," I growled, and went about chasing the squealing children. I felt like a big kid and was having the time of my life. I wished Raylene and I had been able to play like this as children.

Ray

It was a beautiful October afternoon when I arrived back at the Carper's farm. I took the road to the barn, like I always did, to unload provisions I brought from home when I spotted a small group of townie boys on Carper property. They were getting more brazen all the time, leaving liquor bottles and cigarette wrappers on the ground which I had cleaned up more than once. We all knew they were the same thugs who had been stealing, breaking windows, slashing tires, and mocking us, but the Elders had done nothing to stop it except to pray.

When I got out of the truck I heard something sounding like a girl's cry. Sometimes the townies had girls with them, rough girls who smoked and drank. I heard the cry again, louder this time, and I knew something was wrong. Picking up a pitchfork in the barn, I walked to the edge of the woods, coming up behind the thugs. Three townies had a hold of Amy. They were shoving her between them and kissing on her. Her dress was torn from her shoulder. I knew what they had in mind. They laughed when they saw me.

"Hey, Believer Boy, what are you doing with that pitchfork? You gonna turn the other cheek? Come on, join us. One more won't make a difference once we're done with her." They all laughed.

Something in me turned when I saw Amy's petrified face, and I lunged at the one who was doing the talking. I jabbed the pitchfork right in him. I left him there bleeding as I picked Amy up and carried her to the house. The others ran off through the woods quicker than lightning. I yelled as loud as I could, and Amy's mama came running from the house toward us.

"Take her upstairs quickly. I need to see how she is," Sister Carper

161

said in a panicky voice.

I carried Amy to her room and laid her in her bed; she didn't weigh more than ninety pounds. It tore my heart out seeing her lying on the bed weeping.

"Mama, the boys, they were going to hurt me!" Amy sobbed, shaking all over with her long hair in a tangled mess and her bonnet gone.

"Go downstairs and wait for me, Ray, and close the door behind you. If you see the boys, send them to the Graces' farm. I'll collect them later."

I waited in the kitchen for Sister Carper to come back downstairs. Sure enough, the boys came home before their father and I sent them off not answering their questions. I sensed they could tell something was wrong, but it wasn't my place to tell them what had gone on. I didn't have much time to think about what I had done with the pitchfork or what the consequences would be when Sister Carper came back to the kitchen.

"Paul Ray Simpkins, promise me you won't say a word about this happening to Amy. It would be the ruin of her."

"I don't know if I can do that. I need to talk to Brother Carper first. I'll wait for him on the porch."

Sister Carper gave me a piercing glare, then went back to care for her daughter while I waited for her husband to come home.

Brother Carper and I had only a few minutes to talk before the Sheriff arrived. I had stabbed a deputy's son, and he had come to arrest me. I'm glad I hadn't killed the hooligan, though it had been in my heart and mind to do so. Not a mention was made of Amy Carper as I was taken away in handcuffs.

Ray

1977

The first day of my sentence at Mansfield Prison was September 25, 1977. I was eighteen years old. From the back seat of the patrol car, I watched as a small lake and men in striped prison uniforms, doing yard work on the immense green yard, came into view. Guards stood sentry, rifles positioned for easy access. Mansfield was nicknamed Dracula's Castle, probably because it had been a reformatory school at one time. Now it was a prison and had a reputation for being merciless to its cons.

Inside the building the floor echoed with the rattling of the chains on my feet. I was taken to the records room where a deputy gave my commitment papers to a clerk. The deputy had me climb a flight of stairs where we came upon a barred door. The door slammed behind me. The deep clanging of the heavy steel was like nothing I ever heard before. As we walked the length of the cages, the inmates pointed at me, calling me "pretty boy" and "new fish." We continued walking until we came to a place where prison uniforms were given out.

"Got somebody new with you, Shiflett?" The man behind the counter asked.

"Mind your own business and give this inmate what he needs and put a move on it. I don't have all day." I knew then the man behind the counter was an inmate, same as me. I was given two pairs of denim pants, two shirts, a blanket, toothbrush, and soap.

"Have fun in the showers," the inmate behind the counter said. He laughed as Shiflett led me away.

In the bathroom Shiflett ordered me to strip and searched me in the

163

most humiliating way possible, then ordered me to walk slowly under a long row of showerheads, to ensure I was clean.

Once dressed in the prison uniform, my photo was taken with a camera. I'd never had my picture taken before. I asked the guard if I could see it. He let me. I didn't let on to the shame I felt when I saw myself in the photograph.

Shiflett took me to the warden's office. He sat behind a big oak desk and didn't look up when we came n. The chaplain sat in a big arm chair by a fireplace which wasn't lit. He read me the prison's rules and regulations.

"Do you understand what I just read you, Son?" Chaplain Lane asked.

I nodded.

"I need you to answer, Paul. I can't accept a nod for your answer."

"Yes, I understood what you read."

"Tell me about your upbringing. Were you raised in the church?"

"I don't want to be rude; but I've got no answers for you."

"Church services are compulsory. You'll have to decide between Protestant or Catholic services, Paul."

"My name is Ray. I'd like you to call me that," I said.

"You need to decide something, Ray," Chaplain Lane said as his brown protruding eyes searched my face.

"I reckon I'll pick Catholic then. I know nothing about Catholics."

"Catholic it is," Chaplain Lane said as he wrote something in my file.

"Work in prison is a privilege. I want to find something that's suitable for you," Warden Phillips finally added to the conversation.

"I'd like work in a garden." Warden Phillips cut me off as I was speaking.

"Sentence times determine where you work. If you show trustworthiness and dependability you could be bondable. Time will tell."

After being processed, I was taken to my cell. Prisoners whistled and yelled obscene remarks as I walked by. I ignored them. If I responded, they would know they got to me. I was taken to a cell on the sixth tier of the East Block where "the new fish" were sent. After several months I could request a transfer. There were too many levels to fall if pushed to the concrete floor below.

Arthur was my cellmate. He was 51 and serving 25 years for kidnapping and transporting illegal liquor across state lines. He was a small man who walked hunched over and shuffled his feet. His lower lip could almost touch the ground. I never wanted to talk about the things Arthur said happened to him at Mansfield. I didn't want the thoughts in my head. God was surely testing me, for the road I was traveling had become a dark mirror, and I was afraid to look.

Raylene

Brother Carper showed up driving Father's truck with Brother Jamison following him in another automobile. He knocked on the door insisting to see Father. I knew something was wrong, bad wrong. Mother was sitting by the fire in her rocking chair. When the men entered the room Mother started wringing her hands, an expression of worry on her face although, she didn't speak.

"Raylene, go to Brother Farley's. Thaddeus is at his house with the other Elders. Go fetch him now," Aunt Ida instructed me.

I ran the quarter of a mile as quickly as I could. I was out of breath when I knocked on Brother Farley's door. "What is it, girl?" Father questioned.

"There is trouble with Ray, I suspect. Please come as fast as you can."

Brothers Carper and Jamison were still standing in the kitchen when we made it back. Aunt Ida's face had gone dead white with worry.

"We need to talk privately." Brother Carper said, directing his look at Father.

Aunt Ida took Mother back to her room, came back, and made me go outside with her.

"What's this about, Aunt Ida? Please tell me, and don't hold back."

"Don't say I told you child, but Ray hurt somebody. That's all I was told."

The men talked for two hours. Aunt Ida and I were pulling weeds in the garden when Brother Carper and Brother Jamieson left. That evening at supper Father was quiet; even his prayer before the meal was short. I couldn't take the silence and not knowing. "Please, Father, don't shut me out. Tell me about Ray!"

"He's gone from us. He is among the non-believers and evil has come upon him. Ray is being tested as are all of us. We will pray for his safety and return if it's God's will." Father would say no more.

The next day while Father was in the fields I snuck into his room searching for anything I could find about Ray. It didn't take long before I found a letter sticking out of his Bible.

> Father,
>
> I am giving this letter to Brother Carper to give to you. He will tell you what has happened. The townies are sticking together saying I attacked a deputy's son deliberately and no girl was ever present.
>
> I don't know what I can do now except pray. I must pay for my actions. I know Believers do not testify in court so Brother Carper's daughter cannot speak on my behalf. Believers do not file lawsuits or defend themselves against them.
>
> I have talked to a court-appointed lawyer, and he says it would be the townies' word against mine. My case is worsened since the girl cannot testify. If she did, it would be shameful for her and the Believers.
>
> I know this is the way it is and must be God's will. Please pray for me, Father, for I want to return home.
>
> Your loving son,
> Paul Ray Simpkins

Ray

We were awakened at 6:00 a.m. and counted by the guards. Every day was the same. The guards didn't seem to have anything more to do than count us day and night. The third shift guards walked the catwalks shining their flashlights into our cells and rattling our doors, making sure they were locked. Over time I was getting used to it. I didn't like it, but there was no other choice.

Word had gotten out among the inmates and guards that I was a Believer. Most of the prisoners had no idea what that was and didn't care to know. Others thought it was pretty funny and taunted me whenever given the chance.

"Hell, Believer Boy, are you going to burn for what you did?" a con mocked me.

"He's already in hell. Look where he is," another con said, laughing.

"He looks like one of those "holier than thou" types. Look where it got him!"

Everyone got a good laugh, but they only pushed me so far. They knew I had snapped and stabbed a man with a pitchfork.. That gave me a measure of respect in their eyes, believing when push came to shove I would hold my own or die trying. It was hard to ignore their taunts, but I did so by offering scripture in return.

"It says in Proverbs 11:12, He that is void of wisdom despiseth his neighbor; but a man of understanding holdeth his peace." I felt sorry for the prisoners who didn't know what it meant to love their neighbor. Excessive pride and arrogance were doing their talking.

I couldn't let go of the anger I felt or Father's voice in my head. I wasn't scared of the cons; I was afraid I had let Father down, and there wasn't nothing I could do about it in here and they knew.

Raylene

1977

I had never known anyone who had gone to prison. I couldn't bear to think of Ray being locked away in a cage worse than an animal and with non-believers. I worried for him constantly and did not sleep. I couldn't help but pester Father and Aunt Ida for answers.

"Father, please talk to me about Ray. I need to understand what has happened to him."

"There is nothing to tell you, Raylene. What has happened to Ray is God's will. I have nothing more to say about it. Brother Farley is coming to dinner tomorrow. Put your mind on what you are going to prepare," Father said.

The following day, as we were sitting down to dinner, I couldn't help but notice that Brother Farley was sneaking glances at me and it made me uncomfortable. I averted my eyes and concentrated on my food. I had been around Brother Farley many times at meetings, but hardly a word was exchanged between us. This felt different.

"Raylene, the Council of Elders has decided you and Brother Farley should marry," Father said. "The marriage would be in your best interest as Brother Farley is strong in his faith and can guide you in a way a younger man cannot. Trust me that I know what is best for you."

I was horrified. I was only seventeen, and he was close to fifty and missing his right arm! What would it be like to be married to a man missing a limb? I didn't want to marry this man, or any man, but he was a special friend of Father's and an Elder in the church. Although I didn't agree I couldn't say so.

After the decision was made, Brother Farley came to our house several times to speak with Father, always exchanging pleasant words with me when he arrived. He was too old and stern for me. How could Father let this happen? There were young men in the church needing wives. I wanted none of them, but better a younger man with two arms than this!

The minutes of my life seemed to pass with the slowness of all eternity, yet it seemed like no time at all before it was time to marry. I tried talking to Mother, hoping to get her to understand what was about to happen to me, but there was no response from her. I was frightened beyond words. Once I was married to Brother Farley I would have no life except his.

Raylene

1978

My wedding was simple, as I knew it would be. It was worked into the regular Sunday service as not to inconvenience Believers by coming back another day and keeping them from chores. After words had been spoken over us by Father, my husband helped me into his buggy and drove me to his house, the one he had shared with his deceased wife of whom I was now a replacement.

Adam Farley's house was like every other Believer's house; wooden, painted white, with a large kitchen for cooking and preparing food from the garden. All Believers had root cellars for food storage in the winter months.

When I walked through the house for the first time I saw a plain room with straight back chairs for when people came for meetings. The bedroom which I would share with Adam Farley had a high board bed he made before he lost his arm. I wanted to climb into that bed and pull the covers over my head. I wanted to forget where I was and where Ray was. I couldn't accept this was God's plan for our lives!

The wardrobe in the bedroom was small and narrow with two gray dresses, a winter coat, and shawl belonging to his deceased wife still hanging there. Being a practical man, Adam Farley kept the clothes, knowing he would marry again and nothing should go to waste. There were two more bedrooms upstairs for the children who never came to Adam Farley and his wife. These rooms were empty and bare.

Being married to Adam Farley was hard work. He wouldn't let us have an automobile even though some Believers had black cars. With one arm it would have been easier to drive an automobile than a horse and buggy. Some Believers still frowned upon automobiles and tractors, and my husband was one of them.

"Even a Believer can get hooked into the world and be tempted, Raylene. We can never risk being yoked together with non-believers. We must separate ourselves from the sinful nature of the world. We must deny our own selfish wills and submit to the laws of God. I must lead the Believers by example as you will also for you are my wife."

Too many times to remember Adam Farley preached this to me like I was the only member of his congregation and dimwitted at that.

Raylene

My days were long and the same, one day running into another. How I missed Ray and worried for him. I had lost my sister, Sarah Ruth, and now my brother. My work started at five in the morning and lasted well past dark. The wood had to be lit, and it was my job to do the shoveling in of the red hot coals for the cooking of our meals. There was washing, cleaning, gardening, pulling weeds, canning, and sewing to do, as well as the assembling together for worship, foot washing, and communions. My husband pushed me hard, and himself as well, to be perfect before the eyes of God. He expected me to do no wrong and bring no shame upon him.

I hadn't been married long before I was carrying Adam Farley's baby. I was happy about the baby because it would give me something to love. It was a brief but joyous time for me, with well wishes from the others and the seldom seen smile that occurred on Adam Farley's face. He seemed to hold me in a tender regard and didn't expect so much work from me as before.

When my time came, I bled for three days and the pain wouldn't let go. The Sisters came and laid hands on me, praying and anointing me with oil in the name of the Lord. It was the sin of Eve, they said, causing me the pain. Aunt Ida and Sister Harriet attended me, but they had no special schooling in delivering babies other than what had been passed down to them.

"Please get someone to save my baby," I pleaded to them again and again. No one listened. When my baby girl entered the world I didn't hear her cry.

"Give my daughter to me now," I cried out with every bit of strength I could muster.

I held my daughter as she took her first and last breath. Something happened inside me when Sister Harriet pried her from my arms. Grief and rage came over me as my daughter was taken away. I screamed for her to bring my child back to me, but she did not.

I wanted to have my daughter baptized before she was buried.

"It isn't done, Raylene. A person must be of an age to take the vow to follow the ways of the Almighty. A dead infant cannot do this. Our child will not be baptized," my husband spoke softly.

A rage as cold and hard as the white rocks in the creek had moved into my being and did not plan to leave. I couldn't speak but shook for days. I named my baby girl Rosebud because that is what her sweet mouth looked like to me. I kept her name to myself and whispered it often to my heart. I knew the Believers would reproach me that my daughter's death was God's will, so I never spoke of her again. I was all torn up inside having a child. I would never have another.

Raylene

1979

Time passed, but I know not how, as the clock I watched never moved. I went about my chores, ate the little I did, standing in the kitchen. My husband barely spoke as he moved back into the life he had always known. I knew he wanted the child. I also knew he didn't dwell on her death believing it was God's will. But I did not. I needed a doctor to deliver my baby. A veterinarian was sometimes contacted by a Believer if it was something they couldn't handle themselves as not to lose their investment in a horse or cow. No one would get a doctor for Rosebud.

The seasons changed. I was doing Adam Farley's breakfast dishes when I felt myself begin to shake all over. I dropped the plate I was drying. It shattered all over the floor. The dishes were ones Adam Farley had when he was married before. Most of them were chipped and cracked from years of hard use.

"Raylene, carelessness is the work of the Devil," I was admonished.

"I know, Adam Farley," I replied meekly.

I was secretly glad I broke it. One day I wanted to have pretty dishes with pink flowers on them. I wouldn't mind washing and drying endless dishes had there been something pretty to look at. Old, white, chipped dishes were all I had to eat on after Adam Farley finished his food. It felt good to see that old plate break. When my husband went back to the fields I broke another one and then another! When I was finished I got Adam Farley's pants in from off the line.

Ray

1979

When I awoke, I was in the infirmary. I heard the doctor telling the nurse how I had been jumped in the prison laundry. I was fuzzy in my thinking except for being grabbed from behind, pushed to the floor, and kicked repeatedly by at least two inmates. I had been given pain killers and drifted off to sleep.

When I woke hours later the doctor was gone, but the nurse was still there. She told me her name was Leslie, and she looked like an angel. What was she doing in a stinkhole like this? I was tired and needed more sleep.

I remember the pretty nurse checking on me, taking my pulse and helping me eat. She gave me medicine. I slept some more. I was glad I wasn't taken to the prison hospital. I wanted to stay in the infirmary with the pretty nurse.

I was returned to my cell the next day. I held my head high and my posture straight. I looked the other inmates in the eye, but stayed focused on where I was going. I would be aware of my surroundings every moment from now on. I was also focused on Nurse Leslie. I wanted to see the smiling woman again, and I knew where to find her.

Leslie

I couldn't help thinking of the prisoner who was carried in here. He was so handsome and helpless lying on the table. When he finally awoke, I was alone with him except for the guards posted outside the door. When he looked at me with his strong, broad face and hazel eyes, I got butterflies in my stomach. I'd been around many prisoners, but none affected me like this. I asked his name even though I knew what it was.

"Paul Ray Simpkins, and you're an angel," he said, giving me a big smile. "What's a beautiful girl like you doing here nursing criminals?"

I knew it was a line, but when he said it, it was different. It rang true and sounded sincere. Perhaps it was his eyes that locked onto mine or the fact he was young and not as hardened as the rest of the inmates.

What was I doing daydreaming about him? I had school to think about, and my uncle. I wasn't going to end up like my mother. No way.

Ray

"Hello, pretty nurse, remember me?" I said, hopping onto the examining table, happy to see Nurse Leslie.

"Ray Simpkins, it's been a while since I last saw you. Let me have a look at your face and see why you're limping a bit."

"It's nothing bad. I fell down some steps when I wasn't looking." Truth was I had been alone in the stairwell carrying produce from the trucks to the kitchen when a con followed me wanting me to do an unnatural act with him. He didn't fare too well. He tested my farm boy strength, and I got in several hard punches to his gut. I left him doubled over in the stairwell, but not before he had gotten in a couple of licks to my face. I hoped he had enough sense never to try that with me again. It was best to let sleeping dogs lie and not get the guards nor the warden involved. I didn't need to make enemies. At least now the cons knew Believer Boy would fight, push come to shove.

"Before the doctor comes in, may I ask you a question?" This was my opportunity, and I had to make the most of it.

"Depends on what it is."

"Are you a real nurse?" I teased.

She took it seriously. "Not yet. I probably have another year, maybe two, of school. Hopefully, I'll start taking a few classes in the fall. Don't worry, I've been my uncle's pretend nurse since I was a little girl, and hopefully someday I'll be official." Leslie was smiling at me as she spoke.

The guards weren't paying attention to us. There had been a big game the night before, and they were discussing all the plays. I was glad. It gave me time to talk to Leslie and find out more about her. "How is it you ended up in Mansfield working with your uncle, if you don't mind a

178

personal question?"

"I've lived at Mansfield for as long as I remember. I came here after my parents died."

"That doesn't sound too good. What kind of life is that for a young girl?"

"It's not so bad. Uncle and I have a beautiful apartment above the infirmary and the grounds are lovely. The warden lives on the east side of the administration quarters with his wife and daughter. They have a wing to themselves. I know it must be hard for you to imagine, but to me, Mansfield is like living in a beautiful castle."

Our conversation abruptly stopped when Dr. Gusler walked into the infirmary. I wondered when I would have a chance to be with Leslie again.

Leslie

What was I thinking giving a prisoner so much personal information? I couldn't believe I told a prisoner so much about me. Usually I was all about business.

Ray was different, with a politeness and gentleness about him. He wasn't crass like the other men around there. My heart leapt when he came into the infirmary needing care. I found myself opening up to him, something so unlike me. It was lonely here with no one to talk to near my age, who wasn't a creepy criminal or a guard with no ambition but to play up to me, hoping to bolster a no count career by seducing the doctor's niece.

I missed a lot of classes last year with Uncle not being well. Uncle needed to retire, but he wouldn't hear of it. Luckily he let me help out in the infirmary so he had more time to rest. I let him think I needed the experience, but we both knew the real reason was his health. His heart condition worried me, but I was learning more volunteering in the infirmary than I ever would have in school.

Being one of the few females at Mansfield, I was an easy mark, although Uncle had let it be known that anyone bothering with me would face dire consequences. The guards and prisoners kept their distance for the most part. All the prisoners seemed to want was a smile and a kind word. I sensed evilness from Shiflett and Brown, two of the guards. I felt violated and shamed when they offered up their lewd grins even though a hand had never been laid on me.

Ray wasn't like these other men. He had a genuine smile and beautiful hazel eyes. I wanted to know all I could about Ray Simpkins.

Ray

On Sundays my routine was to go to my cell after breakfast, then to chapel service. I told sweet Leslie I didn't want to go, but there wasn't a choice.

"Ray, it's not so bad. Doesn't it break up the time for you?" Leslie teased while I was with her in the infirmary pretending to have a stomach ache.

"I could be having a bit of privacy in my own cell. It's the only quiet time I have to think."

"Perhaps something will change your mind about church."

"I wouldn't count on that, sweet girl, but I appreciate the sentiment," I said softly as not to be overheard by the guard standing by the door.

The next Sunday I spotted Leslie in the chapel. I fairly laughed out loud knowing she was the something she spoke about. Leslie positioned herself so I got a good view of her, although I had to sit in the con section. Leslie was sitting with a few women who worked in the prison. Several times I caught her looking at me, and I grinned real big. She sure looked pretty in her blue dress and little hat. It was nice to see her in something besides her nurse's uniform.

I hung around after the service, acting like I wanted to talk to Chaplain Lane. Leslie did the same. Everybody was gone except for a few prisoners wanting a minute with the chaplain to ask for special favors. There was only one guard, and he wasn't watching.

Leslie walked to the confessional booth, went in, and left the door open. I followed her at a distance. She was sitting on a small bench when

I stuck my head in; there wasn't room for the rest of me. Leslie put her hands around my face and pulled my lips to hers, kissing me long and hard. It was a good thing there wasn't a priest sitting on the other side of that confessional!

Ray

I got jumped again. The word was out that I was a Believer and didn't believe in fighting in spite of what happened in the stairwell. Leslie's uncle, Dr. Gusler, looked me over with Leslie assisting. He left the infirmary telling Leslie I needed to stay in one of the sick rooms overnight and for her to check in on me from time to time.

I held a towel on my mouth which was covered with blood. I had lost a tooth and had two cracked ribs. By the look on Leslie's face I knew the sight of me scared her. She was quiet, studying me as I lay on the examining table. When the guards were out of earshot, Leslie lowered her face to my ear and began to talk softly.

"I never want to see you like this again." Leslie had tears in her eyes. "I know some of what goes on here, and it makes me sick to think about it."

I moved the towel slightly to cover my mouth. If the guards looked at me, they couldn't tell I was talking. I used one hand to briefly stroke Leslie's cheek, then dropped it to hold her hand beside the examining table where the guards couldn't see.

"I can take care of myself, sweet girl. There's no need for you to worry. Just because I'm a Believer doesn't mean I'm going to let any of them get a drop on me."

"Tell me all about being a Believer. I really want to know," Leslie asked, her blue eyes searching mine for answers.

"It's a different way of life than most people experience. One day I'll tell you more about it."

"Do you promise, Ray?"

"You have my word."

"I need to tell you the truth about something," Leslie whispered gently.

"What is it? You can tell me."

"My parents didn't die. My father ran off when I was a little girl and my mother became a lush. I don't know where my parents are or if they're even alive. That's how I came to live with Uncle. He took me in or I would have become a ward of the state."

Hearing the door open, Leslie composed herself as Dr. Gusler walked into the infirmary.

"Hello, Uncle, and good night Mr. Simpkins. It's time I adjourned to my room and studied."

Lying there knowing Leslie would be sleeping one floor above me gave me plenty to think about. I couldn't keep my mind off Leslie and her no account parents.

During the night something else began stirring in me. I imagined myself pulling the pins out of Leslie's proper bun and letting her long brown hair fall down around her creamy white shoulders. I knew her breasts would be round and full beneath her uniform, and she would be wearing white panties. I wanted to take those panties off her. I wanted to fornicate with this woman, and I was wrong to think so. This wasn't how a Believer was supposed to think, and for this I was ashamed.

Ray

Seeing Leslie at chapel and getting the occasional kiss in the confessional helped get me through the days, but only fueled the fever I felt for her.

Having kept myself out of trouble and obeying the rules, I was now bondable and allowed to work in the prison garden. The warden was pleased with my results, but I knew he would be, because of everything I grew up doing on the farm. I jumped at every opportunity I was given to be outside.

I couldn't concentrate inside the prison walls with all the noise and not knowing if and when I was going to get jumped. It was different in the garden with the sun shining on me and having my hands in the dirt. Part of me felt Father beside me, except now I didn't have to stand on a stump and preach like when I was a boy.

How could I explain what it was like being a Believer to Leslie? I fed her bits of information when she asked questions; being an outsider, she could never understand our ways. Thinking of Leslie made my desire for her grow faster than the weeds I pulled. I had never been with a woman before or even kissed one until her.

Mansfield grew beets, broccoli, beans, carrots, okra, cabbage, onions, radishes, turnips, tomatoes, corn, and potatoes. Once everything came up so did the weeds. I spent many hours picking off caterpillars, cabbage loppers, potato bugs and Japanese beetles. What I liked best was growing corn, which I planted every two weeks starting in early May. I sowed seeds three to four inches apart in rows with three feet distance.

When the plants got to twelve inches, I used a hoe to hill up extra soil around their stalks, making the corn better able to stand strong gusts of wind. To help with pollination I shook the cornstalks when the tassels were shedding pollen. The cornfield made me think of sweet Leslie; just about everything did.

When the corn was at its highest I would have Leslie meet me in the cornfield. I had it all planned out in my mind. Leslie would tell her uncle she was going to town to do some shopping, then she would walk the long way around the prison garden with no one seeing her weave off course.

Leslie

My life forever changed on July 14, 1979. The first planting of corn had finally reached eight feet high.

I entered the cornfield the way Ray instructed me to. No one saw me slip inside the prison garden. Ray assured me the prisoners and guards would be working the fields back to front to avoid the hottest part of the day. By the noontime meal no one would be in the back field. The guards knew Ray well enough to know he worked better alone and wouldn't come looking for him unless he didn't show when they blew their whistle at quitting time.

Ray made it so no one could see us if they came to the back of the cornfield. He planted the corn a certain way to make a special place for us.

Taking my hand, Ray led me through a maze of stalks and into our secret den. I was nervous, my heart beating fast, as I carried a ladies dress bag with me. If Uncle should have stopped me when I was leaving the apartment I was prepared to tell him I had a dress to return to a department store downtown. Over the wooden hanger I had placed a bed sheet so Ray and I would have something to lay upon in the garden. I knew Uncle wouldn't question my returning a dress; he had no interest in such things. Ray helped me spread the sheet, patterned with pink flowers, onto the ground.

"Corn is sweetest the moment the cob is picked," Ray whispered, then kissed me deeply as we fell to our knees embracing each other. Ray touched me with tenderness I had only imagined, and our clothes fell away like shucked corn.

Lying on the hard ground, I looked up at the sky while Ray held me in his strong arms, my head resting on his shoulder. I had never been held by a man, and I couldn't believe the comfort and feeling of peace it brought me.

"Ray, I wasn't ever held as a child as far as I can remember. Do you remember being held by your mother?"

"No, girl, I don't remember it ever happening," Ray said, stroking my hair.

Ray touched me in ways that sent tremors of delight through my body. I ran my fingers over his body, hoping he felt the same sensations as I.

"Lovely Leslie, my beautiful girl, I desire you so," Ray said, looking into my eyes.

Ray turned and lay on top of me, kissing my neck, collar bone, breasts, and lips. I was afraid of what might come next, and I had been too timid to go into the drug store to purchase what we needed. The pharmacist knew Uncle and I would be hard pressed to come up with an explanation of my needed purchase, yet I wanted Ray to enter my body as he had entered my heart, but I wasn't prepared.

"The sowing depth for seed is an inch. When the soil grows hotter I will sow deeper," Ray whispered in a low and tender voice.

"It's probably alright Ray. I just finished my cycle so we should be safe."

"Not today, sweet Leslie, we'll hold and explore each other in other ways. I want no harm to come to you. There have been other rows of corn I've planted such as this. Soon there will be unfurling bright green leaves of corn yet to harvest, so we'll have more times together in the cornfield."

That night as I lay in bed I couldn't sleep. As children, neither Ray nor I had a mother's lap to climb into, nor mothers who wanted to love and comfort us. Now we had each other and that was all that mattered. Ray had fallen in love with me, I was sure, although he didn't say it. The next time we met in the cornfield I would be prepared for Ray's sturdy stalk to be inside me. I would be his little raccoon and he would be my own sweet corn.

Ray

Leslie and I couldn't get enough of each other. Sideways looks at church and the occasional kiss could no longer satisfy either of us.

"Ray, I've figured out a way for us to be together. Now that the weather is getting colder, ask Warden Phillips if you can become a house-boy. You've been here long enough and proven yourself to be a model prisoner with your work in the garden. If he lets you be a houseboy, you can move about the prison mopping and cleaning the halls, the infirmary, and other places. I know he'll consider you."

I put in a request to meet with Warden Phillips. I didn't have to wait but a week when a guard came to get me. The warden was sitting behind his big desk when I was taken into his office.

"Ray, you've proven yourself to be a hard worker and have kept your nose clean. I've gotten good reports on your work in the garden. I'll give you an answer about being a houseboy soon."

"Thank you, sir," I said. I had a good feeling it was going to happen.

It wasn't but a week until I was pushing a mop and bucket on the hall where the infirmary was. When there were no patients, I was allowed to mop inside the infirmary. The guards and cons got used to seeing me and thought nothing of it. I kept my head down and didn't engage in conversation unless forced to by a guard. I wanted to be as invisible as possible. Everything Leslie said was working out fine.

"It's time for the next step," Leslie told me after chapel service.

"When you're mopping, be sure to check the infirmary door when no guards are close by. When I know Uncle will be gone for a few hours, I'll leave it open. Uncle always lets Warden Phillips know when he's going to be gone so inmates can be taken to the hospital in an emergency. When the infirmary is closed, no guards are posted. Always have your mop and bucket with you and act as if you're cleaning the infirmary if you get questioned."

I was taken aback by how well thought out Leslie's plan was. It wasn't but a couple weeks before I found the infirmary door unlocked. The door to her upstairs apartment was between the examining room and Dr. Gusler's office.

Opening the door, I felt a moment of panic. What if it was a mistake that the door was open and Leslie's uncle was home? Breathing deep, I climbed the stairs feeling my way, afraid to turn on the light switch. Softly opening the apartment door, I peered around hoping it was safe to venture in. Looking into the living room, I saw my beautiful Leslie sitting on a sofa reading. She was twirling her hair with her finger as she read; a look of concentration was on her face.

"Leslie," I whispered softly, startling her.

"Oh my God, it's you. Our plan worked." Leslie jumped up from the sofa and ran into my arms.

The splendor of the apartment was something I could not have expected. I had never been in a place as fancy as this. Portraits hung on the walls, and velvet draperies hung with heavy chords holding them back from the windows so the sun could shine in. Shelves of books were everywhere.

Taking me by the hand, Leslie led me to her bedroom which was like that of a woman-child. There were dolls from her childhood, as well as perfume bottles for the woman she was.

Lying in her childhood bed, I took her again, then again. There wouldn't be many times an opportunity like this would present itself. I wanted this woman, and she wanted me.

Raylene

1979

Father and Aunt Ida came to the house to tell us about the death of Levi Ferguson. Adam Farley and I were about to sit down to supper when they came. There was something familiar about the name Levi Ferguson, but I couldn't remember why.

"Raylene, I need you to leave the room while your husband and I talk. Supper can wait for a while. Ida, I want you to stay," Father said.

I went outside and busied myself by sweeping the porch. I was mighty curious about what was going on and didn't want to be far away when I was called back in. There must have been a lot of discussion, for it was nearly an hour before Aunt Ida called for me to come back into the house.

"Raylene, we will be attending the funeral of Levi Ferguson even though he left the Believers many years ago," Father said.

"What has this to do with me, Father? I don't understand," I said, pushing him for answers.

"It was a troubling time for Believers when our country was at war. Levi was a high spirited young man and found it hard to follow our rules. A passion for our country fueled a flame within him, and he enlisted in the Marine Corps. As Believers, we could not condone Levi's decision for it could cause a temptation to arise within our young men to join the military. Levi knew what he was doing and still he made his decision to go.

"Through the years the Council has prayed for Levi to renounce his ways and come back to us, but he had not the ears to hear our prayers. The Elders have talked and we have decided to invite his widow into our faith as we would any widow of a Believer. She needs to be saved."

Aunt Ida cleared her throat as if she had something to say, but I knew she wouldn't. My husband looked at me and began to talk.

"It wasn't long after I baptized your sister, Sarah Ruth, into the church when she ran away and lived with Levi Ferguson and his wife. The Elders voted some years back that Sarah Ruth not be allowed to return to us as she showed herself to be disobedient and disrespectful to our ways, but Levi Ferguson's wife is another matter. Although she's a non-believer she can be taught our ways, and if she accepts them, she would be baptized into our flock where she could marry again and be cared for.

"Your Father believes it is unwise for you to attend the funeral. I disagree, and as your husband I have the final word. As my dutiful wife I expect you to attend the funeral as an example to the Sisters. You're not to be swayed by the sight of Sarah Ruth, should she be there, nor enter conversations with her other than pleasantries."

I had been duly warned.

Raylene

Adam Farley was always one for being punctual, so we were early arriving at the funeral home. I knew Father and Aunt Ida wouldn't be too far behind us. I left Adam Farley talking with the funeral director and went inside the parlor. Flower arrangements and family photographs were sitting on low tables around the room. I busied myself looking at the pictures, then made my way to the casket. I could see Levi was missing his right leg, and there didn't seem to be an artificial one in his pants leg. I wondered if he had one and how he had gotten around if he didn't. Levi didn't exactly perish by the sword, but it did seem the Lord gave him a direct warning.

While standing there, two women came in and stood by the casket. Neither woman seemed to notice me as they gazed on Levi. The older woman leaned on the younger one for support. Not wanting to be rude by staring, I snuck a glance at the younger woman and inched closer to them so I could hear their voices. There was something familiar about the voice of the younger woman. It was my sister, Sarah Ruth. It had to be!

How different she looked from me, wearing a black dress that barely covered her knees, a necklace of pearls, high heels, with a purse clutched under her arm. Sarah Ruth hugged the tearful widow while I stood there not knowing what to do. When the women finished their embrace, Sarah Ruth finally noticed me, her eyes growing wide with recognition.

"Raylene, my God, it's you!" I put my fingers to my lips to hush her, our eyes locked on one another. Sarah Ruth whispered something to the widow, then crooked her finger and indicated I follow her. Sarah Ruth walked before me as I followed her into the ladies room where we made sure we were alone and it was safe to talk.

193

"I can't believe it's you, my own baby sister! Oh, look at you in that awful gray dress and bonnet. I'm so sorry, Raylene. I wish I didn't have to leave you and Ray there with Thaddeus and Ida! Please tell me about Ray and Mama. Did they come with you? Where are they?"

I fell quiet. I had no words to tell Sarah Ruth about Ray, not then anyway, and how did I explain Mother to her?

"Mother and Ray didn't come," was all I could think to say. My head was swimming and I had to sit down. I couldn't take in everything that was happening. My true blood sister, Sarah Ruth, was here, even though she told me that wasn't her name and never was. My sister was Lula May Simpkins, and I was with her now!

"We have so much catching up to do. You were probably too young to remember much of anything when I lived with you. It was to Violet and Levi I ran away and lived until I could take care of myself. Now I'm able to help you Raylene, if you'll let me."

I didn't know what to say. Help me how? I wondered.

"I better go back to the visitation room before my husband misses me. He warned me not to talk to you, but I just had to."

"We'll be burying Levi tomorrow. You will be coming to the cemetery won't you?" Lula May asked me. I could hear the panic in her voice.

"Yes, I'll be there as well as other Believers. Mother probably won't be coming, but Aunt Ida will."

"Mother's not sick is she?"

"No, it's not like that. I'll explain more when I have the words."

"Think about what I asked you and please, Raylene, tell me everything you can about Mama and Ray."

"Until tomorrow then." Lula May stepped forward and gave me a big hug. In spite of Adam Farley's warning I hugged her back.

Lula May

The leaves were dressed in their finest colors, and the air was brisk and cool for Levi's graveside service and burial. Levi had let Violet know he wanted to be buried near his parents in the Waters of God cemetery, which was on a high hill with a dirt path that had to be walked up. Levi couldn't be buried with the Believers, but he could be buried in the small separate cemetery for children and infants who hadn't been baptized. Those who had been shunned were sometimes buried there wanting to remain close to the families.

Arrangements had been made to use Midnight, Thaddeus's horse, to pull the casket to the cemetery. Midnight was so old all his hair had turned white, just like with old people. Midnight was the horse the Believers used for funerals as he moved slow and steady, just right for pulling the dead.

I was praying the whole time Midnight wouldn't die pulling Levi up the hill. I didn't think anybody in this group could carry Levi up the hill or Midnight down. Everybody there looked old as dirt. I reckon pretty soon the rest of these folks would be dropping like flies.

The Brothers and Sisters, the few there were, stood on one side of the casket, while we stood on the other with Levi and Violet's friends and neighbors. Raylene looked like an old woman standing next to Adam Farley. How my heart broke for her. This was no life for the little sister I remembered, and where was Ray? What had happened to him?

I tried to put my mind back on the kind words Preacher Early was saying about Levi, but I found it impossible to concentrate. Violet had tried to get Levi to go to church with her, but he never did. When I was in town I sometimes went with Violet, knowing it meant a lot to her,

195

but I wasn't one for church going. More often than not I was on one of my airline trips, which was always a good excuse for not going. Preacher Early was a kind man, and Violet thought the world of him. That was all that mattered.

When Preacher Early stopped talking and said the final prayer, Violet and I threw handfuls of dirt into Levi's grave as well as the red roses we had bought from the florist. Friends walked by and respectfully threw in handfuls of dirt, but not the Believers, who just stood and watched. It sickened my heart to think of my sister married to the likes of Adam Farley.

I wondered what Thaddeus and Adam Farley thought of me standing tall and proud in front of them! I looked their way hoping to catch their eyes, but they never glanced my way except for Raylene, who gave me a quick and shy smile.

When the service was over we were all to go to Levi and Violet's house for a shared meal. I wondered why Violet was allowing Believers into her house. I decided to ask her as we walked to the car.

"The Believers were important to Levi. He had many good memories of growing up in the church. He'd like that they came to his funeral and are coming to our house for a meal. Sometimes I believed Levi would have gone back to them if he hadn't met me, although he assured me he wouldn't. Do you think Levi is looking down on us now?"

"I'm sure he is, Violet, and you can bet he's smiling."

Arm in arm, Violet and I walked down the hill, supporting each other. How I wished Mama had been here today. I hadn't seen her in years. Raylene had only been able to share a little with me in the ladies room, saying Mama was locked inside herself. She hadn't been able to tell me anything about Ray, and I was getting a bad feeling. I wished I was walking with Mama now sharing my thoughts and feeling, like I was with Violet. I would always love Violet and Levi for the many things they had done for me, but I still yearned for the mama I had when I was a little girl.

Violet and I made our way down the hill and got into my car. I drove my TR7 convertible with the top down. I wanted the Believers to see me this way, a strong and independent woman.

Believers followed me in their black trucks and horse and buggies. Thaddeus had taken Midnight home; it was too far for the old horse to make it to Violet and Levi's pulling a wagon.

When I pulled onto the gravel road leading to Violet and Levi's house, I was flooded with memories. It was as if I was five years-old again.

Raylene

When Adam Farley and I got out of the buggy it was like a million dogs jumped all over me, probably because of the dead deer parts all over the yard. The women I had never been allowed to associate with were getting out of their cars trying to keep the dogs from tearing their stockings or dirtying up their pretty dresses as they walked across the yard. It was hard for them to do, walking in high heels carrying their special funeral dishes. The rest of us, in our gray dresses and manly shoes, had no trouble walking. We were used to dealing with country dogs, giving a swift kick when needed.

After what seemed a long while everybody made it over all the dog poop, deer parts, and beer bottles into the kitchen. Lula May took me by the arm when my husband wasn't looking and walked me to the parlor where Violet was greeting people who had come to show their respects.

"Raylene, I've wanted to meet you for such a long time. It's a sad day for me, and I'm grateful you've come. You have your mother's pretty eyes and cheek bones. I hope you and I will get to know each other well," Violet said, her lips trembling as she spoke.

"I'd like that, ma'am, but it will probably not be allowed unless you decide to be a Believer."

"Levi would roll over in his grave if I took up with them. No, girl, I'll be right here if you ever need me. I know this house isn't what you expected, coming from where you do. Levi wasn't one for fixing things up, particularly after he got sick. My Levi liked a little nip. I'm sure you can tell that from the yard. I turned a blind eye knowing how hard it was for him to leave the Believers, knowing he couldn't go back, especially with me, and there were his terrible war memories."

198

"The beer bottles and mason jars in the yard will give the Believers something to talk about for some time," Lula May said with a chuckle.

Through her tears I saw Violet smile, then Lula May and I moved away from Violet as a line of people had formed, wanting to talk to her and offer condolences.

The Sisters were busy in the kitchen setting out the food they brought. Aunt Ida brought a ham from our smoke house and a large container of potato salad. Cakes, pies, and other dishes were sitting everywhere, brought by Violet's friends.

The Brothers were talking on the front porch with men not of our faith. It was interesting to notice how the Believers and non-believers got along on such a day as this. No one was paying the least bit of attention to me.

"Let me show you where I used to play with Mama and Violet when I was little," Lula May said, taking my hand and leading me to stairs in the living room which led to the attic. I couldn't help notice her painted nails, so pink and pretty. My hands were rough and calloused from hard work. It felt good to be holding my sister's hand, but I was embarrassed by my own, and pulled it away.

"What's wrong?" Lula May asked me with concern in her eyes.

"It's my hands. They're so rough next to yours." Lula May reached down, took my hands in her own, and kissed them.

"It won't take much to make them nice as mine. One day soon we'll take care of them. Now let's sit at the table, by the attic window. It's where I used to have my tea parties."

Lula May became more and more beautiful as we talked. Her hair was short, red and curly. I knew the color wasn't natural, but it sure was pretty. I vaguely remembered Lula May having hair the same color as Mother's. My own hair felt drab and heavy under the hair net, hidden by my bonnet.

"I used to have such fun with Mama dressing the beagle pups in these old doll clothes. I wish you could have known her the way she was then." Lula May's face turned solemn as she held up a tattered doll dress. "Mama, Violet, and I used to play with all the old toys up here. This was my special place to come and play make believe."

"I would have liked being here and playing with you and Mother. I can't remember her being any way other than how she is now."

"She doesn't speak, Raylene?" Lula May asked as tears moistened her eyes.

"Almost never, she just rocks in her chair."

"Doesn't she ever talk about my daddy or me?"

"I can't recall. Ray's older and might remember more. It's hard to know what goes on in Mother's mind. I imagine right now she's sitting in the rocker in the kitchen." The tears welling in Lula May's eyes spilled over. She wiped them away with the back of her hand and changed the subject.

"Let me take your hair out of that bonnet and brush it like I did when you were little. I used to love doing that for you," Lula May said, taking a hair brush from her purse.

"I can't do that. Long hair is a woman's pride, and it says in Corinthians that every woman who prays with her head uncovered dishonors God."

"You and I aren't going to be praying. There's enough of that going on downstairs. You don't judge me because of my hair and clothes do you?" Lula May questioned me.

"I think I'm supposed to, but I don't believe I do. In fact, I like how you look." I surprised myself with my answer, mostly because it was my own thought and I believed it to be true.

"Then why don't you leave, Raylene? I'll help you if you'll let me."

Something warm and loving spread all through me when she said that. It was as if Mother's hand was on my shoulder. I let Lula May take my hair out of the bonnet and brush it out long. Lula May showed such tenderness as she brushed my hair, I was overcome with emotion. This was what I had been missing in my life; loving touches and talking with my big sister. This was how family should be. I was sobbing as Lula May pulled me to my feet and held me until I cried out my tears.

"Things are going to get better for you Raylene. We've found each other, and I'm not going to lose you again."

"Do you promise, Lula May?"

"Yes, I promise. Now let's get you out of that dress and go to someplace safe to talk. I don't want anyone coming up here and interrupting us. Adam Farley and Thaddeus wouldn't like us talking, and being around the Sisters makes me feel creepy and won't any of them talk to me."

"Their husbands won't let them," I answered.

"They're afraid I'm a bad influence, I might put ideas in their wives' heads to leave like I did. I'm going to my car and getting my suitcase. I have it packed for my next four-day airline trip. I have fun clothes for my layover that should fit you. We are about the same size, but who can really tell with you wearing that horrible dress."

Lula May left me in the dusty attic filled with old boxes and mouse droppings. Still sitting in a child's wooden chair, I looked around at the discarded toys. I wondered what it would have been like for Ray and me to have lived here.

When Lula May returned she had me put on a pair of Levi jeans with a yellow shirt. This was the first time I had ever worn a pair of pants, and it sure felt funny. I called a halt to Lula May putting make-up on me, knowing this alone could cause my eternal damnation, at least in Adam Farley's eyes.

Lula May reached back into her suitcase.

"Raylene, take the *Cosmopolitan* magazine with you. It will tell you a little of what goes on with women our age."

"We aren't supposed to know about the outside world, only our own. Adam Farley and Father tell us what we need to know."

"That's just plain rubbish. Have you ever read a newspaper or listened to the radio?"

"No."

"Raylene, that's no way to live. Have you heard anything about the Vietnam War?"

"No," I said sheepishly, as if I had done something wrong.

"I have a transistor radio in my suitcase somewhere. Let me find it."

"If I get caught with these things of yours I'll get into serious trouble with Adam Farley."

"Well then don't get caught. Hide them someplace safe. I'm going to bring you extra batteries for the radio and some news magazines, so you won't be living under a bushel basket."

"Alright," I said, feeling a twinge of excitement. "I'll put the radio in the cabinet behind the dishes. Adam Farley never looks at the dishes. I'm sure I can find a good place to hide the magazines." I startled myself with my boldness.

"Let's go to the woods now so we don't have to worry about anyone finding us talking."

When we were out of view of the house I told Lula May everything I knew about Ray. Tears streamed down our faces as I talked.

"I'm going to find out all I can about this, Raylene. You can count on that."

We must have stayed in the woods a full hour. We were laughing and crying telling each other about our lives. It was good to be able to share my feelings about losing Rosebud with my very own sister.

"How terrible! You should have had a doctor. I could be with my little niece now. I'm so angry with Adam Farley and Thaddeus for making you suffer so. You need to leave the Believers. You can do it, Raylene." I began to sob again, and Lula May held me close. Once my tears stopped flowing we continued to talk. Lula May told me about getting her letter of acceptance from the airline, what the training was like, and how much she loved her job. She also told me she was married for a while, then got divorced!

"I got swept up by a passenger who was smooth talking. I had only been flying a year when I married Robert. He worked in his brother's restaurant in Baltimore. We had to keep it a secret I was married. The airline didn't want married women, and I would have been fired if they knew. One night Robert was drinking and smoking some weed with some of his buddies in our apartment. I heard him tell them he was planning on knocking me up so I had to quit my job."

"Lula May, I don't understand anything you said. What's knocked up mean, and what is weed?"

"Knocked up means pregnant, and I didn't want a baby. I still don't. Marijuana is a drug people smoke to get a high. I've tried it, but don't like it. I do like a glass of wine sometimes."

"I can't believe the things you're telling me! What happened then?"

"Robert told me I had to quit my airline job. No self-respecting wife of his could be an airline stewardess. He would get me a perfectly good job working in the restaurant with him. I walked out the door and left him after three months of marriage. I tasted freedom in my airline job, and no man was going to take that from me."

"But why a stewardess of all things? I couldn't ever imagine getting on an airplane, and I never heard of anybody being divorced before."

"I had to get out of the house and experience life for myself. I hadn't been flying but a couple of years when Martin Luther King, Jr. and Bobby Kennedy were murdered. These were horrible things I'm sure you know nothing about. Life with the Believers protects you, but, it's not worth it. My marriage was a bad mistake, but it was my mistake. No one is going to tell me how I'm going to live my life; I had enough of that growing up with Thaddeus."

I couldn't believe all the things I'd been hearing today. Imagine me divorcing Adam Farley. I felt a thrill of excitement just thinking about it.

Feeling like a small child, I needed to head back to the house fearing Adam Farley would be missing me.

"Raylene, when will I get to see you? I can't lose you all over again. I don't even know where you live. Can I write you?"

"Adam Farley would never allow it. Lula May, do you know where the silo is on River Road? It's not too far for me to walk."

"I do, Raylene; it's not far from where your husband tried to baptize me."

"I'll put three white quartz rocks together close to the silo. We can meet there, or at least leave notes."

"I drive by there every week when I visit Violet. Please keep me informed about Mama and if you hear anything else about Ray. I'll leave messages, magazines, and newspaper clippings for you," Lula May said, squeezing my hand.

"We'd better get back to the house now so I can get into my own garments and out of these sinner's vestments."

Raylene

When we got back to the house Lula May went in first, making sure it was safe for me to enter, then motioned for me to come in. The Sisters were busy cleaning the kitchen and packing their dishes. Violet's friends were still with her so I hadn't been missed.

I was making my way up the steps to the attic when I noticed Adam Farley standing by the fireplace, pulling on his beard, talking to a non-believer. I got mighty curious about what Adam Farley was up to because he never pulled his beard unless he wasn't feeling right with the Lord. My husband's beard was long and white, and like most Brothers, he hadn't shaved since being baptized.

Adam Farley followed the non-believer out the front door, walking right past me and Lula May standing on the steps. I decided I needed to follow Adam Farley to see what he was up to. He probably wouldn't notice me wearing what I was, and all of his attention seemed to be on the man he was following. Lula May stayed right beside me. Adam Farley and the non-believer walked to the back of the house, opened the cellar door, and stepped inside. No one else was around. They left the door open, probably for light, and I crept closer to the cellar door. I had to know what was going on.

Staying as quiet as possible, Lula May and I got onto our hands and knees and peered through the cellar door. The non-believer was kneeling to a bottom shelf on the dirt floor, looking through a long row of Mason jars. I watched as my husband took off his jacket, unbuttoned his shirt, and reached into his shirt sleeve, pulling out a Mason jar where his missing arm would have been. Sitting on a wooden bench Adam Farley placed the jar between his knees and opened it with his one hand. Holding the

Mason jar to his lips, he took a big drink, still wearing his black-rimmed hat. Now I knew why Adam Farley insisted I always tie knots in his shirt sleeve at the elbow.

"I ought not to be doing this. It ain't right with the Almighty," I heard my husband say.

The man laughed loudly. "You're not fooling me, Adam Farley. I've known for years you had a hankering for both kinds of Spirit. Now pay up and I'll put this new jar into that shirt sleeve of yours."

I stayed quiet till then, but I could contain myself no longer.

"Adam Farley, if this don't beat all!" I was laughing so hard I almost wet myself.

"It's only water, Raylene!" my shocked husband cried out at being caught.

"Another sin, Adam Farley." By this time I was having a fit of hysterical gaiety. I had never laughed like that before. Lula May just stood there not saying a word.

Adam Farley came out of the cellar, and left to get our horse and buggy. He returned shortly and I, Raylene Farley, picked up the reins to the horse and drove my husband home as my sister watched us go. He didn't say a word about the blouse and slacks I was wearing or my bonnetless hair.

Ida

It was the day after Levi Ferguson's funeral when Thaddeus hitched up Midnight. He didn't tell me where he was going, and I didn't ask. Thaddeus had eaten his breakfast, so I didn't expect to see him for a few hours at best. I worried that Thaddeus expected too much of Midnight, and before he left with the old horse I told him so.

"Midnight is a member of this family and should be treated as such. It wasn't right you had Midnight pull the wagon up the hill much less with a casket with a full-size man inside it, even if you did walk the hill leading him by the reins. You know his gait is choppier due to his arthritis. It must hurt him bad, probably the same way mine hurts me. He's a very old horse and lived much longer than most. It's untold for a horse to live as long as he has! If Father was alive, he wouldn't let you treat Midnight like this."

"Well, Father's not alive, is he? Midnight is my concern and no one else's," Thaddeus said as he walked out the kitchen door. Watching him go, I wondered when he had become so slope-shouldered and lanky. When did he start looking like an old man? No longer did Thaddeus do chores on the house. The front door had been loose in the hinges for over a year, and other repairs had been left undone.

Thaddeus had gotten where he didn't brush Midnight. Over the last several years I had taken up the chore. I didn't mind, though. Midnight's coat wasn't sleek anymore and he was outliving his teeth, having several gaping holes. "None of us is getting any younger, Midnight, or any better looking. I'm glad I've got you to come talk to." Midnight had a woe begotten look in his eyes. It was as if he was trying to tell me something

I couldn't understand no matter how hard I tried.

It was late morning when Thaddeus came walking into the kitchen saying Midnight was gone.

"What do you mean, gone? Gone where?"

"Midnights gone to the other side. I left him grazing in the upper pasture while I walked to look at an old barn on another farm. When I went back to get him he was dead. I'm going to ring the bell and have the Brothers come. It will be a day's work to dig a hole big enough for his grave."

I cried for Midnight, as he was my dear friend and I would see him no more. I always looked forward to our special times in the barn after the supper dishes were done. When I brushed him, he would turn his head and look at me with his soulful eyes as if he was seeing into the deepest part of me and loved me still.

Thaddeus shed not a tear for Midnight. This was the horse our Father gave to him, yet he showed no attachment to the animal, no grief, no sorrow at his passing.

Raylene

It was Sunday morning, and Adam Farley and I were getting ready for church, the same as any other day, when I noticed his steps weren't as brisk nor did he seem to be in any hurry. He was usually rushing to be with the Brothers.

I knew something was wrong the moment we walked into the church. All the Sisters had their heads bowed down as I walked by them. They knew I had shown my hair and worn my sister's clothes, and now they wouldn't look at me. The Brothers stared at me as if I were Lucifer himself. Brothers Culver and Fritts came toward me, each taking an arm, and forced me to stand before the pulpit. How I wish Ray was here. Ray wouldn't let Brother Fritts and Culver treat me this way.

Father stood behind the pulpit looking at me and not seeing me at the same time. I could tell he was in one of his trances. Over the years Father had become more religious, if that were possible, spending hours on end praying. His hair was white and wild now, and his eyes glowed with a golden scary light. It was like the spirit in him was so strong that snakes were going to shoot from his eyes.

From the wooden box at his feet Father lifted a copperhead over his head with his black gloved hand and began praising God as he looked out into the congregation. My heart began beating fast, for Father now recognized me and began to speak.

"We are put through trials and tribulation in this life and some of us do better than others. As surely as Eve was tempted by the apple, Satan had his way with you, Raylene Farley. It is time for you, daughter, of my flesh, to feel and accept the anointing of the Holy Spirit. Come forward and take this snake from me for if someone preaches and handles serpents without being bitten, what is being preached is true." Father stepped toward me, his arms outstretched, and all I had to do was take the snake. Perhaps he was trying to help me repair the damage from the day before, but I couldn't take the snake, even for him.

The congregation was standing, waving their arms in the air, praising the Lord. "Escape the judgment of God, Raylene. Come to Jesus now," the congregation cried out willing me to take the snake from Father. Not to be outdone, my husband walked to the wooden box, took out a copperhead, and wrapped it around his shoulders.

"We take up serpents not to prove our faith, but to confirm it. Take one of these snakes, Raylene. Take one from your earthly father or from me, your husband!"

Adam Farley and Father stood before me wrapped in serpents. The copperhead was curled and poised to strike. Neither man asked if I had felt the anointing of the Holy Spirit. A cold shiver ran through my heart as my husband continued to speak, his voice getting louder and louder. Watching what was unfolding before them the congregation had become deadly quiet.

"Raylene Farley, was Satan himself within your soul when you showed your hair? Did not the Prince of Darkness have you shed your garments and replace them with the vestments of harlots, flaunting yourself before men, taunting them?" Adam Farley said as his angry eyes blazed into mine.

I stood frozen in fear, unable to utter a word.

"Raylene Farley, do you have faith in the ways of the Waters of God Believers, Guardians of the Word? If so, take this snake from me. I command you to do it now!" Father ordered me.

Never had anything like this been asked of a Believer, for without the anointing of the Holy Spirit one could surely die from snake bite, and I was his daughter!

With all the strength I had I broke free from the grasps of Brothers Culver and Fritts, turned, and ran shame-faced from the church. Stumbling and falling, I ran until I could run no more.

Raylene

I stayed in the woods searching for solace and comfort. Deep into the night I beseeched God to help in my unbelief. Why could I not accept the ways of my father and husband? Why wasn't I like the other Believers and satisfied with my life? My actions had caused much offense, and offenses were not from God but there was no spiritual wickedness behind my actions. It was my husband who sinned, not me. The Elders were trying to make me accept the Believers' ways and to reject the love I felt for Lula May, Ray, Mother, and my precious Rosebud. I couldn't let this happen. I would bend to my own will and not to Father's, and certainly not to Adam Farley's.

An ill wind had stirred up, and prickles of sensation ran up and down my spine. I could feel earthbound spirits and conflicted souls all around me whispering how they hadn't known love and suffered still because of it. I didn't want to be a tormented soul. I wanted to experience love and to have kindness and compassion in my life.

The rain began, and I walked to higher ground, taking cover under a weeping willow. Water poured from the sky, and the creek began to rise as only the devil can do. The Lord thundered from heaven and sent a bolt of lightning crashing down before me. The very earth beneath my feet shook and trembled as the rain beat down without mercy, biting into my flesh as the Holy Spirit ran through me like lightning and did not hurt me, but sent thrills of joy coursing through my veins.

All night I stayed beneath the weeping willow tree. In the early morning the rain stopped, and shafts of sunlight broke through the clouds, causing a gray mist to shroud the early morning light. It was an eerie sight, but comforting as if loving angels had arrived and shoved the clouds of darkness away.

Noah's flood had been visited upon me, and I had been purified. I had been washed in the blood of the lamb. I had been anointed. I held on to the comfort of the Blessed One as I walked home. I would need it in the days to come, for Father and Adam Farley were waiting for me.

Raylene

Adam Farley and Father had made the arrangements. A satchel was packed, and waiting on the front porch steps, when I returned to the house, I shared with Adam Farley.

"Raylene, it is for your own good we are sending you away," Father said to me in front of Adam Farley and the Elders. "Satan had hold of your tongue making you speak untruths about your husband."

I kicked and screamed as the Elders forced me into Father's truck. I was made to sit between Father and Adam Farley so I could not get out. Father drove away from the house as Adam Farley held onto me with his one, but very strong, arm.

"Father, where are you taking me? Am I being sent away to live with another Believer family?"

"Daughter, you will stay in an asylum until you see the error of your ways for wearing the shameful clothes of a nonbeliever, and recant the untruths that fell from your lips."

"I did wear the clothes, Father, there is no denying it, but Adam Farley was drinking white lightning. Tell him what you did, Adam Farley!"

"You are still speaking untruths and I will hear no more about it! After some time away, God be willing, you will see the error of your ways and return to us," Father said, solemnly.

Throughout the whole ordeal my husband did not utter a word.

I did not speak during the drive, knowing if I did, things would go worse for me. I became lost in thought wondering if I had taken a snake from Father or Adam Farley what would have happened to me had I not been bitten? Would my life have changed? I would still be Adam Farley's wife. I would still be wearing this gray dress and bonnet; but I hadn't taken the snake, and I was alive. Ray was outside in the world, even if he was in prison. He would get out one day, and I would see him again. Lula May didn't know what happened to me, but she would when I was back home and could leave notes under the rocks at the silo. Violet wanted to be my friend. I needed to think on these things.

Arriving at the asylum in Staunton, Virginia, I was taken back by what I was seeing as a huge mansion with white columns came into view. Folks were outside walking while others were in rocking chairs on the front porch. Everyone was dressed the same except the men, who looked like they worked there. Several barns, a chapel, and other buildings were on the property. It would take a number of people to keep a place this size operating.

Father parked the truck, and a man calling himself an orderly came down the steps and opened the door for Adam Farley and me.

"We've been waiting for you, Mrs. Farley. Please come this way." My husband closed his hand on my upper arm, leading me up the stairs, not letting go until we were inside the mansion. Father walked closely behind us.

"I'm handing you over to Nurse Elliott. She'll take good care of you," the orderly said.

"Say your goodbyes, Dearie, and I'll take you to the good doctor." Nurse Elliot smiled at the others as she took me firmly by my elbow.

"Pray, repent, and follow the Believers' ways, Raylene. We'll return for you when you can be the obedient wife God intended you to be," Adam Farley said, as he and Father walked toward the door.

"Do not count on that!" I said loudly as I was led away by the nurse. I had never spoken like that before. I had drawn on a strength I never knew I had but would need in the days to come.

I was taken to a large paneled room where Nurse Elliott introduced me to Dr. Cooper, a middle-aged man with a pointed chin, wearing wire-rimmed glasses. He was sitting behind a large wooden desk. He reminded me of an old hoot owl, the way his piercing brown eyes looked at me. I could tell his shirt was stiff as it smelled of starch. There was an odor of shoe polish in the air.

"That will be all, Nurse Elliot. You can leave us now," Dr. Cooper said, dismissing her.

"Raylene, I had a long telephone conversation with your husband and father, so I have an understanding of why they brought you here. Those who care for you think your decline is related to losing your baby and this has led to your stubborn disobedience of your husband and father. It's my suspicion that you're suffering from debility, which is an overall state of weakness brought on by grieving, stressed nerves and emotional turmoil. Rest and relaxation with tonics, air, exercise, and a daily dose of cod liver oil often does the trick. If it doesn't, we have other treatments to try. Let's get you settled in, and I'll see you again in a week."

Dr. Cooper didn't ask me a single question. It didn't seem to matter to him how angry I was being forced into the asylum. I bit my tongue, for I was afraid of what he might do to me if I spoke out. To keep from losing control of myself, I thought of Lula May. I imagined her standing beside me holding my hand, giving me strength. While Dr Cooper talked, I wondered about Father and Adam Farley using a telephone and how that came to be. Believers didn't use telephones.

Nurse Elliot came back for me and had me change into the asylum uniform. I was more than happy to be rid of my dress and bonnet. I looked like every other patient, but I didn't care. No one would take me for a Believer, and I was glad.

The first week I observed everything around me, even though I had sleepless nights. How dare I be treated like this, but I was afraid to speak out. I didn't want to be forced to take pills like many of the other patients, so I complied with everything I was told to do. Too many of the women sat in rocking chairs all day, staring off to who knows where. It scared me and made me think of Mother. I dressed myself in the morning and made my bed before breakfast.

I had a small room to myself. I had no lamp for when it was dark. The only light spilling into my room was moonlight from my small bedroom window. The floor in my room was scratched and gouged. The plaster walls looked as if someone had tried to claw their way out, leaving deep blemishes. The heavy iron bed was made up with sheets that were worn bare and a thin green blanket. I didn't care, because Adam Farley wouldn't be climbing into this bed, and for that alone I was grateful. Looking out my window from the third floor, all I could see were hedges, walls, and locked gates.

I tried to be helpful in small ways like clearing the table in the dining room. I didn't talk to anyone and only answered the questions I was asked by staff. I was always sweet and polite. I had been there ten days when I was taken to Dr. Cooper's office again.

"You seem to be settling in well, Raylene. I've gotten good reports on you. Let's give you a little more time to get adjusted and we'll talk again later." I hadn't said a word to the good doctor. He did all the talking. I didn't want to stay here with the crazies, although they didn't bother me except to make me worry about Mother. I prayed that Thaddeus would never bring her here.

The orderlies didn't mess with me like they did with some of the other patients, as I was no bother to them. I stayed to myself and didn't need to be told what to do. I kept my distance from the nurses with their jingling keys and clipboards. I didn't want to give the nurses or orderlies any reason to write something down about me. I spent many hours alone working the jigsaw puzzles in the common room.

After two weeks I was taken so see Dr. Cooper. "You seem to be improving Raylene. How would you like to walk the grounds?"

"I'd like that very much."

"As long as you are not a threat to yourself or others I see no harm in it. The fresh air will do you good. You need rest, Raylene, and good food. After a while you'll see clearly and be able to go back to your husband," Dr. Cooper told me kindly.

I would rather have been bitten by a rattlesnake than go back to being Adam Farley's wife. Having all this time with no chores nor being told what to do or what to believe, I was thinking and feeling things I had never experienced before.

Ida

Not a drop of rain had fallen for weeks and the dirt had become harder than rocks. The grass was yellow-brown and our crops were dying. Heat lightning lit up the sky night after night. I waited for rain but only white clouds floated by.

Sweat was dripping off the end of my nose as I dug potatoes. I wiped my forehead, and the dirt from my hands felt gritty on my skin. It was a warm day, too hot to be digging, but this was a chore that needed to be done. I was doing this for Raylene because she wasn't here to do it herself, and there was no telling how long she would be gone. I'd be sore tomorrow, more from getting old than the physical work itself.

Leaning forward with my hands on my knees to catch my breath, I went back to digging. I had dug three bushels, and that would have to do. I put a bushel of the potatoes in the wheelbarrow and pushed it to Adam Farley's house.

I opened the heavy door to the root cellar and stepped into the darkness, feeling the packed red dirt beneath my feet, carrying the bushel basket. I hadn't thought to bring a flashlight when I left the house that morning, so I had to feel my way to the potato bin.

I hit something with my foot and heard glass break, then I smelled it. I knew what it was. *White Lightning*. Raylene hadn't lied after all.

I sat on that bushel of potatoes and cried.

Raylene

The male patients threw rocks over a low wooden fence as a part of their treatment. There was a whole pile of rocks for them to throw. Some of the rocks were small, but some were as big as hens. When the rocks were all thrown over the fence, the men put them into a pile. The next day the men would throw the rocks back over the fence and make another pile. This went on day after day. I must have watched men throwing rocks for a week before I got the idea that I wanted to throw rocks, too.

I walked over to the fence and picked up the biggest rock I could throw and threw it. No one stopped me. I picked up another rock and threw it for Rosebud. Every day I went into the yard and threw rocks over the fence. It felt good to throw those rocks! The orderlies just watched. It seemed they had no problem with a woman being with the male patients.

Day in and day out I threw rocks and felt myself getting stronger. One day another woman came to the yard. She picked up a rock and threw it, then another. For days she stood near me throwing rocks. She was a red-headed woman and big as a man. After a while she mumbled a few words to me, asking me my name. I asked her the same question back.

"My name is Izzie Brown. Don't let anyone see you talking to me if you know what's good for you," she spoke softly with her head down, in a voice that was deep for a woman.

Izzie and I began having small snatches of conversation when the orderlies weren't watching. She had a hard, strong body. Her hair was short, too. She told me she had taken the scissors to it herself.

"They give me Thorazine each morning. The doctor claims it's for my nerves. When I saw you throwing rocks, I put the pills under my tongue and spit them when no one was looking. I'm feeling clearer now and want to be out here with you."

I didn't know what to say. It was good to have the company. It got so I looked forward to being outside and talking with Izzie as limited as it was. Every morning after breakfast we threw rocks. The staff saw an improvement in Izzie and reported it to Dr. Cooper. Her medication was reduced by half.

"They're all damn fools, and what the doctor don't know won't hurt me none," Izzie said, giving me a lopsided grin. It was good to see her this way. I couldn't understand why she was so cheerful when she saw me. I knew she must suffer terribly living in this place, but that didn't stop her from talking.

"Raylene, throwing rocks is for the crazy men when they get here, 'specially the violent ones. An orderly told me once a man starts asking why he has to throw rocks from one side of the fence one day and to the other side the next, he's on the road to being cured. Do you think we are on the road to getting cured here?" Izzie laughed at her own joke, her blue eyes twinkling.

There wasn't much for me to do after lunch. Izzie had chores, mostly in the laundry. It was easy for her to sneak away, so it wasn't long before we were meeting behind the milking barn so no one would see us talking.

"For over ten years my son has been bringing me here when his wife gets worked up about me living in his house. They need me to plow, plant, and get in the crops. There's no money to hire anybody to help. My husband died years back, but he was no account, so it didn't matter much to me.

"Mary, my son's wife, claims to be sickly; truth be told, she's just plain lazy. She's told my son things that caused him to turn his heart against me. When the hard work gets done, Mary gets to ranting about me being an abomination in God's eyes and tells my son to put me back in the asylum. She and I both know there isn't room for two women in my son's house, and I have nowhere else to go.

"This place is a dumping ground for unwanted women and misfits. I'm here now because of an argument between Mary and my son. She won. Ordinarily I wouldn't be here in early autumn when there's still chores to be done."

"An abomination? That's a strong word, Izzie. What do you mean by that?"

"I have been called a pervert because I loved a woman from a nearby farm and she loved me back. We got caught doing sex things in the woods. I was brought here, and Janie was sent to live with relatives. I never heard what happened to her. It hurts my heart to think about her. She was one of the finest people I ever knew."

I didn't know sex things were possible between a woman and a woman. Izzie told me she and Janie made whoopee. I wouldn't call it whoopee what Adam Farley did to me. There weren't no whoopee in it at all. I didn't hate Izzie for loving someone, man or woman. I liked her, and she was becoming my friend.

Life became new and fresh for me. I was feeling so much better. Every day I awoke thinking of Izzie. I had something to expect, to look forward to. It was Izzie causing me to gain flesh and color to my cheeks. When I couldn't be with her I walked in the garden, sat on the porch, or lay down in my room where I could think of her.

Raylene

As I lay in bed, I thought of the things Izzie told me. Tears streamed down my face, and I wiped them away as I tried to imagine her life. Why were women treated so poorly, having to be controlled, shocked, and drugged? I didn't understand any of it. It made me mad and caused me to throw rocks as hard as I could, with Izzie standing near me, her movements slow and purposeful as she threw. Izzie's long face held a watchful look, always observing what was going on around her, as if she was on guard.

Izzie found safe places for us to meet. She knew the schedules of everyone who worked in the asylum. She knew which patients to avoid for fear they would tattle to the nurses to get special favors. Sometimes Izzie and I would meet behind the doctors' houses or the chapel. She knew places in the hedges we could crawl through and not be seen. We were always on the lookout for gatekeepers, night watchmen, and attendants. I was beginning to care a great deal for Izzie. I had never met anyone like her before.

"May I hold your hand, Raylene?" Izzie said, fixing her eyes on mine as we stood behind the chapel. I felt I was under a spell when our heads came together with a will of their own, causing our lips to touch. A strong current ran directly to my womb, causing me to tremble and shudder. I pulled away, not knowing what to think nor do next. Izzie's hand went to the nape of my neck while her face pressed close to mine.

"It's alright, Raylene. There's nothing wrong with us loving each other." I wasn't so sure.

I didn't see Izzie the next day or the next. I felt unsettled and uneasy from the kiss. I had a growing restlessness and felt as if I was going to pieces. I knew Izzie was waiting for me, wanting me. I knew when I saw her again I would be incapable of resisting the appeal in her eyes. She aroused a yearning in me I had never felt before.

It was several days before I went back to throwing rocks. Izzie smiled when she saw me coming. She moved closer to where I was, and we began talking in low voices so no one would hear. We agreed to meet that afternoon. No one would be at the barn right after lunch. Izzie and I climbed into the hayloft and hid behind stacked bales of hay. The only noise we heard came from the hammering of a determined woodpecker.

"The woodpecker must be a male," Izzie said, causing me to laugh. Then her hand stroked my face gently and she kissed me again.

Izzie began to fumble with the clumsiness of my clothing, and I did not make her stop. Standing naked before her, I let her curious fingers travel all over me, causing me to tremble uncontrollably. Lying on a discarded blanket, I grew in boldness and allowed my hands to wander over Izzie's clothes, then under. Her skin was soft and warm, her kisses deep and unyielding. Izzie's tongue sought out mine, and I cried out in pleasure. A quivering excitement built in my female parts that spread throughout my body. When I thought I could stand it no longer, I felt the soft touch of her kisses make their way down my belly and between my legs. I never knew such a thing was possible.

Izzie rolled on top of me, and we stared into each others' eyes in amazement. Afterwards I lay quiet as if in a dream when Izzie began to speak.

"Don't let anything about this asylum fool you, Raylene. There are people who got put in this looney bin who are now sleeping in graves with blank headstones. That could happen to us if we aren't careful. If they think I've turned you into a homosexual, they'll do things to you, they have done to me, and I couldn't bear it. Dr. Cooper can't know I love you, Raylene. I'd go back to getting electroshocked or even get a lobotomy, and the same might be true for you. I know people here who have had over a hundred shocks, and now they aren't nothing but hollowed out souls."

Izzie and I met at the barn the next day and the next. I touched her warm body, blowing gently into her navel and kissing the insides of her thighs. I never knew there could be so much pleasure touching a woman's body.

"My body is getting old and worn out from farm work and I'll soon be 41 years old. I never thought I'd have a chance to love another woman until I met you, Raylene."

"I don't want to hear you talk about yourself that way. We were made for each other, and that's all that matters." I delighted in caressing and exploring the slopes, curves, crevices, peaks, and valleys of her body. More than that, I loved being held by Izzie and talking the way we did. Being with Izzie released me to another world I could never have known without her.

"Always remember to act cold and mean to me in the dining room. Talk bad about me so no one will suspect us. If they think I like you or have spent time with you alone, they'll up my medication. The first year I was here they gave me shock treatments. I heard tell they first used shocks on pigs. Dr. Cooper was the one who pushed the button and sent an electric current through my brain. He did this to me six times the first two weeks I was here. He told my boy the only way to keep me from being homosexual was through shock treatments. Thorazine isn't much better.

"When I was taking four doses, I couldn't do nothing but sit with the loonies and drool. I've seen people here take Thorazine for years, and now all they can do is smack their lips and do funny things with their tongues. You've seen it, Raylene. You've seen their twitching and jerking and how they can't help it."

She was right. I had seen it with my own eyes. We had to be careful. Not wanting to leave each other, we forced ourselves to get up, put our skirts on, and button our uniforms least we be caught together.

I worried about what would become of Izzie when I left the asylum. I ran our conversations over and over in my mind. Izzie was telling me things I hadn't had the courage to question before. Holding my bed pillow close, I imagined how it felt when Izzie stroked my hair and kissed me. It felt good, it felt right when she did it, not like when Adam Farley laid me in bed and pushed his man part into me. He never kissed me, not once, and now I was glad for it.

I should have known there was something wrong with letting Adam Farley use my body whenever he wanted. Now I knew better. There was a tenderness and rightness in loving Izzie. She was my own true love, and I was hers.

Raylene

After being gone forty days, I was told my husband and father would be coming to get me. Dr. Cooper said I had been cured. I didn't want to leave Izzie, but I knew I must. I worried about Mother and I wanted to get news from Lula May. Izzie took the news better than I did.

"It won't be long before my son comes for me. If we continued on, we'd probably get caught. It's better this way." I knew Izzie was trying to stay strong as we talked behind the barn.

Climbing the ladder into the hayloft, we laid in each other's arms, holding each other closely. I ran my fingers through her hair, tracing my fingers over her face, not wanting to ever forget her eyes, cheeks, and lips. After holding and pleasuring each other, we kissed for what might be the last time.

"Don't ever forget I love you, Raylene. When everything gets dark and mean, remember you and me here in the barn, and I'll do the same."

"I could never forget you. Coming here ended up being the best thing that's ever happened to me, because I met you. We have to believe one day we'll see each other again."

"I pray it happens, girl, as long as it's not here."

I knew I might never see Izzie again and it broke my heart. As I walked away, I turned and looked back at her. Izzie's face was expressionless, as if she was submitting to her fate. I couldn't bear to think of her going through another cycle of pain and doom at the hands of her family. Memories of Izzie would always be my refuge from the world.

Raylene

Father and Adam Farley came for me and were shown into Dr. Cooper's office. All three men were seated, with Dr. Cooper behind his desk, when I was shown into the room by an orderly. No one got up nor offered me a chair. I was left standing like a cow, a dog, a mule.

"Raylene, I have told your father and husband that I believe you to be cured," Dr. Cooper said, looking at me for the first time. "Now is your time to speak to them."

Looking from one to another, I spoke. "It says in Corinthians, For a man indeed ought not to cover his head, forasmuch as he is the image and glory of God; but the woman is the glory of the man."

I told Adam Farley, Father, and the good doctor I was created for Adam Farley even though the words stuck in my craw. After being with Lizzie, I didn't believe a word I said. My husband was no more to me than fallen dead leaves, while Izzie was the budding of life in spring.

As we left Dr. Cooper's office, Adam Farley handed me my gray dress and bonnet, which I promptly put on, feeling an inward dread and emptiness. I would not let these feelings spread to my soul. I would not! I sat nice and quiet on the ride home. I had lied and did not care. Memories of Izzie had been planted in my head. Somehow, some way, I would be with her again!

Raylene

I would not lie down with Adam Farley no more. I would have no part of that business at all. Adam Farley told me it was my duty. I laughed in his face.

The first thing I did when I got back from the asylum was to walk to the silo on River Road. Lula May had left note pads and pencils wrapped in plastic under the white rocks. Since Levi's funeral I hadn't been able to leave her any notes. Today there was a letter, a *Time* magazine and, some newspaper clippings waiting for me.

> My Dearest Sister,
>
> I have found out where our brother is and have gotten a lawyer who will try to get him an appeal. What this means is the case could be re-opened. I do not think our brother got a fair trial and neither does the attorney. These things can take a long time, but there is hope.
>
> I have checked under the rocks hoping to have a message for you. I am worried I have not heard from you since the funeral. Remember, you have people who love you and are here to help you. I have left some articles for you to read about what is happening in the world.
>
> Write me and let me know that you are safe.
>
> LM

My response to Lula May was short, as I wanted her to concentrate on helping Ray and not to worry about me. I hoped the day would come when I could tell her face-to-face about Izzie. Perhaps she would be able to help her, too, but for now that would have to wait.

It didn't take but a day or so before I was back into my old life. I could have worked myself to death chopping wood, keeping the stove fed, and the water hauled from the well, and Adam Farley wouldn't have cared less, at least to my way of thinking. I was glad for work that kept me out of the house. Sometimes I wandered to the creek and threw rocks from one side, then to the other. Thinking of Izzie, Ray, and Lula May got me through the days. I would see them again. I had to.

Raylene

1980

I hadn't been back from the asylum long when Father decided Aunt Ida needed my help. Mother had been doing poorly and was nothing but skin and bones. She had declined greatly during the forty days I was gone. Mother looked like a pale flower lying in her bed, wilting a little more each day.

Aunt Ida had her hands full since Mother wasn't strong enough to leave the bed and relieve herself in the slop jar. It took a lot of time and coaxing to get Mother to eat anything at all, and she made a mess while being fed, making more laundry that had to be done. Sometimes Mother looked at me and I saw recognition in her eyes.

"Raylene, you're back. You were gone for such a long time," Mother surprised me by saying in a voice so weak I could barely make it out. I sat with her, holding her hand. Mother had come back to me, at least for a little while.

I was more than happy to help with the extra cooking and washing. Anything was better than being in Adam Farley's house. It was good to sit with Mother and hold her hand when she let me. Sometimes I brushed her hair. It gave me time to think about Izzie and my time at the asylum. My thoughts were never far from Ray and Lula May.

When Mother napped, which was most of the time, I helped Aunt Ida with whatever I could. In the evenings I went back home and tended to Adam Farley. I knew the real reason I was sent to Father's house wasn't to help Aunt Ida; I was to be watched in the event I was tempted to backslide. Adam Farley had seen me yelling and throwing rocks at the creek and told Father.

It was early winter and we had all been busy with hog butchering, and curing meat. I went to the smoke house looking for Aunt Ida and found her sitting on the floor with a ham by her side.

"What happened, Aunt Ida? Did the rope break? Let me help you string the ham back up."

Aunt Ida looked at me funny as if I had caught her at something, then I spied it, the open box of rat poison on the floor. I about fell over when I saw the damp rag in her hand was coated with D-Con!

"We had rats out here a couple of years back. That's where I got the idea. I've cured small hams with D-Con for Thaddeus the last two years. I haven't given anybody other than him a bite of these hams in case you were wondering. I always had a regular ham for myself and whoever else ate with us," she said, looking at me in desperation.

"But to do such a thing as this! I don't know what to make of it, Aunt Ida. It's not right, that much I know," I said, feeling at a loss for words.

"I haven't had no life except this one, Raylene, and I can't bear it much longer. It was a curse my father put on me when I made that promise to him to care for Thaddeus. So do with me what you will, girl. Tell Thaddeus and Adam Farley and be done with it. They can do to me what they will."

I left Aunt Ida in the barn and took a walk. I came to a fork in the path and turned down it. My throat grew tight as a flock of crows exploded in front of me, scolding me as they flew away. I stopped and put a hand over my racing heart. I felt alone in the world, and so did Aunt Ida.

I kept walking, feeling a sense of dread. Like Aunt Ida, I had no children but Rosebud, and she was in her grave. I didn't have to think long. Father had been bitten by snakes, drank poison, and still he lived. D-con wouldn't make much of a difference.

I now understood how alike Aunt Ida and I were. I would not stop her from what she was doing. When I found Aunt Ida in the garden I made her promise not to give Mother any ham or herself either. She gave me her word.

231

Raylene

1981

It was summer's onset and the strawberries were ripe for picking. I had just walked into the house, after scattering feed to the chickens, and was about to start breakfast when Adam Farley came into the room. I could tell by look of him that he was in one of his lecturing moods, and sure enough he started preaching at me.

"Raylene, remember what your mother did. Remember and learn from her sin. For the curse is on the house of the wicked, but he blesses the abode of the righteous." I felt the scarlet rage of anger creeping up my neck, but I held my tongue.

Mother had gotten a little of her strength back, but she wasn't eating much at all. Father told me it was time to resume my duties at home. I didn't want to leave Mother or Aunt Ida, but I had little say in the matter.

It wasn't long when trouble started brewing again. I couldn't stand staying in the house doing woman's work. I had a hankering, a craving, to stay outside. I reckon it was from my time at the asylum with Izzie. I got to hoeing taters in the garden and chopping firewood morning, noon, and night. My arms and shoulders were getting bigger and stronger every day.

My husband was in the barn working when I put on his overalls and took off my bonnet, letting my long hair flow loose around my shoulders, then I went out into the sweet, sweet sunshine. I hadn't been outside long when Father rode by in his truck. Father pulled up next to me and looked at me with burning contempt. He said not a word, but volumes were written in his eyes. I stared back at him, meeting his gaze, and he rode off.

That evening the Council of Elders came to the house. This time they brought the razor. Brothers Culver and Hall forced my husband to sit in a kitchen chair, holding his hands behind his back. Brother Fritts began shaving off my husband's long white beard as Father quoted scripture.

"If the right eye offends thee, pluck it out, and cast it from thee; for it is profitable for thee that one of thy members should perish, and not that thy whole body should be cast into hell."

"Father, stop this! Can't you see what you're doing is wrong? Adam Farley shouldn't be punished for what I do," I protested.

Father glared at me in contempt and continued to speak.

"Adam Farley, you are not head of your household as you cannot make your wife obey you. You are not a suitable leader and we cannot allow you to be an influence to others. No longer does your beard signify you as a Believer."

I had never seen Adam Farley's face before. Adam Farley had not seen his own face since he was twenty years old. To me he looked as old and tired as day old peeled potatoes.

"Who am I, if I'm not an Elder in the Waters of God no more?" Adam Farley asked the Brothers through his tears.

They did not reply, but turned their backs on him and walked out the kitchen door. That night Adam Farley didn't come to bed. I heard him crying like a baby from his chair in the kitchen, but thought it best to leave him be. The next morning he was out before sunrise. I went to the barn to see what he wanted for his breakfast. I pushed open the door. When my eye adjusted to the light, I saw him hanging from a rafter, then I cut him down.

Raylene

I walked to Father's barn and hitched Father's plow horse to the wagon without asking permission and drove back to collect my husband. It took some doing, but I was able to get Adam Farley into the wagon myself. Covering him with a quilt, I took my husband to the undertaker's.

I didn't want anyone to see him lying dead in the wagon. I knew it would be his wish no one ever saw him clean shaven. I didn't pass any Brothers on the ride; most were working in their fields at that time of day. I was wearing my gray dress and bonnet, not wanting to cause any disturbances with people I might run into.

The undertaker was an outsider, but knew and respected the ways of Believers. He was a big bald man, with kind blue eyes. He had a small business, next to his brick house, selling caskets and headstones. Without asking any questions, he helped me get Adam Farley out of the wagon and into a pine box. Seeing Adam Farley without his beard, he knew all he needed to know. Believers always paid cash, and he knew he would get his money. He and I would figure that out later. I asked him to get in touch with Violet for me. She would, of course, get in touch with Lula May. I wanted to have Adam Farley buried the next day. I felt it was best for my husband to be laid to rest as quickly and quietly as possible.

"Leave your husband's body with me. I want to clean him up good for when he meets his Maker. Come back in the morning and he'll be ready for you."

I knew what Undertaker offered to do was right. Adam Farley's clothes were covered in dirt and straw, and his face was anything but peaceful.

Father didn't say a word when I returned his horse, Old Dan, and his rig. He turned his back on me. Aunt Ida didn't come out of the house. I wondered how I would find out how Mother was from now on. I knew I may never be allowed to see her again. I felt a huge pain come into my heart. "What now?" I asked myself on the way home. Was I still a Believer? No mention had been made of what would happen to me.

The next morning I walked to Father's and again hitched Old Dan up to the wagon and went to the undertaker's to claim my husband's body. Father wasn't there to stop me.

"Come look at your husband for the last time. I've laid him out proper."

He had tended to Adam Farley well. I brought Adam Farley's Bible and black hat with me and put them into the casket with him. I kissed his cheek, then Undertaker closed the lid.

Undertaker insisted on going with me to the cemetery and drove the wagon. There were only four of us at the graveyard including Violet. I knew the Elders wouldn't come. I recognized the man who had given Adam Farley the white lightning after Levi's funeral.

"I feel bad about your husband. Violet called and told me what happened. She said the least I could do would be to dig his grave. Undertaker brought me up here yesterday and told me where to dig," Lightning Man said.

"It's appreciated," was all I could think to say as Violet walked towards me.

"I'm sorry Lula May isn't here. She's on one of her airline trips," Violet said, putting her arm around me.

Violet led us in singing "Amazing Grace" and "Rock of Ages." I read Psalms 23, then prayed for Adam Farley to find the songs and scriptures soothing to his soul.

When the brief service was over, Undertaker and Lightning Man covered Adam Farley with dirt. When they were done, I planted periwinkle on top of him as that was his favorite. Violet gave me time to be alone as she walked to her husband's grave. It was well tended, so I knew she visited often.

I had Adam Farley's casket planted east to west. I wanted his body to rise and meet the rays of sunshine on resurrection day. I was glad there were no Believers there to stop me and have me plant him north to south as the Waters of God Believers do for suicides, evil doers, and non-believers.

I hoped my husband would find comfort, planted on the hill next to Rosebud. It was his undoing to have taken a young woman, such as me, for his wife. I wept for my husband and for myself. I wept for the Waters of God Believers. I wept for Rosebud. Although the Believers were not for me, it was a solid faith for those who accepted it and believed.

Now with my husband dead, Father was the leader of the church.

Raylene

Aunt Ida came knocking on the door. My husband had been dead for over a week, and I had been expecting Father or one of the Elders to tell me to leave the house even if I was Adam Farley's widow. I knew I was a puzzlement to the Elders as to what to do with me.

"Raylene, may I come in?" Aunt Ida said as she stood on the back porch.

"You shouldn't be here. What if a Believer sees you?" I said, opening the screen door.

"I have something serious to talk to you about. Let's you and me sit down," she said as she walked in.

Sitting at the table, Aunt Ida took my hand and looked in my eyes before she began to speak.

"Your Mama died three days ago, Raylene."

"I don't understand. She was doing better the last time I saw her," I said in disbelief.

"I wasn't with her when she passed. I was attending to Brother Culver's young wife. She had a difficult delivery, and I was there for two days. Before I left, I told Thaddeus to have you watch over your mother while I was gone, but I reckon his pride was too big to ask. He didn't check on her between his chores and meetings. I reckon he didn't suspect it was her time to go."

I couldn't believe what I was hearing. How could Father have been so selfish as not to have come for me nor sent someone else to be with Mother? I felt my face burn red with rage as Aunt Ida continued to talk.

"I cleaned your mother up the best I could, but time had taken a hold of her, and I didn't want you or Lula May seeing her that way. I sent Thaddeus to Undertaker's for a casket. I told him to get one with a flowered lining; it was the least he could do. Then he left me alone with her. I didn't feel right dressing your mother in a gray dress and bonnet. She never was one of us, and I didn't want to bury her like she was one. I brushed her hair out long and put a white night dress on her, like she was sleeping, then I took Joseph's silver dollar and put it in her hand. I knew she would like that.

"The silver dollar was in your mother's satchel, tucked down inside a small pocket, when Thaddeus brought her here. Something told me not to get rid of it. When your mother got brain fever she burned hot for days. I lay with her in bed, thinking she might not make it. Then I got the idea to put the silver dollar on her night stand so something of Joseph's could be with her, watching over her.

"In the early morning her fever broke. She got better after I left the silver dollar on the bedside table, although she never was the same, lost the way she was in another world. Sometimes I envied Mamie when I saw that certain peace come over her and the gentlest, sweetest smile, like she was seeing Joseph."

Aunt Ida spoke with such sadness I began to weep.

"After I had laid your mother out proper, I closed the coffin lid and nailed it shut without Thaddeus taking a look at her. I told him there was no point in seeing her the way she was. He didn't push the issue.

"I have something to give you and Lula May. I never felt right calling her Sarah Ruth," Aunt Ida said, taking her hand from her apron pocket.

"Thaddeus instructed me to empty the contents of Mamie's satchel deep into the woods, and bury them, when he brought her here to live. I couldn't do it. It felt wrong. I hid these adornments from Thaddeus in the ticking of my mattress along with the silver dollar. Take your mother's belongings, Raylene. They rightfully belong to you and Lula May," Aunt Ida said, giving me two silver hair clips and a string of pearls. Aunt Ida then handed me a towel with something wrapped inside.

"This flute belonged to Joseph. It's the only thing we have that belonged to him. Give the flute to Lula May since it belonged to her daddy. I wish I could have heard him play it. Joseph was my baby brother, and

I loved him, but no one seems to remember that. I hope it brought him joy," Aunt Ida said with a wistful look.

"There's one more thing, a bank book. Your mother and Joseph had an account and made regular deposits. Throughout the years, when I went to the city market, I would sneak off from Thaddeus and add egg money to it. Give the bank book to Lula May. She'll know what to do. She's the beneficiary on the account. Now I best leave before Thaddeus figures out where I've gone."

Aunt Ida hugged me hard before she left, something she had never done before. I knew in that moment Aunt Ida loved me, Lula May, and Ray in more ways than a heart could measure.

Raylene

A low white mist hung over the pines at Mother's graveside funeral. Lula May, Violet and I didn't mind her being buried in the Believers' cemetery because we knew how carefully and lovingly Aunt Ida had laid her out without Father knowing. Mother was dressed in her white nightgown. Her hair was brushed out long and not under a bonnet. In her hand was the silver dollar of the one man she truly loved.

Lula May, Violet, and I stood apart from the Believers. We were on one side of the grave while they were on the other. Lula May had brought a dark green dress, a matching neck scarf, and ladies shoes for me to wear. They were modest by her standards, but I wasn't so sure. Violet told me I looked real nice, so I took her word for it. I was wearing Mother's pearls and Violet had put the silver hair clips in her hair. I wondered if Aunt Ida could tell we were wearing them.

Father's face was solemn and his voice low as he prayed over Mother, but we couldn't make out the words. He did not look at us, but Aunt Ida did, sending us a smile. Aunt Ida and I had secrets we would never share.

The Believers left after the brief service, eager to get back to farm chores and housework. Aunt Ida was the last to walk away. She turned and blew us a kiss when she wasn't being watched and continued on.

It didn't take long for Mother's grave to be covered, and then we were alone with her at last. Her two daughters and her best friend were together again, and one day Ray would be coming home but the finality of Mother's death had left me shaken. What next? I wondered. How would I go on?

The sparrows stayed silent in the trees as we planted Mason jars in the ground, filling them with the red roses Lula May brought for Mother. When we were finished, the birds shot up like arrows. I couldn't help but think this was a sign Mother's spirit was now free and she had gone to meet Joseph.

"We need to go back to the house now. I have to leave soon. The Elders posted a note on the door yesterday saying I had to be gone in two weeks," I told Violet and Lula May.

"That's all the note said?" Violet asked.

"They didn't say anything about me being shunned. I guess I'm supposed to go away like I never existed."

"What do they think you should do now?" Lula May asked.

"They had no concern for me nor I for them. When I leave that house I will not look back," I answered.

"You are coming home with me and that's all there is to it," Violet said, as she and Lula May embraced me in a group hug.

"There's something I need to do before I leave this place," I said, as we walked onto the porch and into the kitchen.

Lula May and Violet stood back and cheered as I threw every plate, cup, and saucer against the table where I served Adam Farley his meals, then I took the gray dresses, shoes, and bonnets I was forced to wear out of the wardrobe, bundled them, and put them into paper sacks.

"I don't want anything I have ever worn being left in this house. Another Believer will be living here, with a wife no doubt, and I don't want her wearing what I was forced to wear. I won't be coming back here ever again."

That night we had a bonfire in Violet's back yard.

"I vow before you both that I will never wear a dress again," I said as the fire burned my gray dresses, bonnets, and shoes. We had become quiet. I knew we were thinking of Mother. The fire burned brightly as if trying to consume our grief and pain. I had a sense we were all being

241

purified so our new lives could begin.

Waking up to the smell of fresh coffee, I looked around Violet's guest bedroom. I had only lived in Father and Adam Farley's house. This bedroom was different from what I was used to, with yellow walls, flowing curtains, and plump pillows. I stretched out in the soft bed pulling the down comforter up to my chin. Looking at the pictures on the walls I couldn't believe what I was seeing. I jumped out of bed, dressed quickly and went into the kitchen.

"Good morning, Raylene. How did you sleep?" Violet asked as she poured me a cup of coffee. Lula May was already drinking hers, having risen before me after spending the night on the fold-out couch.

"Violet, are those photos of Mother, Joseph, and Lula May on the bedroom wall?"

"They sure are, honey. When Joseph died and your mother left us, I went to the house they rented and picked up their personal things. The trunk at the foot of the bed has your mother's keepsakes. I kept them for a day like this, when her children could go through and claim her things. Lula May has been through the trunk, but we agreed to leave everything just as it is until you and Ray can go through it as well.

"Thank you for keeping her things, Violet. It means so much to me."

"I was glad to see you girls wearing your mother's jewelry at the funeral. I was afraid the pearls and hairclips were gone forever. When Thaddeus came for Mamie and Lula May he made me take the hairclips, pearls and flute away saying they weren't allowed in the Believer's world. It was if he thought they were evil. When I ran back into the house to put things in a satchel, I placed them in the bottom of the bag and covered them with nightgowns, underwear and Kotex. I didn't figure he would search too far when he saw those things."

"Aunt Ida took the satchel, so we never knew it existed. I remember Mama wearing the hairclips and Daddy playing the flute when I was a little girl. They have made their way back to us," Lula May said, as tears rolled down her face.

"There's been quite a few surprises in the last few days and probably more to come," Violet said, shaking her head in wonderment.

After a quick breakfast, Lula May, Violet, and I looked through Mother's pictures and scrapbooks together. Mother had saved ticket stubs of movies she and Joseph had seen, birthday and Christmas cards, and a receipt from a hotel at Myrtle Beach. Mother kept a list of books she read and a few of Lula May's baby toys.

A silver hairbrush and mirror, a locket with a picture of Father on one side and Lula May on the other were in special boxes, along with Mother's plain gold wedding band.

"Your mother insisted that Joe be buried wearing his wedding ring. When your mother was about to leave our house with Thaddeus, she handed me her wedding ring in a handkerchief, before he had the chance to take it away from her. She whispered for me to keep it safe for Lula May," Violet told us.

We closed the lid on the trunk late that morning, with tear streaked faces. We agreed to wait until Ray was with us and we would go through Mother's things with him. We wanted Ray to understand more of the Mother he never really knew.

The next morning Lula May, Violet, and I went to the bank. Deposits Aunt Ida made and interest had added up over the years. Lula May said the money belonged to me and Ray as well as her. When we were finished at the bank, Violet insisted on going to Woolworth's lunch counter to eat, and buying us each a grilled cheese sandwich and an ice cream sundae.

"One of my best memories was bringing your mother here. Now look at me here again with her two girls!" she said, beaming.

When we were finished eating Lula May and Violet helped me buy some new clothes. I had never had anything store-bought before. There sure would be a lot to get used to in the outsiders' world.

Before leaving Pugh's Department Store, Lula May insisted on buying me a set of pink flowered dishes, with nothing chipped.

Ray

I was mopping down the hall, rounding the corner in front of the infirmary, when I saw Shiflett and Brown cornering Leslie. Brown had his hand on the back of her neck while Shiflett was whispering something into her ear. I saw the look of disgust on Leslie's face, and I went off attacking Brown with my fist while Shiflett tackled me from behind. Something took hold of me as if I was in the field again protecting Amy Carper with the pitchfork. It took four guards to take me to solitary.

I knew Leslie wouldn't say anything about the guards bothering her, thinking it would go bad for me if she did. She wouldn't want to draw any attention to what was going on between us. I saw no one except the occasional guard bringing me a meal. I remained in my cell with only cockroaches and an occasional mouse for company. There seemed to be no rules for how long someone could be left in solitary.

I longed for the sight of trees and birds, but mostly it was Leslie I needed to see. Who was I and what was I becoming in this place? Father would be so ashamed of me. I was anxious and angry and could not sleep. I did endless sit-ups and pushups trying to tire myself out but it did little good.

After three weeks I was released and sent back to my cell. When I noticed the letter on my bunk, I thought it was from Leslie and it scared me. She knew better than to send a letter through the post as our letters were opened and read before we got them.

I breathed a sigh of relief when I saw it was from Lula May. She knew where I was! She wrote saying Mother had died and she had been with Raylene at the funeral. Aunt Ida and Father seemed the same, as far as she could tell. Best of all she had gotten a lawyer and was trying to get my case re-opened. Maybe, just maybe things were looking up!

The letter wasn't long, but Lula May promised to write again soon. I felt sorry for Mother passing away and my not being there, but in truth, I had lost her many years ago.

I waited two miserable weeks before asking to see the warden. I hadn't been able to see Leslie since I got out of solitary and it was worrying me. A few days passed before a guard came to take me to Warden Phillips' office. When I entered his office, he did not raise his head to look at me. He seemed to be studying the paperwork on his desk. I stood quiet, waiting for him to speak to me.

"What brings you here, Ray? Tell me, and be quick about it."

"Sir, I'd like to ask permission to resume my duties as houseboy again," I said as humbly as I could.

Warden Phillips studied me hard before he began to speak. "I don't know what caused you to go off half-cocked and attack Shiflett and Brown. They claimed there was no reason for it. You hadn't been in trouble before, so my guess is that you were provoked, though I can't prove it. Dr. Gusler's niece came in to talk to me last week. She claims no one cleans the infirmary better than you and asked if you would be allowed to clean it again. I didn't give her an answer, telling her I would need to think about it. Knowing you want to be a houseboy again, I'm willing to give you one more chance. Don't disappoint me, Ray."

Ray

1981

It was Christmas Day, and Leslie figured out how we could be together for a full hour before I would be missed. Extra visitation from family members was allowed on Christmas. I had never had a visitor, nor did I expect to. I had gotten two short letters from Father talking of God's will. I was getting a postcard about every two weeks from Lula May. They were always from somewhere she had just traveled to. I looked forward to her cards and brief messages.

Today the guards would have their hands full with family members, and they wouldn't be paying any attention to me. Leslie told her uncle she had a sick headache and for him to visit friends without her. I had taken up mopping right after breakfast for the last couple of weeks so today would look like any other day.

Leslie left the door unlocked to the infirmary, and I stepped inside, locking the door behind me. Leaving my mop and bucket in an examining room, I made my way up the stairs to Leslie's living room. I wanted to give her a Christmas present, but there was nothing but cheap stuff in the commissary, and that seemed worse than giving her nothing at all.

When I came through the door of her apartment, I was taken aback by the large spruce tree with the twinkling lights. When Leslie saw me, she reached for a sprig of mistletoe dangling from a red ribbon, which she held over her head. Her eyes were close to mine, so innocent and blue, they made me melt. I held her in my arms and kissed her as her red robe fell to the floor revealing a short red nightgown.

"This is your Christmas present, Ray, it's called a negligee. Now it's time for you to unwrap me, but first you have to have a bit of angel food cake. You said the first time you saw me you thought I was an angel, remember?" Leslie said, feeding me a bite.

"Next time make it devil's food, because that's what you're dealing with now. The sight of you in that negligee is driving me out of my mind, and all I can think about is taking it off of you, " I said, taking Leslie into my arms, kissing her and leading her to the bedroom.

When it was time to leave, I put the mistletoe into my pocket. Between bites of mashed potatoes at Christmas dinner with the other cons, I felt tears sting my eyes, blurring the ham and peas on my plate. I asked permission to go to the john. It wouldn't do for anyone to see me look weak.

I took a long look at myself in the mirror and studied the hardness in my face. The innocent young man who had been sent to Mansfield no longer looked back at me. In many ways I was just another con, and Leslie was a beautiful woman. How could this be? Why hadn't sweet Leslie moved on in her life, finished school, and had a family? Why was this lovely girl waiting on the likes of me? I had nothing to offer her.

That hour I spent with Leslie in her bedroom would get me through the many dark and lonely nights to follow. I would never forget that Christmas.

Ray

1982

I was 24 years old and had been in prison for five years and two months. Most times it felt like ten. Lula May was writing more and I looked forward to her letters of remembrance which gave me comfort. She also gave me updates on my appeal but so far there was little to report.

Lula May told me about her job as a stewardess and the places she traveled and the people she'd met. I got some good laughs from her stories. More important was what she wrote about growing up with her real father, Joseph, and what Mother was like then. She told me how bad it hurt her to leave me and Raylene behind and how much she missed us. Lula May's letters made me feel like I was a human being again. I read them over and over.

I made myself useful in Mansfield. Leslie was the only thing good here, but I found myself being short with her and demanding. I accused her of looking at Shiflett in a way that appeared lustful, to me, although she denied it. She claimed she had to be nice to him because he did her small favors such as bringing copies of *Newsweek* to me and other cons when she asked him to. I didn't like Leslie cozying up to Shiflett for he was an evil man. I hadn't forgotten how he looked at her.

There were notes from Leslie stuck in the magazines Shiflett brought to me. I didn't need Leslie's notes. She was getting too bold in her actions. Leslie should have left here and finished school. It would have been the right thing for her to do, to go on with her life.

More and more Leslie told me she was waiting for me. I didn't want to encourage her, so I stayed silent. I saw the frustration building in her. Leslie would never fit in to the Believers.

I felt like a coward and a cheat for not coming clean with her. I hadn't explained our way of life even though she had asked me many questions. My answers were always brief and fell short. I didn't tell her I planned to return to the Believers and how I grieved for all I lost while in prison.

Sometimes I thought I couldn't take another day. I'd been feeling tired and weak. I didn't tell Leslie, as I didn't want her to pester me about the small cough I had. I didn't want to end up in the tuberculosis ward in the prison hospital. Besides, it was only a small cough. It would pass.

Perhaps the day would come when I, like Father, would be an Elder in the church, and he could be proud of me again. I wanted to go back to the way it was before I ended up here in Mansfield.

Ray

Shiflett came to my cell telling me I was needed in the infirmary. I was surprised to be met by Dr. Gusler. I could tell something was bad wrong because of the redness of his face and the bulging vein pulsing in his forehead. Dr. Gusler told Shiflett to leave but indicated for him to wait outside the door.

"What business I have with you, Simpkins, won't take long. I don't know how you got your hooks into my niece, and if it wasn't for Leslie's reputation I'd have you locked in solitary until you rotted. My niece's good name will not be soiled. I've have sent her away from here and she won't be coming back. Leslie understands I'll make sure you serve time until you're an old man if she contacts you. She knows I don't make false promises."

I knew better than to speak, but stood there humble. Dr. Gusler didn't want anyone to know his niece was in love with an inmate. It would make him look like a fool, but I was confused. Where had Leslie gone and why?

"Leslie agreed to leave quickly if I gave you this letter, though I didn't want to. I plan on keeping my word, as she's going to keep hers." Dr. Gusler handed me an envelope, his hands shaking with rage. Looking at Leslie's familiar cursive, I felt a wave of panic come over me.

"Read this letter while I'm watching you, then I'm going to destroy it. Another thing, you better not get yourself hurt. Your medical attention might fall short." Dr. Gusler glared at me while I read.

> Ray,
> It is undeniable I have been conned by you. It was for the best I cancelled my trip with Uncle as I was not feeling well. Imagine my surprise when I went into the infirmary to

get medicine for my vomiting and heard your voice and a woman's coming from the examining room.

It was unmistakable what was taking place. Shiflett and Brown looked sheepish at being caught in the infirmary. How did you do it, Ray? How did you talk them into getting a woman for you, especially the men whom you attacked while defending me?

When Uncle returned from his trip, he saw my distress. He questioned me, and in my weakened state I confessed to our meeting secretly. I did not mention the woman, Shiflett or Brown. It was too sordid to discuss with him. Uncle insisted I leave Mansfield immediately. He gave me no choice, and I knew he was right.

I loved you and you betrayed, took advantage, and dishonored me. Did you laugh with the cons and guards about what a fool I was? How quickly everything has changed.

Goodbye, Ray.

Leslie

I handed the letter back to Dr. Gusler. He ripped it into shreds as I stood there helplessly watching. Opening the door to the infirmary, he called for Shiflett to come in.

"Walk the inmate back to the cell. Make sure he gets no special favors nor treatment. His days of being a houseboy are over."

Ray

I didn't know Leslie came into the infirmary. I believed her to be out of town for a few days with her uncle. I was mopping when Shiflett told me to step inside the infirmary. Brown was already inside waiting for me.

"Put your hands behind your back, Ray. We gotta put handcuffs on you," Shiflett said, as his eyes flicked with cruelty. His uneven and yellow teeth showed as he gave me a slow and treacherous smile.

"Why are you doing this? What's going on?" I asked as they cuffed me.

"We've been thinking about you, Believer Boy, and thought we owed you a little something for your time in solitary."

"I'd rather you didn't," I said, looking at Brown and his protruding belly; his greasy tie showing the contents of his lunch.

"We're having a little party, Believer Boy. We clocked out at the end of our shift and here we are with you, not even getting overtime. We are going to get you drunk and laid."

Shiflett held my head back while Brown attempted to pour gin down my throat. Coughing and sputtering, I tried to break away. Brown continued to hold my head back while more of the vile liquid was poured into me.

"This little party is for attacking us when we were having a little fun with the pretty nurse," Shiflett said, with a wicked laugh.

"The way he was acting he must be sweet on her," Brown said, smirking.

They laughed while they took turns slapping me around before they brought the woman in from the back room. My present wasn't pretty or even young, far from it. She was nothing but sex, and it showed with her bleached hair and poked out breasts.

"He's probably a virgin. What do you think, Sheila? Here's $20 to give him the works," Brown said as Sheila snatched the money from his hand.

Shiflett and Brown threw me into the examining room, but not before stripping me naked and putting the handcuffs back on. I don't remember what happened after that. When I awoke, I was back in my cell and in a clean uniform. The taste of liquor was still in my mouth, and my head felt as if it would split in two.

The next morning Brown took me outside. "There's something you need to see, Simpkins. In case you decide to talk."

In the prison yard, a dead rooster lay. A piece of twine was tied around its neck with a note that said one thing; "Ray."

Ray

1987

Time passed slowly and I had turned twenty-eight years old. My life was hard, slow and strange. Sometimes I dreamed of summer days spitting watermelon seeds as a boy, blue jays, stars, and harvest moons. Other nights I dreamed of Leslie and woke with tears on my pillow. Where had she gone and did she weep for me? How long would it take before my broken life would change? I no longer worked in the garden. The memories of Leslie and me in the cornfield were too strong and filled me with longing. Mostly I worked in the laundry; the mindlessness of it suited me.

I was surprised when I found a long letter from Lula May waiting for me in my cell. I don't know exactly how she did it, but she got me an appeal. The lawyer she hired managed to get the court to review the case and look at the transcripts. The boy I stuck with the pitchfork healed up and had gone on living his sorry life, much of it spent in trouble with the law that even his daddy couldn't get him out of. Brother Carper's daughter, Amy, now grown and married couldn't bear to think of me still in Mansfield. With her husband defending her, she defied her parents and spoke up as to what really went on in the woods. Just like that my nightmare was over.

Lula May and Violet Ferguson were waiting for me when I walked out of Mansfield Prison a free man.

"Sweet Jesus, it's so good to see you, Lula May," I said, sweeping her up into my arms. Lula May hugged me back and covered my cheeks in kisses before I let her feet touch the ground.

"Ray, this is Violet," Lula May said as a kind looking woman extended her hand to me to shake.

"Ray, I've so looked forward to this day. Your Mother was my best friend, and I'm here to do what I can for her son."

"I know you already from the letters Lula May wrote me. Thanks for coming to get me. Where's Raylene? Is she in the car?" I said, looking around. "I really want to see Raylene." I began to panic wondering why she wasn't there, and I started to cough.

"She's at my house waiting for you, Ray. Let's get out of this jailhouse parking lot. We'll fill you in on everything on the drive. I'm so glad to have you out of Mansfield. With that cough I suspect you might be coming down with something. I want you to know my home is yours until something gets figured out. Right now I don't want you worrying about anything. Get into the back seat with Lula May where you two can talk. Today I'm your chauffeur."

It was a long drive to Violet's place. It took the better part of seven hours, and we didn't stop talking for any of it. Violet and Lula May brought a basket of fried chicken, potato salad, and apple pie but most important they brought a change of clothes for me.

Stopping at a gas station, I changed clothes while the car was being fueled. The pants were a little too big and the shirt a bit baggy, but anything was better than what I had to wear in Mansfield.

"Ray, you look so thin. I am worried for you," Lula May said with concern in her eyes.

"Just get me home to my little sister. You can't believe how I've missed and worried for her. I need to see her with my own two eyes."

When I walked into Violet's house, there was Raylene. I would know her face anywhere. She looked beautiful standing there dressed as a non-believer in a flannel shirt and men's trousers.

"I didn't want to meet you at the prison, Ray. I wanted to see you here for the first time. You needed to get to know Violet and catch up with Lula May on the ride home."

I swept Raylene up in my arms and twirled her around. "We'll never lose each other again, Raylene. I promised you that when you were a little girl, do you remember?"

"I never forgot Ray. I knew you'd come back to me."

Raylene, Lula May, and Violet took good care of me, but they could tell I was sick. I wasn't at Violet's but two days when my coughing got worse and my temperature spiked. Violet and Lula May rushed me to a hospital in Roanoke where I stayed for two weeks fighting off a high fever, night sweats, and chills.

I don't remember Lula May, Raylene, and Violet coming every day but I was told they did, taking turns staying by my side. Often I lay awake, tossing and turning, worried I had tuberculosis and had infected my family. I had someone else by my side at times, although I couldn't make sense of it for days.

"Ray, let me help you," a woman's voice called out.

"Can't nobody help me," I said, out of my mind with fever. "Who are you and what do you want with me?"

"Look at me, Ray. It's me, Leslie."

"Can't be. She left me and went away."

"Ray, it's me, Leslie. I promise it is."

I kept my eyes closed, afraid if I looked, nobody would be there.

The woman's voice continued to talk to me. How could it be? Nothing was making sense. Who was this woman, and why was she talking this way? I opened my eyes and looked at her hard. This woman had lines around her eyes and sunken cheeks. She was painfully thin, not like my Leslie. There was something about her that was familiar and the voice was the same. Maybe she was a ghost woman.

I continued to have night sweats and chills, but the clouds had separated, and I had heard the sweetest sound. Was it really Leslie? My mind strayed through the midst of my illness hearing familiar voices and seeing faces looking down on me in concern.

"You left Mansfield, and you've been here the whole time?" I asked ghost woman.

"Yes, Ray, I have. I kept my promise to Uncle and stayed away from you.

"What happened to you when you left the prison?" I asked her.

"When I left Mansfield I went away for a while, then I entered Roanoke Memorial Nursing School. That's how I ended up here at the hospital."

"All this time and you've been here?"

"That's right, Ray."

"I'll bet you are married now, probably to a doctor."

"No, I never married. But I do have a son. His name is Paul."

When the fever broke and the infection was under control, I was able to understand I didn't have tuberculosis. It was pneumonia and a blood infection that almost killed me. I was on the road to recovery and, best of all, Leslie was real and I had a son. I thanked God for the wonder of it all.

As I improved all I wanted was to see Leslie, to talk to her and explain what happened at Mansfield. After days of begging her to listen, she relented and let me tell her the whole sordid story. I pleaded for her forgiveness and asked if I could see my son.

"I can forgive you, Ray, but I can't forget our history. It's too much!" she said, shaking her head.

"I don't think it's a good idea for you to meet Paul; it would confuse him. He thinks his father is in heaven. I made a mistake by telling you about him, and I can't take it back now. How would you be able to explain a son from the outside world to the Believers?" she said, looking into my eyes.

Leslie was right. I had hurt her badly, and I was selfish in my thinking, but I wanted to know my son. It must have been hard for Leslie to not be married and raise a child alone.

I was finally released from the hospital. I had a lot to think about, and I was still weak. Much had happened since I had gotten out of Mansfield, and I knew there was more to come.

257

Raylene

1987

I couldn't keep living with Violet. With Ray in the house, it was getting crowded even if he did sleep on the couch. Violet didn't seem to mind saying she liked the company. Ray was gone most days looking for a job, and Violet went to work at the restaurant.

I cleaned the house for Violet and tried to make myself as useful as possible, but there wasn't enough to do to fill my days. I didn't feel ready to get a job in the outside world yet. I wasn't sure what I could do. Violet told me to take my time; eventually I could work in a restaurant, as a cashier at a grocery store, or be a sales clerk. When Lula May stayed overnight at Violet's, she slept with me. I liked it when that happened as we usually talked way into the night.

"I've put in to change my airline base. It shouldn't be long before I'll be flying out of the Roanoke airport. There's so much happening with our family I need to be close." Lula May squeezed my hand.

"Don't think I'm ungrateful, Lula May. I love Violet, but I don't want to inconvenience her anymore. I'd like to find my own place to live."

"We have the money in the bank, and I can't think of a better way to spend it. You and I can figure out a way for you to make your own money after we get you settled someplace else."

The moment we walked into the sweet little house with the fireplace and big front porch, we knew we had found the perfect place. There was room for a good sized garden out back and plenty of fruit trees. The best part of all was I could easily walk to Violet's.

Lula May made an offer on the house, and it was accepted. It wasn't any time at all before I was in my new home. Lula May and I spent several afternoons looking for bargains to furnish it with. Sitting on my front porch swing, drinking lemonade, after a long day of garage sales I finally worked up my nerve.

"Lula May, there's something I want you to know."

"You can tell me anything, Raylene, you know that."

"I met a woman while I was in the asylum. I love her, and her name is Izzie Brown."

I told Lula May everything that happened between Izzie and me, even the whoopee part. Somewhere in the telling Lula May started crying and had to go wash her face and get a glass of water. When she came back, her purse was over her shoulder.

"There's no use in waiting. Let's go get Izzie now," Lula May said, taking out her car keys.

We didn't have any trouble finding our way. The directions Izzie gave me to find her son's place were burned into my brain. I had committed to memory the houses, barns, and turns Izzie told me to take should this day ever come.

Turning down the road to her son's farm, I saw everything was the way Izzie said it was. The fences needed mending, and there were deep ruts in the dirt road, making it near impossible to drive during heavy rain. The white framed house hadn't been painted in years and the front porch swing was broken.

A little girl in a torn and dirty dress was playing with a beagle pup, covered in fleas and ticks, in the front yard. She went yelling into the house calling for her mother when we got out of the car. Lula May knocked on the door as I walked to the garden in the back of the house. There I saw Izzie in old overalls and a flannel shirt pushing a tiller. I ran to her, waving my arms. She stood gazing at me as if not believing what she saw, then she rushed to me and fell into my arms.

"Raylene, its been seven long year since I've seen you, sweet girl, but

I never once gave up hope."

"Izzie, go pack a bag, the sooner we get out of here the better," Lula May said, after coming to the back of the house to get us.

"No need. I'm ready to go now."

Lula May, Izzie, and I got into the car and drove up the road.

Izzie didn't look back.

Lula May did not tell me what she said to Mary Brown other than she gave her cash. I didn't ask Lula May how much. I didn't want to know. Luckily, Izzie's son wasn't home. I suspect Mary Brown was happy to see Izzie go, and this was her opportunity to be rid of her for good.

Ray

When I returned to Violet's house, she insisted I use Levi's car until I was on my feet and could get another. "You might as well take it. Levi doesn't need a car where he is, and you'll be needing it to court that pretty nurse at the hospital," she said, smiling at me. I hadn't told Violet what had gone on with Leslie and me in prison. In time I was sure most of the story would come out.

Getting behind the wheel of Levi's Oldsmobile, I took off driving. I still hadn't gotten my driver's license since I had gotten out of prison. Driving without a license made me think back about taking Father's truck and driving to the carnival. I didn't have a driver's license then either.

I was nervous about seeing Father and Aunt Ida. What would I say when I saw them after all this time? Twenty minutes later I was driving around Believers' farms.

I saw Brothers on their tractors, in the fields, and passed a horse and buggy on the road. No one took any notice of me, but why should they? I didn't look as they did, and I was driving a blue Oldsmobile. Probably no one knew I was out of prison. It was strange how everything seemed to have shrunk since I had been gone. Prison had been like a foreign country, but even here I felt out of place.

I took a deep breath, got up my nerve, and drove down the road to our farm. Aunt Ida was in the garden picking cutworms off potato leaves. She stood, looking shocked to see me as I got out of the car. Father came out of the barn and walked over to me without saying a word. He stopped, put his hand on his hips, and looked at me hard. Everything stood still until he spoke.

"Let us sit on the porch and talk. Ida, you will join us." He turned and led the way.

After we sat down Father began to speak.

"When you left us, your place at the table was always set. No one sits there now, and no one ever will." He clasped his hands in his lap.

"As Believers, we live in the rhythm of the rising and setting sun, the rain, and the changing of the seasons. This will always be a part of you, Paul Ray Simpkins, as surely as you are the flesh of my flesh, but you don't belong here anymore. I know my telling you this hurts you. God's will takes time to understand."

In the silence that followed, several crows flew overhead and perched in a nearby tree, cawing loudly as if they had something to add.

How did Father know what I came to ask? Had he read my heart and known I wanted to return to the Believers? I looked first at him, then at Aunt Ida. Neither said a word, and I was afraid to speak up. Sitting in the silence, Father arose, shook my hand, and walked back to the barn. I hadn't been invited into the house. I was being treated like a non-believer.

"I have missed you, Ray, and prayed for you daily." Aunt Ida said with gentleness in her eyes I hadn't seen before.

"I am glad you've returned safely, but Thaddeus is right. Much has happened since you've been gone, and having been in prison, the Elders would never accept you back in the fold." She straightened her back. "The best thing for you to do now is to create a new life with your sisters."

Ray

I could not accept what Father said to me. I brooded, and after a few days, I went back. When Father saw me coming down the road he came out to meet me before I could get out of the car.

"Get into my truck, Ray. There is someplace I have to take you."

He drove me through the hay fields along the edge of Brother Frith's farm, taking a dirt path until we came to an old rundown house and barn hidden by trees and overgrowth. From the looks of the house, no one had lived there in years. The paint had peeled off the boards, the porch was sagging, and most of the windows had been busted out, yet tattered curtains still hung on. I had never come across this place with all the rabbit hunting I had done as a boy.

"Follow me." Father slammed the door as we got out of the truck. "There's something you need to see."

Walking into the barn, I had prickles of fear that caused the hairs on my arms to rise. Father began to speak to me in a deep, dark tone that filled me with dread as we stood in the barn looking at one another.

"For all the good blood that ran through Joseph's veins, bad blood runs through mine. Joseph did little wrong, and my parents were relieved by his kind and gentle ways. They did not trust me to be alone with my little brother.

"My father was busy with farming, so it was easy for me to sneak off to be with Obadiah Himes when my chores were done. Obie didn't follow the Believers' rules and laughed at the Brothers behind their backs even though he was a Brother himself. He took a special interest in me, a boy of thirteen, often telling me we were kindred souls.

"It was Obie and his non-believer friends who caught the black mare and placed her in the stall in this very barn. He was never able to ride the mare without being thrown. I took pleasure in watching as Obie used his whip as the mare fought him, kicking, biting, using all her might to tear the stall apart. Obie made me promise not to tell what happened in this barn nor that non-believers came and bought his white lightning.

"Obie only had the horse a few days when Father followed me and watched our wickedness. I saw him weep at the scattered bones of dogs, cats, and calves that hadn't been gnawed away by mice or drug off by other critters. I had never seen my father angry before. He became a man I didn't know full of rage and tears, yet he was not violent.

"He threatened Obie with going before the congregation and telling what he had witnessed, for now he knew what happened to the missing animals and believed Obie's wife's broken arm to be no accident. Father accused Obie for the bruises he had seen on Sister Caroline and would have Aunt Ida undress her to see if there were more under her gray dress. Obie left that night, not to be seen again. Three months after he left, Sister Caroline gave birth to her daughter Mamie, who was your mother."

"Are you saying Obie Himes was my grandfather?" I asked in disbelief.

"Yes, it's true, every bit of it." He turned his back on me and looked out into the distance.

"There's more to the story. I want you to hear every detail so you will know your place is no longer here. I am doing this for you, son, although you may not know it now."

"Why should I believe any of this? It doesn't make sense. Why are you making these things up?" I said, clenching and unclenching my fist.

"Have you ever known me to lie to you? Surely I have omitted much about my past that no one needs to know. I have worked hard to be better than I was, but I am who I am. I was hard on you as a boy, I know that, and maybe it was wrong. When you leave here today, I want you to move on with your life and have no regrets. See me for the man I am and not the one you thought I was. If you are ready now, I will finish telling you the rest. Are you alright with that?"

"I can't imagine there's more to tell but go on with it," I said, dreading what came next.

"Eventually my father won the black mare over with his kind voice and a coaxing manner. He kept fresh water and oats in her stall and did not try to ride her. Father said the mare was pregnant and did I not know? How did I not recognize her swelling sides? I felt young and foolish before my father's eyes.

"The moon shone full when the foal stood on wobbly legs. We named him Midnight, for that was the hour in which he was born. I was surprised when Father pulled a black leather glove from a pocket in his overalls and told me to put it on. He told me I was to wear the glove from that day on as a remembrance of my cruelty, should I ever think of hurting any of God's creatures again. Wearing the glove would help protect me from the depravity within my soul. That night in the barn, I became a boy split in two."

"I often wondered about the glove, especially as a child. I thought it was to hide some deformity. Why haven't you taken it off? You haven't needed to wear it all these years," I questioned him.

"It is too much a part of me now, and I am known for it. I know people have wondered about the glove and you are the only one to know the truth of it. If you wish to tell others, I cannot stop you. I will now continue with my story. I hope never to tell it again.

"Leaving the house in the night, my father and I went back to the barn. While tending to the horses, he made me sort through the bones, constructing skeletal remains as best I could. For many nights I dug, then placed the bones within their graves. It hadn't rained for days, and the ground was dry. It was early morning, when Father left me in the barn and went home to do the milking.

"I led the mare to the creek to drink. After she finished, she spotted an old cherry tree and began to eat her fill of wilted leaves. I didn't think nothing about it. By afternoon the mare didn't want food or water, and had uneasiness about her as she pawed the ground and threw her head about. By evening she was rolling on the ground, pushing Midnight away. I had never seen a horse do this before. When Father questioned me about what the mare ate, I told him about the cherry leaves. Colic was all he said.

"The mare was heaving so violently we took Midnight away from her. Soon she laid down and wouldn't get up. That's when I saw the shadowy white cloud, half in and half out, rise out of her. Father saw it, too, and said the mare was trying to decide whether to live or die, soon after she was gone.

"Father hauled buckets of cows' milk in his wagon trying to teach the colt to drink as he watched me dig the burial hole for Midnight's mother. I was bone tired with the digging, but Father wouldn't let me stop. With his help we pushed and pulled until we were able to get the mare into her grave then we shoveled the dirt back over her. I covered her grave with quartz rocks I carried from the creek while, in the distance, I saw Father busting up Obie's still with his ax.

"Together, Father and I got Midnight into the back of his wagon. He wrapped him in a woolen blanket trying to contain him as best he could. Father stayed in the back of the wagon holding Midnight while I took hold of the reins.

"We took Midnight to Father's horse, hoping she would nurse him along with her own colt. It took but a day before Midnight was accepted. Father then let it be known Midnight was always to be my horse.

"All of what I just told you, Ray, happened years ago, and now your face is as pale as a dead horse's bones. I cannot imagine what you think of me now and I am not finished with the telling of this tale, for I killed your mother much the same as Obie Himes tried to kill the mare. Do you wish me to go on with the telling?"

Confusion about the man I thought I knew was jumbled up in my head. I couldn't think of what to say or do, but could only nod for him to continue. I felt as if a bucket of icy water had been thrown over me. I couldn't imagine there was more to tell.

"After Sister Caroline died, Ida took Mamie in. I hated the child, for when I looked into her face I saw the green eyes of Obie Himes and cursed the glove I had to wear. As Mamie grew into womanhood, I saw how she and Joseph snuck looks at each other, and I envied those looks.

"Jealousy took hold of me and I wanted Mamie for my own, but she and Joseph ran away from me. When Joseph died, Mamie came back, although she did not care for me. I tried to break the hold Joseph had on her, but I could not erase him from her mind. Demanding sons, I ripped the skin off her soul until infection took her mind, driving her to madness."

"How can you be an Elder, preaching to others, pretending that none of this has happened?" I barely whispered the words. My heart was pounding hearing what he had done to my mother. "What kind of monster are you?"

"I have chewed my wrongdoings day after day, and still I cannot swallow them whole. I live off the poison of my regrets. I was a miserable sinner then, and I am a miserable sinner now. I thought Midnight should outlive me, for he was my father's curse upon me." Again, he stared into the distance.

"Maybe it's the one who preaches the most who carries the biggest load of sin. My time on earth may be short, but eternity is long. So hate me, boy, and be done with me and do not come here again."

I would not ride back in the truck with him, but walked back to Levi's car, thinking of all Father had said. Aunt Ida wasn't in the yard or on the porch when I returned from the long walk, and I was relieved because I didn't know what to say to her. How much of this had Aunt Ida known?

Once I was back in Levi's car and starting to pull away, I saw Father come out of the barn. Standing stoically with his hands by his sides, he did not wave farewell and neither did I.

Looking into my rear view mirror, I drove away from the only home I had ever known as I watched Father shrink away, then he was gone.

I had not told Father about meeting Obie Himes at the carnival.

There would have been no point to it. The old man with the same green eyes as my mother was my grandfather. My thoughts were heavy and dark with confusion. Father lived his whole life knowing the things he had done, all the while acting moral to all while locked in his own wrong deeds. Did he lie down at night and dream of nothing, or did Obie Himes haunt him with stampeding black mares threatening him harm?

I hungered for my old way of life in spite of what my Father revealed about himself. In prison I thought of storms passing over during the heat of the day, the sound of rain on the tin roof, and the frogs croaking as we sat on the front porch together. There was no going back. I had no father now.

Fitting back into any kind of life would have been difficult, but I hadn't expected this. I was lost between what was and was not. I now walked upon a pathless trail. I prayed that God would break open a new world for me.

Raylene

Izzie and I worked in the garden, growing vegetables, fruit, and flowers. We loved our little house and fixed it up so it was special to us. We spent hours sitting and rocking on our front porch, contented as could be.

I left Aunt Ida a letter at the silo telling her that Izzie was living with me. It was a hard letter to write, but I owed Aunt Ida the truth. I didn't expect to hear back from her, figuring she would disapprove, but I needed her to know about the special kind of love Izzie and I shared. I went back to the silo a week after I left the letter. I was surprised to find an envelope waiting for me. I opened it with trembling hands.

> My Dear Raylene,
> It has taken me a long time to learn that love and kindness are all that matter in this world. I am glad that you have someone who loves you and you love back. I pass no judgment on you, girl.
> Aunt Ida

I sat on the quartz rocks and wept. Aunt Ida's life hadn't been easy but she hadn't hardened her heart. She didn't judge me or Izzie. A warm and powerful feeling of love for Aunt Ida came over me that I knew would never go away.

Most people thought Izzie and I were spinster ladies, and that worked fine for us. We had three small bedrooms. One of them was for company, and the other was fixed up like it was Izzie's, though she never used it.

Lula May stayed with us some nights.

One Sunday morning, Lula May asked Izzie and me to go to church with her and Violet.

"I don't know if I'm ready for that," I said, startled by her request.

"It'll be okay. We'll sit in the back row. If it gets to be too much we'll leave, I promise."

I insisted on waiting until the service had already begun before we walked into the church so I didn't have to talk to strangers. We slid into the back pew. Violet was already there waiting for us. Lula May held one of my hands while Izzie held the other. I was relieved there weren't no snakes in this church.

Raylene

"Raylene, I'm going to teach you to drive. I can't be taking you and Izzie everywhere on my days off. What if there was an emergency and I was on one of my airline trips and Violet wasn't around?" Lula May asked.

For two days Lula May had me drive up and down country roads until she was satisfied with my performance, then we were off to the Division of Motor Vehicles to take the test, which I passed the first time!

"The next thing to do," she said, "is to get you a car. There are several dealerships we can go to."

When my eyes landed upon a used black Volkswagen, I knew it was the car for me. We bought it on the spot. Now Izzie and I would be able to go places without being dependent on anyone to take us.

Lula May said that one day she would take me and Izzie on one of her airline trips. I was willing to go, but there was no convincing Izzie to get on an airplane.

"You two go on. I want my feet firmly on the earth. If I were meant to fly, I'd have wings." I knew there wasn't any point pushing Izzie on the issue.

Lula May took me and Izzie to a beauty parlor at Crossroads Mall and had our hair cut and styled, although Izzie was skittish about going. We eventually wore her down. I had never cut my hair before, much less set foot into a beauty parlor. I was amazed by the smells, the many hair style magazines, and the chatter of women getting permanents and hair color.

Izzie just wanted her hair cut short, almost like a man's, but not quite. Her hair was easy to do, and she was happy with it. My hair took longer, and I flinched when they took the first cut and a chunk of my hair fell to the beauty shop floor.

"Shorter," I said, surprising myself. "I want my hair the same length as Lula May's."

My hair came just past my chin. It could be worn pulled back with clips or worn straight. One thing for sure, I wouldn't ever be putting a bonnet on my head again.

For Christmas, Lula May and Violet took Izzie and me shopping at JC Penney, where we got matching pants suits, clothes for working in the garden, flannel pajamas, and warm winter coats with plaid neck scarves. Lula May insisted on buying us clip-on earrings. She tried to get us to pierce our ears but that was going too far. Those clip-on earrings were staying in the drawer in my bedside table.

Lula May would never get Izzie and me looking girlie, no sir. She wanted us to get more clothes but that was all we needed. At least she didn't try to buy us dresses. Izzie and I would have come down hard against that. I haven't told Lula May yet, but I'm not going to the beauty shop again. Izzie would cut my hair. There would be no need to waste good money.

On a warm July morning I saw Father, with his long white hair and flowing beard, as he passed by my house in his truck. Standing in the yard watering my flowers, I waved at him. He pretended not to see me.

Father didn't need to go by my house on his way to sell produce, but he had. I liked to think one day he would weaken and stop. I would welcome him into my home.

I would never claim Father's faith as my own. It would always be a part of me, but only a small part. When gardening, Izzie and I sang songs we learned from the radio. Sometimes we listened to preaching, but after a while we were ready to turn the dial.

In the summer we sold fruit and vegetables to our neighbors. Sometimes we operated a small produce stand. We were known for our tomatoes and the beautiful quilts we made. We got by just fine.

Ray

1988

I was on the outside looking in. My life was different now. I don't know what would have become of me if not for Violet and my sisters. I had been a foolish man. Looking back on my time in prison Leslie had been there for me. She was there for me when I was in the hospital. It was God's plan for her to be my wife and I would do whatever it took to get her back.

I told Lula May, Violet, and Raylene almost everything that went on in the prison, but I didn't mention Christmas Day or our day in the cornfield as they were my own cherished memories. I wanted my sisters and Violet to be on board with helping me win Leslie over. If I had to make a fool of myself and wear her down I would.

"Hey, pretty nurse, you must be an angel," I said leaning on Leslie's automobile.

"Ray! You shouldn't be hanging out at my car when I'm coming out of work. This is the third time this week!"

"I'll be here every night until you take a drive with me," I said, giving her my best smile.

"Will I have to get security, Ray? I don't know if I can trust you. What do you want with me anyway?" she said sternly, but I saw tenderness in her eyes.

"Well, I've been thinking. I'm working in a carpentry shop now. In a year or so I'm going to be able to buy it from the owner. He's retiring and willing to finance it for me. I'm finding my way, sweet girl, and I want a life with you and Paul. I want to marry you and raise a family if you'll have me."

"What about the Believers, Ray? Why haven't you gone back to them?"

"They won't have me, Leslie."

"So you want me now? That's why you're proposing? Uncle was right about you when he warned me to stay away. I wish he was still alive so he could hear this." Leslie's face had turned red with anger. "Do you think this is a kind of proposal any woman would want to hear? You are a stupid man, Paul Ray Simpkins!"

"Please, Leslie. I didn't mean it to come across that way. Please take a drive with me. I want you to know my sisters better," I pleaded. "You didn't get to know them well while I was in the hospital." I moved a step closer to her.

"I've told them about our time in Mansfield except for the intimate details. I want my son to know Lula May, Raylene, Violet, and Aunt Ida. They're his family, Leslie. I'm asking you to marry me because I love you. We can make this work!"

"This is too much, Ray. I don't want to be proposed to because your other plans didn't work out. I will not be second place."

It took two months before I could convince Leslie to take a ride with me and meet my sisters at Violet's house. After several hours of us all drinking coffee in the kitchen, I could tell they were winning Leslie over. It wasn't long after that Leslie relented and invited me to her home to meet my son.

"Go slowly, Ray. He doesn't know who you are yet," Leslie said as we walked into Paul's bedroom. Picking up a ball, I tossed it at Paul. He caught it and threw it back. The three of us went into the back yard and pitched the ball back and forth. After an afternoon of playing with Paul and pushing him and Leslie on his swing set, he looked at his mother.

"Mama, can Ray stay for supper?" Tears poured from my eyes at his words.

"Why are you crying, Ray?" he said and hugged me. How was it possible I could love someone so much?

After several more visits, Leslie and I told Paul I was his father. Leslie and I married soon after in a small ceremony in Violet's living room. Paul was my best man, and Violet's preacher did the service. My sisters pulled out all the stops with a wedding cake and all the trimmings. It was the happiest day of my life.

Leslie and I didn't want a honeymoon. It was more than enough to be together, just the three of us.

Ida

1989

Life was quiet living in the house with Thaddeus. He was often gone for hours, I knew not where. I got to sitting in the rocking chair like Mamie did. Sometimes I would sit in the chair for hours or until words came creeping like shadows, causing me to have thoughts I had never had before. I liked the feeling there were empty spaces in my mind. When the emptiness happened, it was like I had gone someplace else and never left my chair. Sometimes I'd get to wondering if lunacy ran in my blood.

Thaddeus and I shared few words and ate our meals in silence. When he did talk to me, his voice would grow thin and thinner until he was only moving his lips. I reckon this came from me not wanting to hear a word he had to say. Sometimes my grief felt like it would take hold and strangle me.

More often than not, my chores didn't get done and Thaddeus had to fend for himself. Sometimes there were wasps crawling over the dirty dinner dishes I left unwashed in the sink, along with the cracked cup I drank my coffee from.

It was a hot August morning when Thaddeus took off on Old Dan. He said he was going to the hillside pasture to check on his cows and would be returning in time for lunch, wanting to avoid the heat of the afternoon sun.

I'd been snatching weeds from the bean vines for most of the morning and gone on to plucking a chicken and shucking corn. I had just sat down under a shade tree, where it was cooler and not so buggy when a big boom sounded and I saw the lightning bolt come down.

I could smell sulfur and something burning not far off. Lightning had struck a tree or a barn, I was sure of it, for lightning was not uncommon here. The wind and rain picked up quickly, as summer storms do, and moved on within the hour. Thaddeus did not make it home for lunch, but I thought little of it, as he had probably taken shelter with one of the Brothers. By late afternoon I knew something was wrong. I could feel it in my bones.

I was sitting on the porch when I saw Brother Frith come down the road with Old Dan tied to the back of his wagon.

"Good afternoon, Sister Ida. Is Brother Thaddeus in?"

"No, I'm out here waiting for him. He didn't come back for lunch."

"I was down by the creek bed after the storm passed. One of my horses wandered off during the storm. That's where I found Old Dan. I am concerned now. We had better have the Brothers go search for him."

"I'm going, too," I surprised myself by saying.

Brother Frith rang the metal bell just outside our kitchen door, giving the emergency alarm. The loud ringing did not go unnoticed. It wasn't long before a search party was formed.

Just before dark we found Thaddeus's remains near an old deserted barn at what looked to be an animal cemetery. I knew the property had long ago belonged to Mamie's parents, but I did not know who owned it now. What was left of Thaddeus was lying beneath a heavy branch of an old willow tree. His body had been badly burned. Brother Frith covered the body with his jacket.

"When lightning has struck a tree in the past, it will likely hit again. This willow tree has been hit before. You can tell from the burn marks on the ground and on the trunk," Brother Frith said to me and the other Believers who had gathered.

"The grave where we buried Midnight some years back is right over there. It seems fitting Thaddeus should die near his horse," Brother Frith said, pointing to a grave covered with white rocks.

"What's that on Midnight's grave?" I asked, walking to the mysterious dark object. No one answered me as I picked up Thaddeus's black leather glove. A hush fell upon the Believers when they recognized what I held in my hand.

Holding the glove, I looked to the sky to say a silent prayer for Midnight. I hadn't known where he was buried. Thaddeus wouldn't take me to his grave nor tell me where it was.

As I looked to the heavens, my eyes began to make out patterns and shapes, and there he was, Midnight, his spirit hovering, with wings unfurled just above me. The thick sinews along his long neck arched as he bent his head down, our eyes locking together. Our souls met, and I knew at once who his mother was. I had seen her when I was a ten-year-old girl looking out the kitchen window. I felt power, anger, and a tremendous peace all rolled into this other-worldly encounter. I knew Midnight's strife was no more, and neither was mine. He had come to say goodbye and was eager to return to the other side of the cloven night sky.

The others hadn't seen Midnight. Maybe my own world was more real than theirs. I did not find my experience with Midnight peculiar at all, for seeing him was a blessing that had been given me. I did not tell the others I had seen him, for I knew how they would have looked at me.

I packed my bag that very night without saying a word to anyone. I did not want to see or tend to Thaddeus's burned body. I wanted no part of his funeral nor did I want anything in the house. Packing a small bag, I walked to Undertaker's, using a flashlight to find my way.

Being a kind and gentle man, Undertaker asked no questions when I asked him to drive me to Raylene's home. We rode in silence all the way there.

I said a silent prayer when I got out of the truck and walked to the porch. I waved for Undertaker to drive on. Getting up my nerve I knocked at the front door. It wasn't but a moment before the front porch light came on and Raylene answered.

"Aunt Ida, what are you doing here? Has something happened?"

"Lightning has struck, girl, and the promise I made to care for Thaddeus is over. He's now on the other side, and I've come to live with you."

Raylene wrapped her arms around me and led me into the house. I was finally at home with those I loved.

**"The Soil Is The Great Connector Of Our Lives,
The Source and Destination Of All"
Wendell Berry**

Ray

1996

Growing up, I always heard talk of how the farm was the only way to raise children. It is a good, solid life. I was raised on a farm, but now work in town at my own carpentry shop. Leslie is a part time nurse at the local hospital. Our boys go to public school. They have regular chores and help me work in the garden. That's education you can't get anywhere else, watching crops grow and seeing God's hand in all of it.

I want Leslie and my children to know about the Believers. They have no need to know of Father's sordid life. Believers are faith-filled people who disregard personal gain and convenience to help one another. They wield hammers and paint brushes when the call comes.

The Believers could not sustain the life I live now. I had seen too much of the cruelty of the world. Leslie could not have lived the kind of life that would have been expected of her. Without Leslie, I would have never known how great a love can be between a man and a woman. I wanted my sons to witness that.

I bear witness to the Believers' quiet non-conformity, their intertwining faith with farming, and their vigilance to a higher calling not of the material world.

I no longer blame Father for his misdeeds, for who am I to judge? He is with his Maker now and I wish him peace. I have good solid work, a wife, children, sisters, and dear friends whom I love. I am a blessed man.

Death Is Nothing at All
Henry Scott Holland

Death is nothing at all.
I have only slipped away to the next room.
I am I and you are you.
Whatever we were to each other,
That, we still are.

Call me by my old familiar name.
Speak to me in the easy way
Which you always used.
Put no difference into your tone.
Wear no forced air of solemnity or sorrow.

Laugh as we always laughed
At the little jokes we enjoyed together.
Play, smile, think
Of me. Pray for me.
Let my name be ever the household word
That it always was.
Let it be spoken without effect.
Without the trace of a shadow on it.

Life means all that it ever meant.
It is the same that it ever was.
There is absolute unbroken continuity,
Why should I be out of mind
Because I am out of sight?

I am but waiting for you.
For an interval.
Somewhere. Very near.
Just around the corner.
All is well.

AUTHOR'S NOTE

The bones of my story began with a long deceased relative, a strong minded woman, who wore her husband's pants. She refused to take them off when demanded by her husband and church and paid the consequences. I never had a chance to meet her, being born too late, but I wish I had. Stories of her have been handed down by older relatives some living, some not.

Once I wrote the first few chapters, I allowed the characters to write their stories. They took me on surprising journeys as their lives unfolded during my many walks, then through my keyboard. While they are all fictitious and not intended to represent anyone, living or dead, they are as real to me as the words on these pages.

For most of the story, Thaddeus did not speak. I was at work on a quiet Sunday afternoon, when out of the blue he began talking. I was surprised and horrified as to what he had to say. I have moved to a place of compassion for Thaddeus and hope you can to.

The setting of *Lightning Shall Strike* is my beloved Franklin County where my ancestry goes back 200 years. I feel fortunate to live, work, and play on beautiful Smith Mountain Lake in Moneta, Virginia.

Thank you for reading my book. A review from you on Amazon and Facebook would be more than welcomed. If you enjoyed it please consider reading my first novel, *Cahas Mountain,* which is available on Amazon.com.

I want to agive a big thank you to Lakewriters (SMAC), and Tim, for their help and support in making Lightning Shall Strike a reality!

The cover of this book came from a photograph I took thirty years ago of a deserted farmhouse in Hardy, Va. The voice of my characters seemed to come right out of this photograph, complete with crows. All that was added was the lightning bolt!

I am happy to hear from readers and love to talk at bookclubs, library programs and just about anywhere I'm asked!

Please feel free to contact me at: Lindakaylightning@gmail.com
www.facebook.com/lightningshallstrike
www.facebook.com/cahasmountain

I'd love to hear from you!
Linda Kay Simmons

Made in the USA
Monee, IL
25 September 2021